SOLITARY SINNERS

SAINT VIEW PRISON, #2

ELLE THORPE

WWW.ELLETHORPE.COM

Editing: Studio ENP

Proofreading: Barren Acres Editing

Photographer: Wander Aguiar

Original Cover Design: Elle Thorpe

Special Edition Cover Design: Emily Wittig

#2

For Karen, most amazing proofreader and all round beautiful person. Thank you for the hard work you put into all of my books.
Love, Elle x

1

MAE

A madman held my hand, a shiv that still dripped with blood clutched tight in his other. The scythe-shaped birthmark all I could see.

Vincent was Scythe. The man the worst of the worst feared. Legendary killer, and potentially the person who'd taken my sister's life.

Even with smoke surrounding us, a fire billowing somewhere outside my classroom door, and a dead body at our feet, it was Vincent's possessive grip on my fingers that made my legs tremble.

His eyes narrowed into slits, something dark buried deep within him rising to the surface. "That's a good girl," he purred. "I have so many plans for you, Miss Donovan. And the night has only just begun."

The instinct to shrink away and curl in on myself was overwhelming. I swallowed down a scream and darted a look toward the door, not sure if I was praying for Rowe to walk back in or hoping he wouldn't.

Vincent yanked my arm sharply, and a tiny cry of pain

escaped my mouth. He didn't seem to hear it. The panic inside me ramped right up and mixed with the desperate questions about my sister that I longed to yell at him. It all became a swirling chaos, pounding in time with the rapid beat of my heart. But the smoke grew thicker with every passing moment, and the instinct to survive woke up with a body-shuddering jolt of adrenaline.

I had to get out.

But there was no escape from this classroom other than through that door, which probably led straight into an inferno.

Just great.

I fought back a hysterical laugh. How insane to be in a situation where Vincent and his shiv and penchant for murder weren't necessarily the most pressing danger.

The smoke clawed at my lungs, suffocating and raw, demanding my full attention. The roles reversed, and suddenly it was me hurrying for the exit, pulling him along. I hitched up the front of my long skirt, wrapping it around my hand and using it as a barrier between my skin and the metal doorknob. Whether it was hot or not, I wasn't sitting here, waiting to die with a psycho my only company. With a quick flick of my wrist, I had the door open.

Only to be met with a face full of thick, acrid smoke, and the scorching heat of flames to my left.

It burned my lungs, and I dropped low while coughs racked my body.

"Miss Donovan! Come on!"

I peered through the smoke at Vincent's pleading face. His eyes were wide, his grip on my hand stiff but no longer cruel.

Scythe was gone, and the young man I knew from my class was back.

Thank God.

I scrambled back to my feet and let him drag me out into the hallway. Any sense of relief disappeared. The flames were barely ten yards away, curling lazily along the floor and up the walls, blocking the corridor to the infirmary almost entirely.

Someone stood on the other side, his shoulders strong and broad through the fire, his face too handsome to be real, even when smudged with ash. Our gazes clashed and held, and my name ripped from his throat in a smoke-choked roar.

"Mae!"

Rowe.

Two women stood behind him, farther away from the flames. His shout caught their attention, and Tori burst into tears, Perry yanking her back when she lunged closer.

"Miss Donovan!" Vincent pulled my hand again. "Come on!"

But I couldn't stop staring at Rowe. His gaze seared me more than the heat from the fire did, the agony in his eyes wrapping itself around my heart and squeezing hard enough to break.

I wanted to fight my way through the blaze and throw myself into the safety of his arms. But my gaze flew back to Tori's terrified, tearstained face. Dammit, she'd only come here to help her priest bless the dying prisoners and now she was in danger of joining them. She had a husband and a baby at home. The longer I stared at

Rowe, wishing I could get to him, the longer she was in danger.

"Go!" I screamed to Rowe. "Keep them safe." I reluctantly stumbled back a few steps, dragged along by Vincent. The flames rose taller, and panic for Rowe and Tori pushed out any desire to save myself. "Dammit, Rowe! Leave me! Go!"

Then I forced myself to turn around and follow Vincent. I ran after him, around the corner and out of sight of Rowe, knowing he wouldn't move until I did.

At least Vincent had snapped out of whatever murderous rampage had come over him. I ran blindly through the empty corridors, all the prisoners obviously steering clear of the smoke and sheltering elsewhere. But Vincent ran with purpose, making turns left and right, taking us deep into the belly of the prison.

"Where are we going?" I panted. Trying to run while breathing in air that wasn't exactly clean was doing a number on my lungs.

"Kitchen."

I stopped. "Wait." The kitchen had to be full of prisoners. Like the infirmary, surely that was the first place they'd go in a riot. The last thing I wanted was to be surrounded by dangerous men hyped-up on power and aggression. "Why the kitchen?"

He glanced back over his shoulder as he forced me into a jog again. "I like being around the knives."

Oh God. My blood, heated from running and adrenaline, suddenly turned cold. I'd been lulled into a false sense of security. Even when Vincent wasn't in full-blown psychopath mode as his alter ego, he still wasn't mentally stable. And neither of his personalities were letting me out of his sight.

We ran some more, the corridor walls an unending sea of beige, broken up only by doors with large letters spelling out each section's name.

Vincent faltered at Gen Pop A.

"What's wrong?" I peered backward down the hall. The threat from the fire didn't seem as immediate, the air clearer in this section.

"Heath's in there."

I stared at the doors. The windows had been blacked out by something—I couldn't imagine where the prisoners would have got spray paint from, but it could have been boot polish. I wanted it gone. I wanted to scratch it off with my nails just so I could see what was going on inside. But the sounds numbed me with fear. Yells that reminded me of war cries, mixed with the crashes and bangs of furniture being thrown around. The chants of the men inside—as dangerous and unpredictable as the one who held my hand now—sent chills down my spine.

But I couldn't just walk past, knowing Heath was inside.

I lunged for the door.

Vincent yanked my hand. "No! There's nothing we can do for him right now." He pulled me away and into the food hall, while I fought against him, trying to get back.

It was a useless effort. Jayela, with her years of police training and strong from hours at the gym, would have fought him off. But that had never been me. I could teach a five-year-old to read, but none of those books had held any information on how to disarm a psychopath. My skill set here was sorely lacking. So where Vincent went, I went.

And he wanted to go play with the knives.

Fan-fucking-tastic.

The food hall and kitchens were set up much like a high school cafeteria, but right now, it looked as if a tornado had ripped through it. I widened my eyes at the carnage. Tables were overturned, trays, plates, and cutlery strewn about the room. One prisoner had the back of the chair gripped in his meaty fingers as he repetitively slammed it against a window. The noise thudded through me, and I jumped at every bang. The glass in this place was made to withstand that kind of assault, but for how long? The bars on the outside would stop him from escaping, so the destruction he caused now was just for the pure fun of it.

Another man I didn't recognize looked up from eating sugar direct from a packet. A slow grin spread across his unattractive face. "Well, well, well. What have you brought us, kid?"

Vincent didn't say anything. He just tightened his grip on my hand and led me toward the kitchen.

The man stepped in front of him. "What? Didn't your mama teach you how to share your toys?"

We couldn't go around him, with overturned tables and chairs blocking the path. Vincent stared up at the bigger man. "She's not a toy."

The man cocked his head to one side. "Could have fooled me. She looks good to play with." His beady gaze rolled over my body hungrily.

Unbelievably, I found myself inching closer to Vincent.

So it was in full, horrifying detail, that I watched Vincent raise his arm, shiv still clutched in his fist, and ram it into the bigger man's eye.

A howl of agony lifted over the din. All gazes turned in our direction, glancing over me, then Vincent, then to the man writhing in agony on the floor, weapon still lodged in his eyeball.

Quiet fell over the room. Vincent ran his fingers back through his hair, and stepped over the man on the floor like he was a crack in the sidewalk. I had no choice but to follow.

It was only as we reached the kitchen that the whispers started up.

"Did you see the mark on his hand?"

"Do you know who he is?"

I knew.

The men who had taken over the kitchen walked out without a word, giving us a wide berth. With only the two of us in the meal preparation area, and the door locked, Vincent finally let go of my hand.

I watched him move around the large, industrial space, pulling open drawers and rifling through cupboards. One thing was clear—Vincent's reputation preceded him. I blurted out the question that had plagued me ever since I'd seen that mark on his hand. "Did you kill my sister?"

He paused with his arms full of plastic bags. "What's her name?"

A lump rose in my throat. How many women had he killed that he needed a name in order to answer the question? I tried to find hope in the fact he could have killed me a dozen times over by now if he'd wanted to. So far, he'd done nothing but protect me. But I needed to know. The man was ruthless. Vicious. He could kill and maim in cold blood and not think twice about it. "Jayela Donovan."

He mulled her name over for so long I felt the need to add extra details. "She was murdered in my apartment. In her bed. She has navy-blue walls, with police certificates in frames."

"Her throat slit?"

I swallowed down the lump. "Yes."

He shrugged. "Sounds like me."

With that he went back to his task, filling bags with food and other equipment, like we'd just had a Sunday afternoon chat about the weather while sipping coffee.

A silent tear dripped down my face. "Why?"

He didn't answer. He passed a bag in my direction. "Hold this, please."

I did as I was asked, fingers trembling while I pried apart the plastic opening and held it out in his direction. He dumped armfuls of food inside and then motioned for another bag.

"Why are you doing this?" I asked. "The police are going to storm in here any minute. Just eat what you want now while you can."

He shook his head, not slowing in his task. "No. Riots can last for weeks."

"Weeks?" I squeaked out. It was one thing to keep Vincent talking and on my side for minutes, or even hours until the riot squad got here. But I couldn't keep this up for any longer than that. He'd realize we weren't on the same side. I'd say the wrong thing and end up with a shiv in my eye.

"Don't look so worried. You'll be gone by then."

I froze. "What does that mean?"

Vincent yanked open a drawer and grinned with delight. "Ah! Exactly what I was after."

He pulled out a sharp silver knife, the blade glinting in the overhead lights as he brandished it through the air, making the same swiping motion he'd used when he'd slit DeWitt's throat.

There was no need for him to explain any further.

I knew what gone meant.

2

ROWE

*N*ot again. Flashes of a life I'd left behind crashed over me like relentless waves, smashing down on a man who couldn't swim. Not being able to get to Mae felt a lot like drowning, only worse because I'd already gone under once before. I'd barely managed to put my life back together then. I didn't think I had it in me to do it twice.

A palm cracked across my cheek, the sharp bite of pain bringing the world around me back into focus. Flames seared my skin. Sirens pierced the air. And a woman screamed in my face.

"Rowe! You can't help her if you're dead. Move!" Perry frantically clutched at my arm, trying in vain to drag me away from the fire.

Mae was gone, and Perry was right. If I stood here any longer the smoke would overcome us before the flames did. I turned and ran, boots stomping on the floor. I didn't need to tell Perry or Tori. They both followed, the three of us sprinting down the hall, shoulder to shoulder, the blaze picking up pace behind us.

I barked sharp words into my walkie-talkie. "Fire in the corridor outside the schoolroom. Requesting immediate assistance."

I let go of the button and waited for the warden to spit back a response.

There was nothing but the sounds of our labored breathing.

"What's going on?" Tori's face was splotchy with exertion, but she wasn't stopping. She kept pace with me and Perry, looking to the two of us for guidance.

I wished I had some to give. But without communications, I was blind. Any corner we turned could be a trap.

I pulled up short at the end of the corridor, and Perry stared at me. "Which way? They'll be guarding the main doors."

She'd been employed here longer than I had, but her work was very much centered around the infirmary. She'd likely never been much past that wing of the prison. My plan of waiting this thing out in Mae's classroom was long gone. Her room was probably completely ablaze by now.

I hit the button on my walkie-talkie once more. "Warden, you there? We need immediate backup. You can't wait for the cops. Get people in here now."

"Pritchard?"

Relief washed over me. "There's a fire in the corridor outside the school rooms. Why aren't the sprinklers going on?"

The warden let out an uncomfortable-sounding

cough. "We're aware. However, the sprinklers are currently...not available."

"What the hell does that mean?"

"Inmates tampered with the detection units, so they were temporarily turned off. Seems the system wasn't reset."

A fresh gust of smoke filled the corridor, and I bent over, the smoke not as thick closer to the floor. "Then manually turn them back on! We can't fucking breathe in here!"

"We're trying."

"Try harder. I've got two women with me, and I need to get them out. Where's clear?"

"Nowhere. I don't know. Nobody is responding to radios, and most of the CCTV is out. We have to assume they're working their way through the prison and that all sections might have been breached."

"I've got civilians with me."

As if to prove the point, Tori let out a racking cough and pulled her shirt up to cover her mouth.

"Jesus, fuck. That's going to kill us in the press."

I stared down at my walkie-talkie like it had suddenly grown a head. Like I gave a shit how this looked to the media. No matter how they tried to spin it, this entire thing was a disaster from start to finish. "The guard's office in the West Wing. There's an exit into the yards. Get people over there, ready to receive."

The warden's words were gruff. "No one in, no one out."

"Explain two dead women to the newspapers then!"

Perry shot me a sharp glance, and I wished I could take the words back, but they were the truth. Untrained civilians in the middle of a riot was a disaster waiting to happen. Especially women. I felt sick at the idea of a prisoner even laying a single finger on Mae.

"Goddammit, Rowe. Quit busting my fucking balls. It's crazy out here. I've got no one on the inside talking to me, and no backup from the cops yet. I'm trying to stop you all burning to crisps. I can give you one guy on that exit, but that's all."

"We need more than that!"

"It's all I can promise right now. So if anyone follows you, we're royally screwed. You do not request that door to be unlocked unless it's clear, you hear me?"

It was the best I was going to get. "Roger that."

"But, Rowe? I mean it. That door doesn't get opened if there's even one other body in that room. If the prisoners have commandeered any of our communications equipment, they could have heard this entire conversation and know what we're planning."

He was right.

We'd just painted targets on our backs.

3

HEATH

I was no stranger to the fists of other men. Growing up in Saint View, you learned how to fight as well as how to take a punch. I was good in a ring. Bigger and stronger than most men, but still agile enough to dance around them, ducking and weaving and avoiding their mistimed swings.

My father had taught me that.

But being great in a one-on-one fight would only take you so far on the streets. When the stakes were raised, and fights became one versus a pack? It didn't matter if you were a pro level or a complete beginner. Unless you were armed, you were going down.

I had no allies in this place. No one to have my back.

I'd thought I could go it alone, keep my head low, and mind my own business until I could prove my innocence. That had been a mistake. I was probably going to die here, forced to my knees on the dirty concrete floor of Gen Pop A, with a hyped-up crowd of thugs around me. I'd go down as the man who'd killed

Jayela Donovan, with no opportunity to prove my innocence.

Sharp pain splintered through my shoulder as my arms were pinned behind me. My scalp protested my hair being yanked back, and I braced myself for the blow I knew was coming.

Randall threw his thick fist into my midsection once more. "You could have been a king in here, bro. Instead, you're the loser."

He was right. I was. But not for the reasons he thought. All Randall and DeWitt cared about was the glory and the power that running this place brought them. They got off on the other men looking up to them and kissing their asses. They lived for the tiniest glint of fear in a guard's eye.

All I was living for was the occasional glimpse of Mae.

She was the only thing that made sense through all of this.

Fuck, I regretted not kissing her. In her apartment that night, I'd been so close to doing it. Holding her in my arms had just felt surprisingly right. She was soft, and warm, and so incredibly beautiful. She'd taken my breath away. But we'd been so drunk, and I couldn't take advantage. But what had stopped me when I had her cornered in that prison bathroom? What had stopped me from taking her face between my hands and giving her what we both wanted?

I was an idiot.

I deserved every punch.

Randall's fist slammed into my cheek, whipping my head to one side.

"Did you hear me?"

I heard him. I just wasn't going to give him the satisfaction of responding.

His fists rained down, over and over. A cut opened up on my cheek, and through a swelling eye, I saw my own blood across Randall's knuckles.

"Enough."

Randall paused in his blows and stared over his shoulder at whoever had spoken. "Excuse me?" His laugh filled with fake amusement when he recognized whoever it was intervening. "Look at you, trying to be the big man. DeWitt will be back any minute, and he ain't gonna be in the mood for a smart-mouthed kid who doesn't know his place. So run along now. Nothing to see here."

From my spot on the floor, I couldn't see past Randall. The blood from my cheek trickled down my neck, wetting the collar of my uniform.

"I said, *enough*. Let him go."

My heart sank when I recognized the voice. Vincent. He was a good kid, and probably the one person I actually did like in here. Standing up for me was honorable, but it was going to get him killed. Fuck. I didn't need another death on my conscience. "Vincent. Don't," I protested weakly.

"DeWitt is dead. I slit his throat."

I blinked, shock slicing through my gut. What the fuck? The kid didn't have it in him, he had to be all talk.

Though DeWitt had been oddly missing since this whole thing started.

But there was just no way. Vincent was so mild-mannered and quiet. The thought of him overpowering DeWitt, who probably had fifty pounds on the younger man, was impossible.

Randall scoffed. "No you didn't."

He took the words right out of my mouth.

Suddenly I was glad it wasn't me who'd uttered them.

Vincent had Randall's arm twisted in a punishing hold, and the bigger man down on the floor in less than a second. His knees hit the unforgiving concrete beside me, his eyes wide with shock and pain. "What the f—"

Vincent leaned in, a glinting silver knife that seemed to have come out of nowhere held to Randall's throat. "I don't lie about my kills. The man is stone-cold dead on the schoolroom floor, and unless you want to join him, tell your friends to let mine go."

The guy holding my left arm loosened his grip and took a step back. "His hand...the birthmark...It's Scythe."

The guy on my right dropped me like I'd electrocuted him. "We didn't know..."

I shook out my shoulder, rolling it, testing it to make sure it wasn't dislocated.

Vincent hissed in their direction. "Now you do."

The two of them scuttled off into the chaos of the room, abandoning Randall entirely.

I stared up at Vincent, wondering who the hell this man was.

He gave me a half smile. "Time to go, friend."

4

MAE

*W*ith my eyes slammed tight, I sucked in shallow breaths, trying to calm my racing heart. For the second time that night, I was locked in a storage closet. But unlike the one in my classroom, this one reeked of cleaning chemicals. The fumes stole the air in the cramped space, barely big enough to conceal me, a dirty mop in a bucket of sludge my only companion.

I twisted the door handle, but it was useless and locked from the outside. My heart pounded a thumping beat right through my body, keeping pace with the seconds that ticked by, my panic increasing with each one.

This was my chance. And I was going to do everything in my power to take it. I rammed my shoulder against the door, over and over again, and screamed until my throat grew hoarse.

"Help!" I pummeled my fists until I had exhausted every ounce of energy.

With aching arms, I slumped onto the exit, physically

desperate for a break, but my head screamed at me to keep fighting. I was going to die in here. Either the fire would reach me, or Vincent would come back, fully in serial killer mode and slit my throat. Panic clawed its way up my spine as the walls closed in, hot and suffocating.

The door gave way.

I stumbled out into the hall, strong arms breaking my fall.

"Mae?"

My heart stopped. No. That couldn't be right. The smoke or the cleaning fumes had to be getting to me. Or maybe I was dead already. I stared up at Heath, taking in the cut on his cheek and his black eye. It didn't matter. He was no less devastatingly handsome. My heart started up again, beating for him the way it always had.

That was how I knew. My body recognized him even when my brain was confused. I gulped back a sob filled with relief.

His sharp focused gaze darted all over me, disbelief etched into the way his perfect lips parted. "Are you really here?"

"Are you?" But he was. He was warm and solid and alive. I twisted my fingers in the rough material of his shirt, nodding as fast and hard as I could, reassuring him that yes, I was here, too. I had no idea how he'd found me, but it didn't matter. There was no one I wanted more in that moment.

I pulled his head down and pressed my mouth to his.

He didn't hesitate. His lips opened, his tongue seeking entrance, and the rest of the world faded away. The faint smell of smoke was replaced with the scent of him. The biting fear disappearing with his taste. His arms tightened around me until I was crushed to his hard chest, and in the midst of a prison riot, with a fire burning out of control and a madman killing in cold blood, I'd never felt safer. Relief fueled our embrace, one I might have stayed in forever if I could have.

An uncomfortable throat clearing broke us apart, and I nearly jumped right out of my skin to find Vincent standing a foot away, watching us quietly.

He shifted his plastic bags full of supplies into one hand, his gaze flicking over me and then landing on Heath. "Sorry to interrupt, but we really need to get a move on now we're all together."

I clutched Heath's hand tight, taking half a step behind him. "I don't understand. What's going on?"

Vincent frowned at me. "I told you. I have plans for you."

"Plans to kill me."

"What?" Heath pushed me entirely behind him and glared at Vincent. "Talk, kid. That better not be true."

I peeked around Heath's muscled biceps.

Vincent recoiled, like I'd struck him with my words. "I never planned to kill her. Why would I do that? I have no idea what gave you that impression."

"You shoved me in a cupboard. You locked me in."

"Yes," Vincent replied, like I was a little slow for not putting the pieces together. "I couldn't have you in Gen Pop while I got Heath for you, could I? That would have been irresponsibly dangerous of me." When he sighed it was laced with exasperation. "You're a bit of a magnet for trouble, Miss Donovan. I'm not sure if you're aware of that."

All I could do was blink. I was a magnet for trouble? That was rich coming from him. "You got Heath for me?"

Vincent's cheeks turned pink. "For you, and for him."

"Why would you do that?"

"He's my friend." His gaze flickered up to meet Heath's. "I do feel bad about the injuries you sustained in my absence, though. I do apologize and hope you can forgive me for that."

Heath eyed the silver knife in Vincent's hand. "Sure, don't even mention it. Not your fault."

Vincent nodded like that was a job taken care of. "Good, good. I knew you wouldn't want to leave without Miss Donovan. But we really do need to get going now. Better we do it now before things get even messier. DeWitt had no idea what he was doing in organizing this riot. It's a bit of a joke really, but we'll make do."

Heath didn't move to follow him. "Leave?"

Vincent smiled broadly. "Of course. You're up for the death penalty, Heath. You can't stay here."

"What are you proposing? That we escape?"

Vincent held up his bag of supplies once more. "Precisely. Trust me, I know what I'm doing."

My mouth dropped open, and it was the schoolteacher, the woman who always had to follow the rules, who came out. "He can't do that, Vincent. And neither can you."

I scolded the crazy man with the knife like he was a kid on the playground.

Vincent's eyes narrowed.

Okay, that had not been a smart move.

Heath must've seen it, too. He put his hand up in a stop

motion, placating the younger man. "Hey, hey. It's fine. She just doesn't know the plan like you do. You're right. We can't stay here, so let's get on with it. Where are we going?"

Vincent smiled again, and I let out a breath.

"The guard's office in the West Wing. They said over the radio that they're getting some women out through there. Only one extra guard on the outside if we move quick enough. That's our best shot on short notice."

Hope lit me up from the inside. "That could be Rowe, Perry, and Tori."

Heath spun around to stare at me with big eyes. "Tori is in here, too? Fucking hell. Was the warden having a freaking tea party that I wasn't invited to? You're not supposed to be here either."

"I came in early to organize my room and get some tests ready."

Vincent glanced over with interest. "Trigonometry? I've been studying."

I gave him a weak nod, even though I could barely remember what was on the tests. I just didn't want to push his buttons any further.

Heath ignored him entirely, though, and ran his hand through his hair. "At least Tori's with Rowe." He tightened his fingers around mine. "Okay. Let's go. We can't go through Gen Pop A. Not with Mae, you're right about that. There's too many men in there. They might have been willing to back off and give me up, because you took them by surprise, but I couldn't guarantee they'd do the same for a woman."

Bile swirled in my gut at the thought of what might happen to one woman alone in a sea full of men who hadn't been near a female in months or even years.

"We'll go around through Gen Pop B. There's an entrance on the other side." Vincent nodded decidedly and strode in that direction.

Heath followed, tugging me along with him.

I stared up at him, waiting until Vincent was a few steps ahead. "Hey," I whispered. "You know you can't do this, right. If you escape, you really have committed a crime. We'll get you out legally."

"I know," he hissed back. "But are you going to tell him that? The man with the knife?"

He had a point. Instead, I opened my mouth to tell Heath that Vincent had all but admitted to killing Jayela. But a piercing scream cut me off.

A feminine shout that struck fear in my heart.

I spun in a circle, trying to work out where it came from. "That's Tori. Jesus, Heath. That's Tori!" I pulled away from him, sprinting for the closest door. The one to Gen Pop B.

There was no more dancing around the hornet's nest. We were going right through the middle of it.

5

ROWE

Five minutes earlier

"I need something to use as a weapon."

I glanced over at Tori, all five feet of her at best, and continued on with our slow journey down the hallways, taking the back passages to the General Population wings. "To do what exactly? You're pint-sized."

She gave me a dirty look. "I'm short but I'm feisty. Just try me."

I couldn't help but grin at her.

Her eyes went wide. "Whoa, put that thing away."

"What thing?"

"That smile. I see what Mae meant when she said you were stupidly attractive."

"You're only noticing that now?" Perry asked.

Tori shrugged. "It's been an eventful evening."

"Are you two seriously discussing this right now?" I shushed both of them, continuing our steady trip closer and closer to the west wing of the prison. Inside waited our target, the guard's office. That was what I needed to keep my mind on. But a few steps farther, I glanced over at Tori. "Did she really say that?"

She grinned, her teeth white against a face streaked with ash.

I tried not to let that please me and instead refocused my mind on the job. "We're going to have to go through either Gen Pop A or B to get to the guard's office."

"Don't suppose either of those are nicely empty of murderous prisoners," Perry muttered, creeping along beside me.

The three of us froze as someone ran across the corridor that joined ours. He didn't turn our way, though, and Tori let out an audible sigh of relief.

"Hey," I told her. "I'll get us out. I promised Mae I'd look after you. I don't break promises. Gen Pop B is smaller. We'll go through there. If we're lucky, maybe they already got the doors open and most of them will have emptied out."

Tori nodded, but Perry shot me a dubious glance.

I knew how it sounded. One guard, and two women versus an entire prison full of inmates. But what choice did I have? We could hide, but I had no idea if the sprinklers had ever come on around Mae's classroom. Until I knew for a fact that fire was out, I couldn't risk staying inside. A chill shuddered down my spine. Nothing terrified me more than the thought of being burned alive.

I squeezed my eyes tight for a moment, willing away the horrific memories that threatened to flood in. I couldn't let that happen. Those memories had held me hostage for years. They'd kept me from getting out of bed some mornings.

They'd kept me from living.

I wasn't watching anyone else go out like that. Hiding just made you a sitting duck.

I'd get Tori and Perry to the pickup point. I'd make sure no one followed. The last time I'd sat and waited it out had ended in tragedy. This time, I knew better.

Then I'd find Mae. Because I wasn't leaving this place without her.

The beige hallway had never felt longer, and it was suspiciously quiet. From farther down, muffled shouts drifted on the air, and I was glad I'd decided on going through Gen Pop B. Colt was in A, though. The thought made me sick. The noises coming from that direction were horrific, and I could only pray he was safe somehow. I wished I could clone myself. I wanted to be everywhere —here for Tori and Perry. With Colt in Gen Pop A. And overwhelmingly, with Mae, wherever she was.

I stopped the two women outside the door to Gen Pop B. The door was already ajar, but not enough to see inside. "The door to the guard's office is straight to your right." I focused on Perry and the swipe tag still dangling around her neck. "I don't know if you have clearance here. Swap cards with me, and I'll watch your backs. Move quick."

"I feel like we're in a bad action movie," Tori murmured.

I frowned at her.

She shook her head. "Sorry. I make inappropriate comments when I'm nervous. Let's do it."

She stepped forward before I could stop her.

"Dammit, Tori." I pushed Perry ahead of me and then went in after her, head low, and waited for the roar of the prisoners when they spotted us. All we had on our side was the element of surprise. If we could get to the guard's office quick, maybe that would be enough.

Tori stopped. "Huh. There's no one in here."

Perry and I both stopped, too. She was right. The room was completely empty. It housed around forty prisoners normally, and there were certainly signs of that—mattresses flipped off beds, clothing and books strewn about the floor. And blood...a trail of blood that led right where we needed to go.

Tori stared down at it. "That doesn't look good."

But Perry strode ahead and scanned my card on the lock. Her fingers flew over the keypad, punching in the access code.

I caught her hand before she hit enter. "Wait!"

She shook me off and pinned me with a glare. "That's a lot of blood."

"Could be a prisoner."

"Does it matter? That much blood on the floor means an artery has been cut. That person could be bleeding out right now while we're standing here debating whether it matters if that person is worthy of being saved or not."

Fuck. She was right. I let go of her hand. "I go in first."

"Deal."

The panel let out a beep, and the tiny lights above the pin pad turned green. I opened the door.

The smell of blood hit me before the sight of it did. The sharp tang hit my nostrils, bitter and metallic. A prisoner leaned over a guard on the floor, the pool of blood spreading out around them. The prisoner jumped up as soon as he saw us, scuttling away.

I ran for him, shoving him up against the wall.

"I didn't do it. I dragged him in here for safety, that's it. I swear!"

"Bullshit!"

He held his hands up in mock surrender. "I swear! The guy has a kid... I couldn't just watch him die."

Perry looked up at me from where she'd dropped to the floor beside the bleeding man. "Rowe! It's Colt."

My fingers loosened on the prisoner's shirt, my gaze straying to the horrific sight on the floor again. I'd never seen a man's skin so sickly white, made worse by the striking contrast with Colt's dark hair.

My stomach lurched as his eyes rolled back. I forgot about the prisoner entirely and fell to the floor beside Colt's barely moving body. "Fuck." I hovered my hands over him uselessly. "What can I do?"

Tori's scream was the instant I realized I'd screwed up. The prisoner pinned her to his chest, his arm around her neck.

Perry glanced over her shoulder, but she had her hands pressed to the wound in Colt's leg, trying to stem the flow of blood.

I lowered my voice. "Let her go. Just walk out, and we'll forget you were in here."

The man shook his head. "I ain't going down for what happened to him."

I spoke to him like he was a startled horse. "I get it, I get it. You were trying to help. I'll make sure I write that up in my report. Just let her go."

For half a second, I thought I'd gotten through to him. His gaze darted toward the door, but then it flew open, cracking back off the wall.

Bodies filled the doorway, and adrenaline flooded my system. Fight or flight.

Until my gaze slammed into Heath's. It held for half a second. Then slid to Mae standing behind him, eyes wide.

I only let myself feel the relief for the tiniest of moments. Instinctively, I knew Heath would protect Mae in the same way I would. And that protection extended to her best friend as well.

In unison, we rushed the prisoner holding Tori.

Heath went straight for the man's throat, shoving him against the wall once more. While I went for the arm he had around Tori's neck, wrenching his wrist back.

He yelped in surprise, or pain. I didn't care which, and Tori followed up with an elbow to his midsection before she darted away. "Asshole!"

But her bravado broke when Mae engulfed her in her arms. A sob burst from her chest, and she trembled while Mae held her.

"I'm sorry," the man choked out, around Heath's grip on his throat. "I wasn't going to hurt her!"

I took a step back, breathing as hard as if I'd run five miles. Adrenaline coursed through my body, shaking my fingers, and I clenched them into fists so no one would see. I was the only guard here and I needed to get the doors open. Even more so now that I had Mae and Colt. We could all leave safely. But I couldn't do that with a room full of prisoners. "Let him go."

Heath glanced over at me, a question in his eyes.

I forced out the words I knew I had to say. "Prisoner. I said, let him go."

A muscle ticked in Heath's jaw. "That seriously how you're going to play it?"

I had no other choice. We weren't suddenly on the same side because we'd had a moment where we'd read each other correctly and worked together. I needed to regain control of the situation. "You heard me."

Anger burned in Heath's expression. Slowly, one finger at a time, he released his hold on the man's throat. But his gaze never faltered from mine. It was a show of defiance even as he did what I'd commanded.

The prisoner scuttled for the door this time. "Too much drama in here," he muttered as he pushed past and disappeared into Gen Pop.

That left Heath and I staring at each other, neither of us willing to back down.

Without looking at them, I barked out orders. "Mae, Tori. Get over by the exit."

Mae let Tori go, but when she moved to follow her, hands clamped down on her shoulders. It was only then I noticed the young guy from her class, Vincent, behind her. He was the one she'd been with on the other side of the fire.

"She stays with me," he spoke up.

I narrowed my eyes at him and opened my mouth to put him in his place.

Heath cleared his throat, catching my attention. He gave a subtle shake of his head.

"It's fine, Rowe. I'm good here." Mae pleaded with me silently, her eyes saying more than words could have.

I paused, picking up on their cues. What the fuck was going on?

Tori didn't catch the vibe, though. "Mae, no. Come here."

Silver glinted at Vincent's side, and a slow, rolling silence fell over the room as we all saw it.

The knife.

Vincent kicked the door closed behind him. "No more interruptions." He pinned me with a glare. "Get the exit open." Like it was an afterthought, he tacked on, "Please."

I shook my head. "I can't do that."

Vincent tilted his head, his dark hair falling in his eyes. "Can't you?"

"He knows you can," Mae said quietly. "He heard you on the radio."

Fuck.

But maybe I could use that as a bargaining chip. "I'll open it when you let Mae go."

His fingers tightened on the knife handle. "Miss Donovan stays with me and Heath. We're a team. And looks to me like you don't have a choice about opening that door. Your friend is losing a terrible amount of blood over there. We can wait, but he can't. You wouldn't want his death on your hands, now, would you?"

I dared to glance down at Perry and Colt. Colt was completely out, and Perry had her fingers deep in his wound.

She looked up at me. "He's right. He's going to die if we don't get him out now."

Indecision ripped me in half. I couldn't let prisoners escape. Without the proper reinforcements outside, they could get well away before a dog squad was brought in to find them. The woods weren't far and would be easy enough to lose themselves in. Though I had growing doubts about Heath's guilt, Vincent was armed and dangerous.

But Colt wasn't even old enough to drink. And he had a family. I wasn't letting him die in here like this. Not when there was an alternative.

I hit the button on my walkie-talkie. "Warden."

Vincent waved the knife in my direction. "No telling him we're here, now," he said quietly, knife punctuating every word.

I went to argue, but Mae frowned at me and mouthed, "Don't."

"Rowe? You at the pickup point?" the warden's voice rumbled down the line.

"We need an ambulance." I didn't want to let them in. I didn't want to put another person in the way of danger. But I had no choice.

"Already got one on the door. How many you got with you?"

"Three women. Three guards," Vincent supplied, before I could hit the button. He pulled two jackets from the rack by the door and tossed one at Heath.

Heath looked like he'd rather shove the jacket back at Vincent, but Vincent was already shrugging his on and motioning for Heath to do the same.

"Say it," Vincent growled at me. The knife flashed again.

Normally, my access card would have opened the external door, but in a full lockdown, there was only one override. There was nothing I could do but fill my voice with confidence I didn't feel, and lie. "Three women, three guards. Open the door, Warden."

The lock popped, and a medic rushed into the small

space, pushing Tori flat against the wall to let them pass, and trapping me, Heath, Mae, and Vincent at the opposite end of the room. Tori glanced at me, and I jerked my head toward the door. She was the only one close enough to the exit to make a run to freedom and she needed to take it.

She glanced at Mae and then shook her head at me.

For fuck's sake. Her loyalty to her best friend was going to get her killed.

The paramedics talked frantically between themselves and Perry, loading both Perry and Colt onto a gurney, since she was plugging his wound with her fingers. They barely looked in our direction. The gurney bumped out into the freedom of the night beyond, and I rushed after them, grabbing Tori by the shoulder and shoving her out after them.

I blinked into the darkness on the other side, my eyes adjusting quickly.

The yard was full of cops. A riot squad in full gear, still at a distance but ready to take down any prisoner who stepped a foot outside those doors.

The warden had come through.

Vincent I didn't care about, but he held Mae like a shield.

And Heath... Fuck. I wasn't going to let him walk out there and be slaughtered. He wasn't like the others.

I wrestled with my need to get Mae to safety. But the reality of that slipped away by the moment, Vincent's hold on her never faltering.

I had to let it go. I slammed the door shut and pressed down the talk button on my radio. "Lock it down."

"What? No!" Vincent pushed forward, dragging Mae

along with him. He yanked the door open once more, then shut it just as quick. He glared at me. "There's cops out there! They said there'd only be one guard." He shoved Mae toward Heath and came at me with the knife raised. "You knew! You tipped them off!"

Vincent's eyes flashed with unimaginable anger. I opened my mouth to speak as the clunk of the locks reengaging sounded. I was unarmed and backed into a corner. The knife came toward me, slowly and menacing, threatening a slow and painful death. "I didn't—"

Heath cut me off. He stepped between us, back to me, facing Vincent.

"Hey, wait. He saved you. He shut the door so you couldn't walk out there into an ambush. Can't you see that? He's one of us. Right, Officer Pritchard?"

What?

Mae nodded hard. "He's with us, Vincent. He protected us."

Vincent paused, arm hovering. "He ruined the plan."

"He didn't. The cops did. Come on. Put the knife down. We can work out a new plan."

"Those cops were ready to take the place."

"All the more reason to not be standing here holding a knife to a prison guard's throat then, huh?" Heath suggested gently.

Vincent lowered the knife an inch. "Solitary."

Heath frowned. "What about it?"

"No one will be there. Everybody hates it. Not me. I like the quiet. I think better when it's quiet. And I need somewhere safe for Miss Donovan while I collect the things I need."

Heath nodded. "Then that's where we'll go. Just put the knife down, okay?"

Vincent looked over at the knife in his hand like he hadn't even realized it was there. "Oh."

He dropped his arm. Mae let out a sigh of relief.

But I didn't feel it. Because locked in solitary would just be swapping one hell for another.

6

LIAM

*B*aseball was the last thing on my mind while I drove to practice. Normally I loved to train, and it was the one thing that broke up my work week, but tonight I couldn't keep the stupid grin off my face.

Mitchell, one of my teammates, glanced over at me from the passenger seat. "Why are you grinning out at the road like you just won a million bucks? We're already five minutes late, and Coach is going to have us running laps, so I don't see much to smile about."

I glanced over at him. "Who's to blame for that? I was at your place on time. It's not my fault you left me sitting in the car for ten minutes."

"I had something on!"

"What?"

"My girl." Mitchell sniggered and thrust his hips up from his seat. "Had her right on top of me. I ain't no thirty-second show like you, bro."

That scored him a dirty look. "Is that seriously why you were late?"

"Yeah." He laughed.

I couldn't help but laugh with him. "Finish faster next time, huh? Or you can run my laps for me."

He leaned forward and turned up the radio, bopping his head in time with the song. I went back to smiling out the windshield, mentally replaying my night with Mae. I'd had daydreams about her ever since I was sixteen, but none held a candle to the real thing. I'd woken up with her in my bed this morning and immediately called in sick to the office. I'd had women beg me to do that the morning after, and I'd never once considered it for a moment. Mae hadn't asked. She hadn't even been awake when I'd gotten out of bed, made a whispered phone call, then gotten back in beside her. I'd tucked myself around her, her ass pressing against my cock, my fingers splayed out across her belly, fingertips brushing the underside of her full tits.

She'd rolled over, golden hair spilled across my pillow, and stole my breath. The feeling that punched through me wasn't just lust, though I had pulled her panties down and slipped my morning erection between her thighs. But when she'd moaned, pushing back against me, and taking me inside her body, new, stronger feelings rose through the arousal haze.

Real feelings. More than the crush I'd had on her. More than the desire to get her off. They were emotions that wrapped themselves around my heart and squeezed until this stupid grin on my face couldn't be removed.

Mitchell went quiet for a moment, and I thought he was just enjoying the song, but then he let out a laugh. "I should have realized earlier."

"Realized what?"

"Your good mood. You ain't never look like that unless you got laid. Who was it this time? Aleah? Georgia? Oh, oh, no, wait, I got my money on that chick who did the thing with her tongue. What was her name. Lola?"

"Louann," I supplied. "But no. Shut up. It's none of your business."

Mitchell actually looked hurt. "What do you mean? You, Liam Banks, playboy of the century, aren't going to spill the details of his latest conquest? Who are you and what have you done with my teammate?"

I reached across the center console and shoved him. "That's not true."

Even as I denied it, I knew that it probably was. I did sleep with a lot of women, and rarely more than once. I'd never really thought twice about sharing the details with my teammates. We'd all played together for years, and a lot of them were older, and married with kids. They got a kick out of my wild stories, and I'd always been happy to be the center of attention.

But there was no way in hell I was going to share with Mitchell or anyone what had happened with Mae. I was still trying to process letting someone in like that. When had sex ever been something more than a means to an end? I always made sure the women I slept with were properly and completely satisfied. Every time. But it had only been physical. A primal thing where getting laid was the end goal.

Mae had broken something wide open in me last night. Something I didn't want to close up, even though it was immense and powerful and maybe a little dangerous.

I could fall for her.

That's what it boiled down to.

Maybe I already had.

The thought was terrifying and exhilarating all in one. I put my foot on the gas and took the last turn into the baseball fields, ready to get out on the diamond and smash some balls into the outfield.

Mitchell's off-key singing died off, and the announcer took his place. *"First, to breaking local news. A riot has broken out in the Saint View Prison."*

I froze, key still in the ignition.

Mitchell opened his door and pulled his bag from the back seat while I dove for the volume button, cranking it up.

"Reports are only just starting to trickle in, and we'll keep you updated as more details come to light."

Mitchell palmed the doorframe and leaned back inside the car. "You coming?"

"Get out."

"Huh?"

I waved a hand at him frantically. "Get out! Get out!"

He took a hurried step back, and the moment the door closed, I slammed the gearshift down into reverse, backed out of the parking spot and then the fields as well. Dread welled in the pit of my stomach, a dark, churning fear starting up that had nothing to do with me and everything to do with the woman I'd spent last night with.

Mae was at the prison. She'd kissed me goodbye at lunchtime, and even though I'd tried to drag her back to bed, she'd insisted she needed to go to work early.

"No, no, no," I muttered to myself, speedometer well over the limit and tires screeching as I screamed around corners, heading out of Providence and into Saint View.

It wasn't far, but the miles felt like they ate up hours. I drove recklessly, blindly, and when the gates of the prison loomed, I stomped hard on the brakes, parking crookedly in my hurry to get out. I ran toward the front entrance where a crowd was building, but then flashing blue and red lights caught my eye. Compelled, I changed direction, heading for the back of the complex where an ambulance waited, the paramedics lined up behind a row of riot police.

I rifled through my pockets, finding my phone, and hit Mae's number, praying she'd answer while also knowing it was probably in her locker. It went to voicemail, her cheery greeting out of place with the panic and mounting tension in the air around us.

There was a ripple of activity from the police while snipers got into position. I had no idea if they were a comfort or completely disturbing. "What's going on?" I asked a woman watching on.

She shrugged. "No idea. I just came for the show."

Though I knew it was human nature, when someone I cared about was on the inside, her words sent anger coursing through my body.

"Doors opening for extraction in three, two, one..."

The paramedics' boots on the concrete and the clacking of the gurney's wheels bouncing over cracks and stones drowned out my questions. They disappeared inside, and there was no other movement. No one in. No one out.

I wanted to scream. I wanted to storm out of the shadows and demand that the police tell me what was going on. But I couldn't move, paralyzed with fear that the person the paramedics brought out would be Mae.

The doors finally opened, but there was no flash of golden hair. The paramedics crowded the gurney, blocking my attempts to make sure it wasn't Mae they worked on. A small, dark-haired woman ran blindly, head down, but as she reached the back of the exercise yard and the police who ran to catch her, she lifted her gaze.

"Tori!" I shouted.

She stopped and turned my way, her eyes wide and wild even from a distance, face covered in soot. But she recognized me, and a sob shook her shoulders.

I moved stiffly at first, as if my body was trying to hold me back. My head roared questions, and then denials, not wanting to know the answer. Police stopped me from getting too close.

"Where's Mae?" I yelled. "Tori, please! Is it her? Is she hurt?"

Tori shook her head, but I had no idea which question she was answering.

The paramedics finally reached the ambulance, an auburn-haired woman perched over a patient, her hands covered in his blood.

His blood. A man in a guard's uniform.

I breathed a sigh of relief, but it was short-lived.

Because two men I cared about worked in that prison. I'd been blinded by my fear for Mae, but as the gurney rolled past, and I took in Colt's ashen face, my stomach flipped. "Shit, no. Colt..."

"You know him?" one of the paramedics asked me.

I nodded quickly. "I'm his lawyer. I got him the job here...is he going to be okay?"

She didn't answer, and that in itself told me everything. She either didn't know if he'd make it, or she knew he wouldn't. Either way, her silence wasn't good.

I gripped the door of the ambulance. "He can't die. He's got a family. A baby..."

"We're going to do our best to make sure that doesn't happen. Does he have any allergies or medical conditions?"

I shook my head, racking my brain. "I don't know...I'll call his partners. But his mom works at the hospital. Willa McCaffery."

The woman's head snapped to me. "He's Willa's son?"

"Yes!"

She grimaced, then shut the door in my face.

The slam jolted through me, and I watched in stunned silence when another ambulance arrived, and the riot guards handed Tori in. They immediately fitted her with an oxygen mask, coughs shaking her slim shoulders. I rushed to where she sat on the back of the ambulance, grateful the police now seemed too occupied with what was going on in the prison to worry about what the ambulances were doing. "Where's Mae? Did you see her?"

She pulled the mask aside to speak, and frantic frustration rose in me when I had to wait for her to cough before she could answer. "Still inside. I couldn't get her out. There's a guy with a knife. He wouldn't let her go."

Bile rose in my throat, and I spun to stare up at the huge, impenetrable building. "I need to get in there," I choked out. "Fuck! If anything happens to her, I'll—"

Tori grabbed my arm and spun me around to face her. "Hey. She's strong and she's smart. Nothing is going to happen to her."

I shook my head, knowing full well that no matter how intelligent and capable Mae was in any other situation, that right now, with a prison full of dangerous men on the loose, none of that would make any difference.

Sickening images flooded in. Mae cornered by a roomful of men, intent on taking what they pleased from her body. The body I'd worshipped just hours ago, the lips I'd kissed as if I'd needed them to breathe. The thought of anyone hurting her turned me inside out until I was sure the pain I felt inside was as physical as being tortured.

Tori pressed her nails into my arm. "Hey. Breathe before they force you onto one of these masks as well. Rowe and Heath are with her. They aren't going to let anything happen to her. You just need to hold it together in the meantime."

My heart still pounded, but a tiny bit of my panic subsided.

I knew how I felt about Mae. If I'd been inside, I would have done anything to protect her.

So if Rowe and Heath's feelings were even half as strong as mine, they'd get her out. Without a single hair on her head being harmed.

7

MAE

*V*incent's grip on my arm was never-ending. It didn't hurt, but it was a constant presence nonetheless, and one that kept Rowe and Heath in line. Vincent's favorite knife was a lingering threat neither of them seemed willing to tackle head-on. I didn't want them to. Though he terrified me, Vincent didn't appear to want to hurt me or Heath. Rowe was another story, but for now, Heath had convinced him we were all on the same team.

The corridors to solitary were more crowded than when we'd come through earlier. More men ran past, a few slowing down, taking interest in me. Vincent put a stop to that by holding up the knife, and they scuttled away without a word.

Rowe stiffened at my back and moved in closer. I was sure he was thinking the same thing I was. That the pure number of men we were passing meant that this riot was only gaining momentum. More and more sections joining as time ticked by. Besides Rowe, I hadn't seen a guard the entire time, and though we knew there were police on the outside, none of them had made an attempt to enter. I had no idea what they were waiting for. Everything seemed to be taking hours, though it had probably only been thirty minutes since Vincent had slit DeWitt's throat.

The only good thing was the fire had to be out. Otherwise the entire building would be ablaze by now. It was a relief to know I probably wouldn't die of smoke inhalation.

Vincent led the way into the solitary confinement section, yanking open a heavy door and pushing me in ahead of him. I jumped at a shuddering thud to my left. A face was pressed to the tiny glass window, the man's fists beating against the door, while he screamed a bout of incomprehensible language that might not have even been English.

I shrank away, heart pounding.

Vincent wasn't bothered. He strolled without flinching down the middle of the corridor as new horrors started up from behind the doors of the other cells. Howling. Screaming. Crying. Men desperate to get out. Some yelled death threats, promising violence if we didn't free them.

"At least they had the sense to keep these doors locked," Rowe muttered. "Psych ward is overcrowded, and a lot of them ended up in here."

I flinched away from a hysterical scream on my right, and Vincent squeezed my arm reassuringly. "This is why I brought you here. These men are dangerous. But you'll be safe when you're locked inside."

Fear crawled its way up my throat at the thought of

being locked in one of those tiny rooms. "You don't need to do that," I pleaded. "I can help with whatever you're planning."

"No. It will be quicker if I go alone. Officer Pritchard and Heath will stay with you. You'll be fine."

He took in my expression. "You believe me, don't you?"

I agreed quickly, not wanting to upset him again.

He led me right to the very end of the corridor, and for that, at least, I was grateful. The noises from the other prisoners were dulled back here, but when Vincent pointed to an open cell my panic started up in earnest. The room was claustrophobic. I was sure if I held my arms out, I'd be able to touch the wall on both sides. There was a bench with a padded mat to one side, and the toilet at the far end. But other than that, it was just bare gray walls with only a small window covered by bars for light during the day.

I wanted to turn around and run but I knew he wasn't going to let me go.

Vincent waited until Heath and Rowe followed me in. "Look after her. I'll be back soon."

None of us said anything. We just watched Vincent pull the door closed behind him. For a long moment I just stared, willing my legs to not give out as the adrenaline that had fueled me since the beginning disappeared.

Heath caught me. His strong arms wrapped around me, holding me up. He crushed me to his chest, pressing his lips to the top of my head. "Shh. It's okay. I got you. He's gone."

My flight-or-fight response had kept me from fully

feeling, kept me from really letting in the danger of the situation. There hadn't been time. It had all been a single-minded focus to get away from DeWitt, to stay on Vincent's good side, to get Tori and Colt to help.

I couldn't hold it together anymore.

Heath cupped my face, wiping tears away with his thumbs, before lowering his head and kissing my lips.

It was exactly what I needed. I soaked in his strength, gulping in great, heaving lungfuls of his scent and letting it soothe my frayed nerves. His tongue ran the seam of my mouth, and I opened for him, just wanting everything around us to fade away.

At some point soon, the cops would come in. Once that happened, I wouldn't get to do this again until he was released. Nobody knew how long that would be, and I didn't want to regret not taking the moment while I had it. Whatever we had right now, in this tiny cell in the middle of a hellhole, was all I had to get me through until we got him out.

"Get off her."

I wrenched away from Heath and spun to stare at Rowe.

He wasn't looking at me, though. He stared Heath down, rage glittering in his eyes.

"Rowe, don't," I protested. "It's fine—"

"It's not. He's a prisoner."

I clenched my fingers around Heath's. "He didn't do it. You know that."

Rowe's shoulders were stiff, as unyielding as his stick-in-the-mud personality. "Until it's proven in court—"

My irritation bubbled over. I crossed the tiny gap between us and shoved my palms against his chest. "Why do you always have to be such a stickler for the rules? Just...stop. Can't you give him this one thing? Can't you give *me* this one thing? Bend the rules one damn time, Rowe!"

"It's not about the rules," Heath interrupted.

I glanced up at him. A muscle ticked in his jaw. His gaze didn't leave Rowe's, though, neither of them willing to back down.

Rowe ground his molars. "Tell me what it's about then, Michaelson. Since you seem to think you know it all." He finally looked at me. "You can't seriously expect me to stand here and watch while a prisoner feels up a woman. Should I stand here and watch him fuck you as well?"

I blinked at the harshness of his words and the cruel tone in his voice. That wasn't like him. We gave each other a hard time, but he wasn't normally mean-spirited.

Heath's gaze raked over Rowe in a slow roll, taking him in and sizing him up. "You're jealous. You want her, too."

Rowe froze. That same spark of energy—an unbridled desire—burned in the air around them. My gaze bounced between them, and I realized Heath had hit the nail on the head.

Only, with the way they stared at each other, I wasn't entirely sure it was me Rowe wanted.

I stepped between them again and put one hand on Rowe's chest, more gently this time. "Is that true?"

He wrenched his gaze away from Heath and stared down at me. He didn't say a word, confusion and indecision replacing the fire in his eyes.

"Is it true?" I whispered again. My heart thumped

unevenly.

There was something between Rowe and me. Something that had been there since day one. It had been kicked and beaten and shoved down, neither of us willing to act on it, but that chemistry just bubbled away, simmering beneath the surface.

"No." He went to turn away.

But it was too late. I'd seen it. The lie. The flash of disappointment.

I reached up, touching the side of his face, and forcing him to face me. "Liar."

He jerked away like I'd branded him, the desire in his eyes turning to anger once more. He looked as though he wanted to pace, but the tiny cell with three of us inside gave him no room to do so. He threw his hands up in frustration instead. "Fine, Mae. What do you want me to say? That I care about you? That I want you? That I can't stand the sight of his hands on you because I wish it were me? You made your choice. You're with him. Or Liam. Fuck, I don't know. I don't get to do that with you. I get it. But I'm not going to stand here and fucking watch."

I faltered, a stupid daydream shattering into smithereens. Because he was right. My head had been filled with ideas of the three of them—Rowe, Heath, and Liam. Liam had encouraged them by being open to the idea of sharing. And seeing Colt happy with his family had lulled me into the idea that a four-person relationship could work. Somewhere along the way, I'd gotten lost in those daydreams, not really thinking about the fact that Heath and Rowe wouldn't feel the same.

"Kiss her," Heath growled.

I spun around, staring at him with big eyes.

Rowe tensed. "No."

Heath took a step toward him, until the two of them were chest to chest. Heath had an inch of height on Rowe, both of them towering over me, but Rowe didn't back down. His fingers clenched into fists at his side.

"Kiss her," Heath growled again. "Quit fucking around and pretending you don't want her. It's written in every inch of your body right now."

"Why?" Rowe spat back. "What do you fucking care?"

"Because I know you want to. And more, because I know she wants you to." He paused, and the tension between the two men thickened until it was practically palpable. "And because I want to watch."

Rowe and I both stared at Heath. My stomach flipped, and my head spun in dizzying circles. But overwhelmingly, it was the heat that had me in a tailspin. It flashed up from deep inside me, hardening my nipples, tingling my clit, and opening up a yearning ache inside me that begged for Rowe to do it.

His breaths turned ragged, ripped from his lungs like Heath's words had sucked the air from the room.

In one move, he made his decision. Rowe spun on me, pushed me up against the wall, and lowered his head.

I gasped as his big body crowded me in, his solid chest pressed to mine.

"Is he right? Do you want me to kiss you?"

I swallowed, drowning in the depths of his dark eyes. His lips were so close to mine that our breaths mingled. I went to see past him to Heath, but Rowe blocked my view. "Don't look at him. Tell me you want it."

"I want you—"

His lips slammed down on mine. He wasted no time,

opening his mouth and seeking entrance I was all too happy to give. I dug my fingers into his shoulders, clutching him to me, and closing my eyes to fall into the kiss. He stole my breath, and the gaping hole of need inside me worsened into a chasm. Our tongues dueled, the kiss deep and wet and mind-blowing.

With a groan of frustration, Rowe pulled away. For the tiniest of seconds, he closed his eyes, squeezing them tight. Then he ran his hand through his hair and turned to Heath. "Happy?"

Heath didn't say a word.

The main door opened with a bang, shattering the moment. The prisoners started up their complaints once more as boots thumped down the hall. I braced myself for Vincent's reappearance, while I tried to catch my breath after Rowe's kiss.

It was only when the fully masked riot squad officer peered through the tiny window that I remembered Vincent wasn't even wearing boots.

"Mae Donovan?" the officer yelled.

I nodded. "Yes! That's me." I flashed him my ID badge.

He pointed a gun at the window. "Prisoners! Get to the back of the room."

Heath immediately did as he was told. His pinkie finger brushed mine when he moved past, and I grabbed his hand. "Heath..."

He squeezed my fingers back but then let me go. "End of the road for you, sweetheart."

I suddenly didn't want to leave. Not without him.

The riot officer tapped his gun against the glass once more. "You! Move back."

Rowe frowned. "I'm a guard. I need to get out, too."

"Where's your ID?"

Rowe went for his tag, patting his chest where it normally hung. Then he closed his eyes. "I gave it to Perry in the guards' office." He turned to the officer. "I've lost it. I'm Rowe Pritchard." He gestured to the uniform he wore. "Obviously a guard."

"Not without ID. We've got half the prison running around in guard uniforms. The only person I'm authorized to bring out is Mae Donovan and guards with ID."

Rowe gaped at him. "So what? I just sit here in a jail cell with a prisoner?"

"Until we can confirm you aren't a prisoner yourself, that's exactly what you do. Sit tight. I'll get someone up here ASAP."

He wouldn't meet my eye. He moved to the back of the room, standing shoulder to shoulder with Heath. But while Heath's gaze sought mine out, Rowe wouldn't look at me at all. He stared down at his feet. The officer spoke into his radio, and then the mechanical click of the deadbolts sliding free sounded. The door swung open, and two men stormed in. One grabbed me by the arms.

Though I'd been waiting for this moment, it had suddenly come too soon. I held Heath's gaze, dragging my heels, until the very last second.

That last second belonged to Rowe. But when his gaze met mine, I almost wished it hadn't.

His eyes were like stone. Hard. Cold. Unfeeling.

Nothing like the man who'd just kissed me. When I was hurried through the prison and out a side exit, I didn't even know existed, I wondered how I could have feelings for two such different men.

8

LIAM

*O*utside the prison, a swarm of people circled the main entrance, held back only by flimsy police tape. Two officers stood together nervously, jumping at every shout, their gazes bouncing around the crowd, hands hovering over their Tasers.

I pushed my way to the front of the crowd made up of reporters and family members.

"What's going on inside, Officers?" the woman next to me called. "Is it true inmates have taken all sections of the prison? That a complete 'Nobody in, nobody out' emergency protocol has been instated?"

The officers looked her way. "I'm not at liberty to say."

"What about the smoke coming from the south wing? Any word on what that was?"

"Smoke?" I asked her.

She nodded and pointed to the far end of the building. "There was smoke reported at that end earlier, but whatever was on fire must have been put out because it didn't get any worse."

Mae's schoolroom was in the south block.

"Hey!" a man yelled to my left. "We have a right to know about our family in there!"

The officer cast a stern glare at the man. "Settle down. As soon as we know anything, we'll pass on the information. Let us do our jobs."

No. That wasn't good enough. I tugged at the collar of my shirt, my skin beading with sweat despite the night air. My heart hammered against my chest. "What about the employees? Are there any casualties? My...."

My what? I'd wanted to say my girlfriend. But that wasn't true. "Mae Donovan. She's the prison teacher and she was scheduled on tonight."

"Buddy, I don't know anything. I keep telling you that —" He cut himself off and pressed two fingers to his earpiece. He listened for a moment, then stood a little straighter. "Right, everybody needs to move back. We've got officers bringing out casualties."

"You're bringing them outside the prison gates?" the reporter questioned.

"It's a civilian."

My heart sank. And even before two masked riot police came running down the path with a woman between them, I knew it would be Mae.

Cameras flashed around me, lighting up the dark, and a ripple of shocked conversation moved through the crowd.

My feet moved as if on autopilot. I broke the tape and ran for her, gaze running all over her body searching for injuries. "Mae!" Her name fell from my lips on a hoarse shout.

The police came at me, Tasers at the ready. "Get back!"

I blinked and dug my heels into the grass. I held my hands up like they were about to arrest me. "Whoa. Whoa. I'm her..."

There it was again. That urge to claim her as my own. My gaze met Mae's.

"...lawyer."

It killed me to say it. I'd never hated the word more.

"That true, Miss?"

Mae nodded slowly. "Yes. Please let him through."

The officers stepped aside, letting me pass. I ran up the slight incline while she argued with the riot police until they let her come to me. We met in the middle of the hill. She stared up at me, face streaked with ash, tears making two tracks through the grime.

All pretense of just being her lawyer went out the window. I wrapped my arms around her while she buried her face in my chest.

"Are you hurt?" I murmured into her hair. "The police said they were bringing out casualties."

She shook her head against my chest. "I'm fine. I just want to go home."

That I could do. We skirted the crowd with my arm around her shoulders, shielding her from the press.

"She can't leave!" one of the cops yelled. "We need to question her."

"Not tonight you don't. Lawyer, remember? She has rights, and we're using them."

The press lost interest as we moved farther away from the prison. I rubbed her arm soothingly and steered her toward my car on the street.

She was quiet when she got inside, slowly pulling on her seat belt, as if it hurt her to move any quicker.

"Are you sure you're okay?" I asked. "Do you want to go to the hospital?"

She shook her head, pulling her legs up beneath her, and staring out the window.

The miles flew by on the way to her apartment, but the closer we got to her home, the more worried I became. I'd never seen Mae so quiet. So withdrawn. Her skin was pale and clammy, and it killed me not to pepper her with questions about what had happened.

"My things are still at the prison," she murmured. "They hustled me out before I could even ask to grab anything."

"Superintendent will have a spare key, right?"

She nodded, and after a short conversation with an older man who lived on the ground floor, we took the elevator to her apartment, keys clutched tightly in her grip.

She rested her spare hand on the knob and poked the key toward the lock, but her hand shook so hard she couldn't insert it.

"Here. Let me." I put my hand over hers, steadying her grip and inserting the key.

The door swung open, but Mae just stood there staring at her empty apartment.

"You're really worrying me," I said quietly. "The hospital..."

She shook her head again. "Can you stay? Please?"

My heart lurched. "Of course." I locked the door behind us and then led her to the couch.

She stared blankly at the wall, our breaths the only sound in the otherwise silent room.

After a long moment, the silence got to me. I couldn't take it anymore. I pushed to my feet. "No. You need a doctor."

She snapped her head toward me and then reached for my hand. "I'm sorry," she whispered.

I sat back down and gripped her hand tighter. "Just talk to me. Please. I don't know what happened in there, but if they hurt you—"

"I watched a man die. And there was a fire..."

I blanched. "Jesus, Mae. I don't even know what to say to that."

"None of it even seems real. And you know what I feel worst about?" She stared up at me with big eyes. "I kissed Heath." She let out a near hysterical-sounding laugh as she shook her head, then lowered it, hunching over to wrap her arms around her knees.

"Okay," I said slowly.

She glanced at me in surprise. "Is that all you're going to say?"

What else was there to say? That my heart was snapping in two, but that I knew this day would come? I'd been a stand-in for Heath this entire time. She'd come to me in love with the man. I knew that. And yet I'd taken a little for myself. I'd let myself have a tiny part of her, even though I knew her heart belonged to someone else. I'd pay the price now, but I wouldn't make her feel bad about it. I'd gone in with my eyes open. "You're in love with him."

"I think I always have been."

I raised one shoulder, trying to be casual. "You had to take your chance. I get it."

She lifted sad eyes to me, and I couldn't stand it.

I didn't want her pity. "Don't worry about it."

"I feel like I betrayed you."

I shook my head hard. "Never. We had some fun for old times' sake. But I knew your heart wasn't with me. It was fun while it lasted." Even though it killed me, I shifted a little so we weren't touching. "Maybe we can actually be friends now, though?" I had to force the words out. "Might be nice if it wasn't our school reunion before we meet up again."

She frowned. "Is that what you really want?"

I paused. I wanted to scream that no, of course that wasn't what I wanted. I'd never wanted to be just friends with her, but friends was better than not having her in my life at all. I knew all about what it felt like to want someone and not have them feel the same way back. "I want whatever makes you happy."

She buried her face in her hands once more. "Why say that, Liam? I kissed Rowe tonight, too. Does that change your response?"

Heat flushed through me at the thought of her kissing both men. "We talked about it..."

"But talking is different to actually doing it."

I shook my head, and I couldn't help it. The over-whelming need to touch her won out over common sense. I put my hand on her thigh, squeezing it gently. "Is this why you've gone all quiet? Because of who you kissed tonight?"

"I feel like shit about it."

A little relief seeped in. "Fuck, Mae. When I heard

there was a riot at the prison, all I could see was someone hurting you. Someone forcing themselves on you. All I care about is that you're safe. Not that you kissed Heath. Or Rowe. The only reason I could breathe while you were in there was because I knew they'd find you."

"You're okay with them protecting me?" Her eyes were watery when she looked up at me.

I nodded.

"Could you be okay if they were more than that?" Something changed in her tone.

The fear seeped away, and desire crept in.

Heat flushed through me. We'd joked about it before, after she'd dreamed of the four of us together. But this felt different. This felt real and raw. Honest.

"I don't know."

Her gaze dropped to the floor. "I understand."

"Tell me."

Her head lifted once more, frown firmly etched on her face. "Tell you what?"

"Tell me how you felt when you kissed them."

Her breath caught. "Scared," she admitted. "Relieved. And then...hot."

I pictured it in my head. The three of them, danger swirling around them but lost in the touch of each other. "If you could have, would you have taken those kisses further?"

"Liam..." She stared at my lap, her gaze resting on my dick thickening behind the sweat pants I'd worn to practice.

"Tell me, Mae. I need to picture it. The three of you."

"Yes," she whispered. "I would have taken it further. I wanted them to."

I didn't miss the way her nipples strained hard behind her shirt. I inched closer, running my hand up her leg, fingers dipping between her thighs but stopping short of touching her center. "Close your eyes," I whispered. "Then tell me what you wanted them to do."

Her breath came out in a shudder, and her dark lashes drifted down, fanning out as her eyelids closed.

"He kissed me." She didn't specify which man, but it didn't matter. She leaned against me heavily, her thighs parting a little.

I massaged her leg softly, inhaling the scent of her. "Here," I asked, nosing up her neck before letting my lips touch the sensitive part behind her ear. God, her skin was soft.

"No," she whispered.

I let my lips trail down her jawline, until I hovered over her mouth. "Here." It was less of a question this time.

Her lips parted. "Yes."

"Did he kiss you soft and slow?" I leaned in and touched my lips to hers. It was barely a featherlight caress, but I kept it up, teasing her lips with my tongue until she opened and let me devour her. Our tongues slid together, a slow, sensual roll that had blood rushing to my dick. I kissed her until I wanted to lay her out and make love with her.

I forced myself to pull back. She was breathless, her gaze unfocussed. Her fingers snaked into the hair at the nape of my neck and tugged me down to her once more. "Heath kisses like that. Like he wants to wrap me in cotton and protect me from the world. But Rowe kisses like he wants to burn it down."

"Show me."

Our lips crashed together. Her tongue pressed into my mouth, hard and hot, and her groan of need told me exactly what she wanted. In a second, I had her on her back, soft couch cushion beneath her while my weight pinned her down. I plundered her mouth, giving her the heat she wanted. My erection ground against her leg, thickening and straining inside my pants, begging to search out her core.

"Liam," she moaned.

The sound of my name on her lips spurred me on. They weren't here to give her what she needed. But I was. I'd be here for as long as she'd let me.

"Where did you want him, Mae?"

She only kissed me harder.

"Did you want his mouth on you?"

She didn't answer, but fuck, I was dying to do it. I dug my knees into the couch either side of her hips and yanked up her T-shirt. She scrambled to pull it off, but I was too impatient to undo her bra. I slid the straps down her arms and flipped the cups down, exposing her perfect tits.

Her nipples strained toward me, two sweet peaks just begging for my mouth. I pinched one between two fingers, while dragging the other into my mouth. She gasped and struggled with my shirt buttons, fighting to get them undone around what I was doing.

I didn't care about me. I just wanted her. As much of her as she'd let me have in case this was the last time.

I licked and sucked and then switched to love on her other breast. She was more than a handful. She spilled over my hands, and I ran my tongue over every inch of her swells, loving that she was soft and curvy.

I moved down her body, peppering kisses across her soft belly, pausing at the elastic of her long skirt. Her fingers stroked through my hair, nails scratching across my scalp which only bolstered my erection.

"Did you want his fingers between your legs?"

Her groan of arousal was nothing compared to the way she writhed beneath me, spreading her knees. I yanked her skirt down, taking her panties with it. My fingers drifted over the neat patch of hair at the junction of her thighs and delighted in the sweet pink of her slit beneath. I leaned down and kissed her again while my fingers found her slick heat. I coated them in her arousal, pressing two of them up inside her with ease, then rubbing it into her clit. She ground against me, gyrating her hips, searching for my fingers to fill her again. I gave her what she wanted, thrusting them deep inside her, brushing her G-spot, before sliding out to work her clit.

Three more times I did that, until little cries of pleasure fell from her lips and her pussy widened enough to take a third finger.

"No," she moaned.

I stopped immediately. "You don't like it?"

She blinked her eyes open. "I love it. But that's not what I was thinking about when he was kissing me."

She pushed me back, and I stood to let her up off the couch. My hot gaze swept her body, watching while she undid the bra band around her middle and let it fall to the floor. She was so gloriously naked while I was still fully clothed, apart from a few buttons she'd managed to work lose. Like some goddess born from the earth, she closed the distance between us, her rounded hips swaying when she walked. She gripped my collar and brought her face close to mine. "I wasn't thinking about him touching me. I was thinking about me touching him."

Heat flared in her eyes and she dropped to her knees on the soft carpet, her tits bouncing with the impact.

I groaned as she freed my dick, my pants and underwear pooling around my feet. She gripped my base with one hand and my balls with the other. I hissed and thrust my fingers deep into her hair, wrapping the silky lengths around my fist when her mouth closed over my tip.

"Fuck, Mae," I bit out, fighting the urge to thrust deep and fast into her warmth. The idea that she'd been thinking about doing this with Rowe or Heath only spurred me on. I closed my eyes and imagined her on her knees in front of the three of us. My dick kicked at the thought of her as eager to please us as we would be to please her.

There was no jealousy in the idea. Just heat, and pure, unyielding desire to make her scream.

I opened my eyes, and my gaze met hers. Her cheeks hollowed out, sucking me off, her head bobbing and her hand working in unison. But her pleasure was my pleasure. And though I loved her mouth around me, I wanted her just as turned on.

"Put one hand between your legs, Mae. I want to see your fingers shining with how wet you are."

She moaned around my cock and eagerly dropped one hand to her snatch. She pushed her fingers between her folds, yelping as she touched her swollen clit, and pressed them up inside herself. Her eyes rolled back, and on the verge of coming myself, I pulled from her mouth and got down on the carpet with her. I kissed her hard, encouraging her back onto her ass and then onto her back. Her legs spread wide around my hips, and my cock lined up at her entrance.

My knob slicked through her juices, but I paused short of pushing inside her. "I want to fuck you bare."

What I didn't say was why.

But I knew.

I wanted to mark her. Spill myself inside her so I could pretend she was mine. Even though I knew her heart was elsewhere.

"Yes," she moaned. "I want that, too. Please."

But the responsible side of me won out. "I'm clean, but birth control..."

She shook her head. "I can't... You don't need to worry about it."

I didn't need to question her. I trusted her with everything I had, and if she said we were good, then I wasn't going to waste another second. I hooked my arms beneath her knees and threw her legs over my shoulders. Then I plunged in deep, sinking inside her.

She clamped down on me immediately, crying out as her orgasm barreled into her. A manly pride washed over me, that she'd been so ready she could come that fast. I gave her a moment, thrusting slowly while I fought my own urge to come. God, she was tight when she came. Her internal walls were like nothing I'd ever felt before. I'd never gone bare with a woman. I was always so careful and had never trusted anyone the way I trusted her. I always wore condoms because in the back of my mind, there was the thought that I could knock a woman up if I didn't. Then I'd be linked to a woman I didn't know for the rest of my life. What if she was an awful mother? What if she wouldn't let me see the child and I became the deadbeat dad I'd grown up with? Or grown up without since mine had never been in the picture.

Mae was different. And my head was full of crazy thoughts about her.

Thoughts that her having my baby would be the best thing that ever happened to me.

Her moans of pleasure brought me back to the moment, and I realized she was close to falling over the edge again. Her legs trembled, and I picked up the pace, pounding into her harder and faster. My fingers found her sensitive bundle of nerves and pinched it between two fingers, squeezing then releasing in time with my thrusts into her core.

Her eyes opened wide, shock all over her expression. "I'm going to come again. I didn't...I can't..."

"You can. Come, baby. Let go."

Her back arched as if she'd been electrocuted, and the scream she let out was pure music to my ears. I fell into the abyss with her, closing my eyes, sparks dancing in the darkness. My cock buried deep in her pussy, I came with a yell of my own, words that made no sense but all portrayed the same one feeling.

That she was everything. Everything I'd ever wanted. Everything I'd ever need.

And that if she wanted me, Heath, Rowe, or any other man, I'd give it to her. Because all I could think about was making her happy. Making her whole again. She needed them, and I needed her. I just prayed there'd be a spot in her heart for me, too.

9

ROWE

*T*he door closed with a solid thunk, and I rushed forward, pressing my face to the cell window. I watched until the riot police hustled Mae around the corner and out of sight.

She didn't look back.

I couldn't blame her.

Anger swirled deep in my gut. It was a buildup of everything that had gone wrong tonight. The guilt over Tori being grabbed by an inmate. The fact I'd left Mae alone and then couldn't get to her when a fire threatened her life. That I was here in a cell with Heath instead of out there, doing my damn job.

Every muscle in my body wound tight, stiffening until I was sure I'd explode if something didn't give.

I roared into the silent room, slamming the heel of my hand into the door. "Goddammit!"

"Settle down."

I spun around and glared at Heath, sitting on the bed mat and leaning against the wall, hands tucked behind his head like he didn't have a care in the world. His eyes were closed, as if he were sitting out on some porch, face turned up to the sun. My gaze strayed to the way his biceps popped in that pose, but all too quickly the anger fire consumed all errant thoughts. "You knew," I spat out. "Didn't you?"

He cracked one eye open. "I know a lot of shit, Pritchard. So you're going to have to be more specific."

His relaxed attitude only pissed me off further. "You knew what was happening here tonight. You and DeWitt and Vincent. Who else was in on it?"

He opened his eyes and sat forward slowly, his palms coming to rest on his thighs. His broad shoulders stretched the ugly orange of his prison-issue clothes. "No. I didn't know."

"Bullshit," I yelled. "This thing moved too quick for you all to not be in on it. You must have been planning this for weeks for it to go off so effortlessly. I hope you fucking enjoyed it. Because you know what's going to happen now?"

He didn't say anything, but his entire posture stiffened, and his fingers curled into the material of his pants.

I laughed, the sound hard and bitter. "No, of course you didn't think about the consequences, did you?" I cracked my knuckles. "Let me tell you. Here's what happens after a prison riot, no matter how long they go on for. We get back the control. Sure, you have it now. But you won't hold it. You can't. At some point, you run out of food. Or they cut the electricity and water. Or they storm this place with so many police officers that you're outnumbered four to one."

Heath's eyes glittered as he pushed to his feet. "Don't

lump me in with them like I belong here. I don't."

I took a step closer so we were eye to eye. "You forget I've read your rap sheet. So whether or not I believe you killed Jayela Donovan is irrelevant. You might have Mae fooled but you're no saint."

His fingers clenched into fists at his sides. "I'm so sick of this. What the fuck is your problem? You've had it out for me since day one."

"No more than any other prisoner."

His hand came up to my shoulders and shoved me. My back hit the cold wall, and Heath followed in until we were chest to chest. "Fuck you. You've had it in for me from the moment you realized there was something between me and Mae. It's got nothing to do with what happened in my past. Admit it. You're jealous as fuck of what she and I have."

"You have nothing! What the hell can you do for her, locked behind bars with no out in sight? You might have stolen a kiss tonight, but she kissed me, too, asshole."

"Because you didn't have the balls to do it! I've been watching you pussyfoot around her for weeks. Grow a pair, Rowe. Go after what you want." He glared at me, a challenge in his eyes.

"You have no fucking idea what I want." The words slipped out before I could really think them through.

Something changed in the air around us. It charged with electricity, sharp and stinging. I drew in a breath, trying to fill my lungs, but it was suddenly as if I'd forgotten how.

Heath didn't let up for an instant. "Then tell me."

His gaze dipped to my lips.

The lock on the door disengaged, and I snapped my

head to the right as Vincent came back in. He stopped and dumped an armload of supplies on the floor at his feet, a huge grin plastered across his face before he registered the room.

His gaze flickered over me and Heath, inches away from each other, chests heaving. I straightened uncomfortably, heat flushing through my body at the thought of where that argument had been going. Vincent had to be able to read the situation and understand what might have happened if he hadn't walked in.

I knew.

"Where's Mae?" Vincent asked quietly.

Heath dragged his gaze away from me and turned it on the younger man. "The cops took her."

"No they didn't." Vincent shook his head. "No. I left her here. Safe with you."

"She's still safe," Heath said quietly. "They got her out. That's what we wanted, right?"

But Vincent shook his head, his eyes narrowing. "No! We were all supposed to go together." He turned his dark eyed gaze on me. "This is his fault. He wasn't part of the plan."

The anger inside me roared again. I knew my instincts had been right. Heath had been in on the whole thing. But Mae had planned to help them? That was a punch to the gut.

Shame heated my cheeks. What an idiot I'd been. I'd known all along that her motives in working here hadn't been just about giving the inmates the education they deserved. I'd been wary of her and Heath's relationship from the beginning, but I'd ignored my gut and let myself like her. Let myself care about her.

I was a fucking fool.

Heath stepped between me and Vincent. "Not his fault, Vincent."

Thumping boots sounded on the concrete once more, and then a heavy fist thumped against the door. "Inmates against the wall! Rowe Pritchard, you're authorized for removal."

Heath's gaze met mine.

I was a fucking idiot. They'd both played me like a fiddle. I should have known better. "You heard him," I ground out. "Get against the wall." Then in a louder voice I told the riot squad, "They're armed."

When the police stormed in, it was nothing like when they'd brought Mae out. In seconds, all three of us were pinned against a wall, my cheek smushed to the cinderblock while I was patted down.

Barely a foot away, Heath stood completely still in the same position, staring at me with his golden-flecked stare. His expression spoke all the words his mouth wasn't saying. It screamed of unfairness and betrayal. But fuck him. That one moment of attraction didn't mean I owed him anything. He'd planned a prison riot in an attempt to escape. If those weren't the actions of a guilty man then I didn't know what were. And Mae had helped him. I'd have to report her, too.

Fuck this. Fuck the whole thing. I hated all of it. Most of all I hated that my body was still somehow drawn to his, even though my brain knew better.

When the riot squad led me away, I told myself to not look back.

And hated that I couldn't do it.

10

MAE

Screams echoed down the hall.

They woke me from sleep, my mouth dry, and the undeniable nausea of a hangover turning my stomach. I peered through the darkness, trying to work out where I was when the screams came again.

"Jayela," I whispered, suddenly recognizing my room and the screams that came from the other end of our apartment. I stumbled out of bed and ran blindly down the hall, crashing into the walls in my hurry to get to my sister.

I threw her bedroom door open, her navy walls and white trim familiar. I'd helped her paint those walls the weekend we'd moved in. But even in the darkness of the night, something felt off. Dark spatter covered the paint we'd so painstakingly applied, and something deep inside me knew it wasn't just a shadow.

The scream came again, catching my attention, but this time it was more of a gurgle. My gaze snapped to the bed, and my sister's eyes, wide and pleading, hands reaching for me.

My feet wouldn't move.

I was as pinned down as she was, watching the whole thing play out, no ability to stop any of it from happening,

The man hovering over her, silver knife in his hand, looked over at me. He smiled, his white teeth shining in the darkness. "Hello, Miss Donovan."

"Mae!"

"Don't touch me!" I jerked against the grip on my arms, and it immediately disappeared.

Nothing like how Vincent had held me. When I'd tried to get away from him, he'd only held me tighter.

A light flicked on, and I blinked in the brightness.

Liam hovered on the other side of my bed, his features etched with worry. His knees dug into the mattress, his chest bare, hair tousled with sleep. "You were dreaming...I didn't mean to..." His expression was so tortured. He jabbed his fingers through his hair. "Shit, Mae. I never meant to scare you."

I launched myself across the bed at him, wrapping my arms around his neck and holding on.

The tension flooded out of him immediately, and he put his arms around me, his warm skin so comforting beneath my palms. I ran my hands up and down his back, but it wasn't enough. I needed more to take away the memory of that dream. To drive out the horrifying images of Vincent murdering my sister.

They weren't real. But Liam was. I pulled back and lifted my oversized T-shirt over my head. I wore nothing beneath it but panties, and when Liam engulfed me in his arms once more, the skin-to-skin contact of our bodies was overwhelmingly more comforting than when there'd been clothing between us. I pulled his mouth down to mine and kissed him deeply, tasting him, relishing in the fact he made me feel safe and cared for.

"Hey," he murmured against my mouth. "Talk to me."

"Vincent...one of my students...he admitted last night to killing my sister. I dreamed I saw him do it. I walked right into her room and saw her last moments."

"Fuck," he muttered. Then he kissed me again, knowing what would help without me having to say it.

I just needed him. His hands. His tongue. His body. I needed him on top of me, blocking out the rest of the world, narrowing mine down to nothing but us.

Everything else was too hard. Too big.

Last night had been about Rowe and Heath.

This morning Liam was all I wanted.

"I need you," I whispered. "I can't stop seeing it. The dream...it was too real."

His lips brushed the shell of my ear, and a shiver ran down my spine. "It wasn't real. This is. You and me, okay?"

I nodded, closing my eyes when his palms skated down my sides, his fingers tucking into my panties and dragging them down my legs. Tears welled behind my eyelids as I fought to free my mind from the horrors in my head. But I wouldn't cry any more. That wasn't the release I was after.

Liam knew. I ran my fingernails over his scalp while he moved down my body, bypassing my breasts and heading straight for my core.

The first lap of his tongue was heaven. Wet and warm,

soaking my center and setting off pleasure receptors that lit me up from the inside. His fingers massaged the tight muscles of my thighs until I relaxed and let my legs fall out, completely displaying myself for him in the low glow of lamplight.

His tongue circled my clit, building the anticipation, then when I didn't think I could wait a second longer, he sucked the tiny bud, flicking it until my arousal coated his tongue.

"You taste so damn good."

I believed him. I stared down at him between my thighs and watched as he worked my body to the brink of orgasm. His fingers thrust up inside me, one at a time, and alternated with the flat of his tongue. Each stroke drove me higher, our gazes met, and he watched me watch him.

"I want to blow your mind," he whispered.

But I heard the words he wasn't saying.

I want to take your nightmare away.

I want to take away all the bad things that happened.

I can't do any of that, but I can give you this.

I nodded. Giving him permission to work my body in any way he wanted.

I gave him my trust.

He lowered his head and then pressed his finger deep inside me. He rubbed it over my G-spot tantalizingly, waiting for my hips to rock. When I lifted my ass, seeking more, he caught me, holding me still so he could put a pillow beneath me. His finger trailed a leisurely path around my inner thighs, while I trembled in anticipation. I wanted to urge him on and at the same time, I wanted to enjoy every second.

Because every second he drew this out was a second I didn't have to think about anything else.

He licked through my folds slowly, building me up again at this new angle. His tongue worked my sensitive flesh over and over, licking high up over my clit, then lower, to thrust inside me. Then lower again, spreading me wide where I'd never had a man's tongue before.

My eyes flew open. "Liam!"

He grinned up at me from between my thighs. "Mmm?"

"I...um..."

"You're really fucking cute when you blush."

I didn't need to put a hand to my cheeks to feel how hot they were.

Liam placed a kiss on my inner thigh. "Question is, are you blushing because you're embarrassed? Or is that pink in your cheeks there because you liked it and that surprises the good girl inside you?"

He lowered his head and did it again.

His tongue flickered over my ass, and I nearly jerked off the bed when sensation, longing, and a very real need for more hit me like a sledgehammer.

"Which is it, Miss Valedictorian? No one has ever touched you there, have they?"

There was no use lying about how vanilla my sex life had been. Until him, I'd never really done anything much more than missionary position in a bed. I'd definitely never had a man who seemed delighted by the prospect of tonguing my ass, just to get me off.

I'd never had anyone care about my pleasure the way Liam did.

"No," I admitted. "I've never even... My ex wasn't into that..." That blush heated my cheeks again.

"A complete anal virgin? Fuck me. That's hot. And those other guys don't know what they're missing. I'd give anything to take you there right now." He trailed his finger from my pussy to the puckered star below, rubbing my arousal there until I relaxed.

When he added a finger to my pussy, I closed my eyes and let go. The sensation was too much. His mouth on my clit, one finger deep inside my body, the other rimming my ass.

It was like nothing I'd ever felt before. An overwhelming sensation to be touched so intimately in three places at once and by a man who was so damn sexy he made my legs tremble even when he wasn't deep inside me. He drew it out, licking and teasing me for what felt like an hour.

Every time I got close to orgasm, every time those feelings intensified, he backed off, slowing it down.

The third time he did it, I wasn't letting him stop. I rolled my hips up, spread my legs as wide as I could, giving up any semblance that I didn't want him in every way possible. I was so wet, so needy and aching to have him inside me. I wanted his dick in my mouth. I wanted it in my pussy. His constant attention on my ass had me wanting him everywhere and needing more than just a featherlight touch. I grasped the back of his head and held it where I wanted it. "Liam, please! I need to come."

He chuckled against my clit, the vibrations only revving me up more. He slipped two fingers tight inside my core for me to ride. My hips bucked and rolled, but each slide wasn't enough. I ground against the finger he held gently on my ass, pressing down harder.

"Your body is saying you want more, baby. But I need to hear it from your mouth, too. Tell me where you want it."

"My ass. God, Liam. I want to feel you there."

He groaned out loud, and so did I, not recognizing the words even falling from my lips. I was the good girl who got straight A's. I was the sweet schoolteacher. I was the little blonde baby who had always been protected by her badass older sister.

I wasn't this woman, splayed out across her bed, begging for a man to fuck her in the ass.

Except there was no shame in it with Liam. Liam made it seem like the hottest, sexiest thing in the world. And God, I wanted him.

With his fingers deep inside my pussy, he added an extra to my ass. I shouted at the intrusion, but it was because it felt entirely too good. I rode his hand, screaming his name, begging for him to let me finish.

Fireworks lit up behind my eyes, and I grabbed my breasts, squeezing my nipples as I found my edge. I fell over it, freefalling into a world of pure pleasure and pulsing nerve endings. I'd never felt anything like it. I could make myself come with a vibrator in less than five minutes. It did the job, but it was nothing like having an orgasm at the hands of someone who knew what they were doing.

And oh my God, did Liam know what he was doing.

He lapped at my clit, riding out my pleasure, wringing every last drop of me out until I was sure I'd go blind if he kept it up any longer.

I had to physically push his head and hands away for fear he'd just keep going and build me straight back up into a double.

He got up and disappeared into my bathroom, coming back a minute later with a warm, wet cloth. He pressed it between my legs and put his lips to my ear. "You were so fucking wet, Mae. Your arousal is everywhere. I've never seen anything so hot. You're incredible."

His lips covered mine, his tongue plunging into my mouth, tasting of me. But I kissed him back, sinking into it and relishing in how good my body felt.

I was still floating on a cloud of bliss when something occurred to me. I rolled onto my side to find him watching me. "You didn't... I thought you were going to..."

"Take your perfect fucking ass? Not today. I need to work you up to that. Or we do..."

I froze. "We, meaning..."

"Me, Heath, and Rowe. "

I stared at him in shock. But he just kissed my lips then got up, disappearing into the bathroom once again. The shower started up, and I desperately needed to join him, but I lay there for another whole minute, just thinking about his offer.

*L*iam was on my phone when I got out of the shower. I padded back into my bedroom, my body still singing with the aftereffects of my orgasm, and a new round of longing that lit up as I watched Liam talk wearing nothing but his underwear. He glanced over at me, and I cheekily dropped my towel.

His eyes widened, and he mouthed something that looked like, "Are you trying to kill me?" before turning around and facing the wall to finish his call. I giggled, the sound a surprise. It had been too long since I'd felt light enough to laugh. But the long shower had helped me put a few things together in my mind.

Last night had been awful. But it had also brought some closure. I still didn't know why, but at least I knew who had killed my sister. And once we went to the police with everything Vincent had told me, Heath would be free.

My heart lit up at the prospect of him walking out of those prison gates, maybe even as early as tonight.

I'd be there, waiting on the other side. With Liam at my side.

The thought made me dizzy.

I picked out clothes, while Liam finished his call. He put my phone down on the bedside table and watched me shimmy into my bra and panties. "That was Boston."

"Was he calling to say the riot is over? They got it under control, right?"

Guilt swamped me when I realized I'd spent all morning having mind-blowing sex while Heath and Rowe could still be locked in that solitary cell.

The pure selfishness of that realization was startling. "God, I can't believe I'm only just asking that now."

Liam shook his head. "You had a traumatic experience. You needed a minute to just be. Don't beat yourself up over taking what you need."

I knew he was right, but the guilt remained.

"That's not what Boston wanted to tell me anyway. He was calling to tell you he quit the police force last night."

My mouth dropped open. Boston, my sister's strait-laced partner, a man who seemingly lived and died by the law, had given it all up? "Are you sure you heard him right?"

Liam nodded. "He wants to talk to us. I told him we'd meet him for breakfast in fifteen minutes."

Thirteen minutes later, Liam and I were seated at a window table in a little café on the edge of the Providence/Saint View border. I ran my fingers along the edge of the white tablecloth, before taking an unsteady sip of water. I had no idea why, but nerves rattled my body. Things had been off with Boston ever since Jayela's death. He'd been hiding something, keeping secrets to the point I'd considered him a suspect, even though my heart wasn't really in it. Deep down, I knew Boston. He loved my sister, and he never would have hurt her.

But his actions lately were unsettling to say the least.

"Did he give you any indication of why he quit?" I asked Liam.

Liam tapped his fingers on the tabletop, gaze pinned to the doorway. "No. But you can ask him yourself. He's here."

I followed Liam's gaze and tried not to gasp. Boston made his way through the small room, edging around other patrons eating their extravagant breakfasts, and slumped into the seat across the table from Liam and me.

I didn't even know what to say. Every question that came to mind sounded incredibly rude in my head and would have sounded worse out loud.

Liam had no such qualms. "You look like shit, man. What the hell happened to you?"

Boston looked as if he'd aged ten years since I'd last

seen him. There were dark circles beneath his eyes, and a weariness to his expression that spoke of trauma. On instinct, I reached a hand across the table and gripped his. "Are you okay?"

Weariness seeped from his every pore. "I don't even know where to begin. Let's just say that last night wasn't only adventurous for you guys at the prison." His gaze raked over me, but not in the way that Liam's did. Boston's was in a brotherly fashion, full of concern. "I heard you were stuck in there for a while. You okay?"

"Fine. Heath had my back." It was a testing comment. Boston's police department had been the ones to arrest Heath in the first place. I'd fought and argued with Boston, begging him to listen to me when I told him that Heath had nothing to do with it. Boston had refused to listen.

He nodded now. "I'm not surprised."

"You're not? Last time we talked about this, you were pretty convinced that Heath was the scum of the earth."

He sighed heavily. "A lot has happened since then. That's why I'm here. I quit last night. It's not even worth going into all the reasons why."

"Does it have anything to do with a sassy strip club owner?" Liam asked. He shrugged at my inquisitive expression. "What? She asked me for his number. And you don't say no to Eve if you want to keep your balls intact."

I'd met Eve once, when Liam had taken me to her club. That night had ended in a spray of bullets and Boston showing up, absolutely fuming. We'd left with him and Eve at each other's throats. But obviously it hadn't ended there for them.

Boston breathed out a shuddering breath. "The Cliffs-Notes version includes a pin the penis on the politician party, a dildo with my name on it, and a night where I thought I'd lost everything, so it's not one I want to rehash right now. Another time. Maybe one when Heath is out." He stopped any further questions with a look. "Getting back to the point —I know Heath didn't do it. That's what I wanted to come here for this morning. I'm sorry for my part in his arrest, and I want you to know that even though I'm not on the force anymore, I'm going to do everything I can to get him out."

"Well, hopefully that won't be necessary."

Boston raised one eyebrow in question.

Liam filled him in. "One of the prisoners confessed to Mae last night. We're headed to the police station after this to make a statement."

Boston sat up eagerly. "No shit? Who?"

"Vincent Hanover."

"Why does that name sound familiar..."

"He's got gang affiliation with the Saint View Sinners," I added. "He's some sort of hitman. He's young, and slight, looks like some emo high school kid. But I watched him kill and injure men in cold blood last night. It didn't faze him at all."

Boston's thick eyebrows knit together. "Wait. You don't mean Scythe?"

"Yes."

He shook his head slowly and pulled out his phone.

I squinted at him. "What's wrong?"

"Something doesn't fit with that. I need to call my partner." He glanced up from his phone. "Shit. Ex-partner, I guess. It's gonna take me a while to get used to that." He pressed his phone to his ear, and Liam and I exchanged a glance while we waited.

Boston tapped his fingers on the tabletop. "Richards. You at work, already? I need you to find out the intake date for Vincent Hanover."

He went quiet for a moment, one eyebrow raised at whatever was said on the other end, then thanked his ex-partner, promising to talk to him soon.

Boston levelled me with his steady gaze as he put his phone back in his pocket. "Vincent Hanover was in the holding cells at Saint View Prison the night Jayela died. He was picked up early afternoon the day before."

Shock punched through my system. I shook my head hard. "No. He admitted to it."

But then I played the conversation back through my head, and I realized I'd kind of put words in the man's mouth. He'd never actually admitted to killing Jayela specifically. Just said that the way she'd been killed sounded like him. There'd been no confirmation that he'd taken her life, and when I'd questioned him over why, he'd had no answer.

Because he hadn't done it.

Anger and frustration welled up inside me, and I gripped my fingers around the table's edge to keep from lashing out and backhanding the glasses of water across the room. "I thought... Dammit. Dammit!"

Liam put his arm around me, drawing me into his side.

Boston gazed at me with pity. "We are going to find out who killed her. I promise you that. I won't stop searching. Not until I find out who did this."

"How? Seriously, Boston. You quit the force. So now you're as unequipped to deal with this as I am."

Silence settled in the busy room, the other diners turning to stare at us with wide eyes like they'd never seen someone have a breakdown in the middle of an eating establishment. But I didn't know how much longer I could do this for. Getting a lead, thinking we had this worked out, and that Heath could walk free. Only for that hope to be smashed to smithereens minutes later.

But Boston saw these kinds of breakdowns all the time, so he spoke like I hadn't had an outburst at all. "There's something we're missing. Something that isn't fitting together."

"What about the cop?" Liam asked. "The older guy?"

"Johnson," I supplied.

Boston shook his head. "I won't rule him out, because he certainly has motive and opportunity. But I don't know, Mae. I think we have to search wider. I think we're getting hung up in the wrong places. I don't want to be like the cops. They've closed this case based on information that was right under their noses. It was too easy. Even Johnson is too easy. There's gotta be more."

He ran his hand through his hair. "I don't know that either of us knew Jayela as well as we thought we did."

His words stung. I wanted to deny them and scream in his face that I knew my sister. All we'd had was each other while we were growing up. Our mother was dead. Our father didn't give a shit. Jayela was my whole world.

But had I been hers? When had she ever spoken to me about personal things? She'd talked about work, her career ladder, the people's lives she'd saved. The stories had all fallen from her lips every single night, dominating her conversation. But when had she ever spoken about anything beyond her job?

It was only now that I realized her personal life was mostly a mystery to me. I assumed she hadn't had one. But maybe I was wrong.

"I want to put an ad in the local paper. I want to ask anyone with any information about Jayela to come forward," Boston said.

"Offer a reward," I told him. "I don't care if we get inundated with fake calls. I need to know what happened to her. I want any little detail any person can provide. And I want them all investigated. Every single one. Somebody knows what happened to her. Somebody knows why. I need to know, too."

11

ROWE

They kept me at the prison late into the night, while sirens wailed and people rushed around outside a makeshift tent that had been hastily erected. I stared out the gap, hearing the commotion as if it were happening far away instead of just on the other side of some thin canvas.

The warden snapped his fingers in front of my eyes, forcing me to focus on him. He stared at me, waiting for me to answer a question I hadn't heard.

"Sorry, what was that?"

"Is there anything else you want to tell us?"

The only thing I had left to say was that I suspected Mae and Heath of knowing about the riot and planning to use it as a distraction while they escaped. Yet I couldn't bring myself to say the words out loud. In the heat of the moment, those thoughts had made total sense. But now, hours later, with a clearer head, I struggled to see the sense in them. I couldn't believe that Mae had that in her. She was good to her core. And despite Heath's current situation, he'd had my back last night. Was I really going to throw him under the bus when he'd put himself between me and a knife?

The warden sighed heavily and sat back against his chair. He crossed his arms over his barrel chest like I was a disappointing kid. "Forget it. You need to go home, get some sleep and a shower, then get your head in the game. I need you back here first thing tomorrow."

No.

Coming back to this hellhole was the last thing I wanted to do after what had gone down tonight.

I must have said it out loud. Either that or I'd shaken my head because the warden held a hand up in a stop motion. "Look, I get it. You probably saw some shit in there, and we'll get counselors in or whatever. But I need you back here tomorrow. The riot squad are locking the place down right now, but tomorrow they'll be gone, and it'll be on us once more. All hands on deck. Capiche?"

I lifted my head wearily. "And if I say no?"

"You won't."

I hated that he was right. I barely did anything outside the four walls of this place. There was very little in my life these days except work and baseball, where I mostly sat on the bench because I continually missed practice.

I pushed to my feet, carrying the knowledge of my pathetic existence as heavy as the weight of royally screwing up. Each step was as difficult as having sandbags strapped to my feet, but eventually I made it to my car, which I drove on autopilot back to my house in the woods.

It was almost a surprise to get there in one piece. I

didn't remember stopping at red lights or paying any attention to other cars on the road. I didn't remember taking the turnoff. My head was too full of regrets.

Regrets, Mae, and Heath.

I slammed my car door closed harder than necessary and trudged to the front of my cottage. The porch swing that had once boasted colorful cushions now swung sadly in the shadows, no cushions or color in sight. Just the rough wood, aged by weather and neglect. Every time I walked past it, I remembered that I really needed to sand it back and varnish it. But I never did. What was the point? I no longer wanted to sit out here in the summer, grilling on the porch while friends and family talked and drank and enjoyed themselves.

They were all part of a life I didn't have anymore.

One I'd lost because I'd fucked up.

I'd learned nothing. I'd gone and done the exact same thing all over again last night.

My cabin was dark on the inside, and I didn't bother hitting the lights as I let myself in. I went straight for the bathroom, turned the water on, and for half a second, I considered not letting myself turn the heat on at all. I didn't deserve that comfort when I had very nearly cost people their lives tonight. But in the end, I cranked it up, hating the dirt and grime from the prison caking my skin more. I wanted it gone. Washed down the drain with suds. Maybe if I was lucky, it would take some of my sins with it.

I scrubbed shampoo through my hair, rinsed it, then stood there, water pounding on my back, head pressed to the shower door. I closed my eyes, but that was a mistake. All I saw was Mae. The smug little smile she gave me if she thought her teasing had hit the mark. And the way her long skirts swayed around her hips and ass when she walked. If I tried to shove her out, it was Heath's face that crowded in. Him way too close to me. Our breaths mingling. His gaze so intense I didn't know what to fucking do with it. I groaned into the steamed-up bathroom and gave up trying to push either of them away. Needing to feel something, I gripped the base of my cock.

I wouldn't allow myself to move for a long moment, and it was fucking torturous. I filled my head with images of Mae kissing Heath, and then her kissing me. My erection grew without me stroking it, until I was hard and adjusting my grip to allow for how thick I was.

God, she was so beautiful. Her mouth soft, her taste dragging me under until all I could think about was licking every part of her. I relived her kiss, committing to memory the way she'd felt in my arms.

I hadn't kissed anyone in so long. She'd been different, but that was good.

I didn't want her to feel the same way Rory had felt in my arms. I couldn't do that sort of love again and survive it.

I gave in and stroked my cock, squeezing my eyes shut while I worked myself. The water fell down around me in the darkness of my bathroom, splashing onto the tiles at my feet.

I imagined Mae in here with me. Her pressing up on her toes the way she had in the prison. Her mouth opening beneath mine, the intensity between us driving through me, and pushing her up against the wall. The tiny gasp as she felt my dick, thick and hard at her stomach.

I stroked myself harder, faster, knowing this was wrong and that I didn't deserve it, but unable to stop it now. I hovered on the brink, desperate to come, but something stopped me. Something held me back.

And I knew what it was, I just didn't want to give in to it.

Heath.

Fuck.

My balls clenched and then emptied into the spray of the showerhead.

I stood there for a long time after, but the release had done its job, clearing some of the fog from my brain. When the water ran cold, I stumbled out, drying off with a threadbare towel I'd left hanging on a rack yesterday, and then made my way to my bedroom.

I let the towel fall on the floor and dropped down onto my mattress beside it, not bothering to find sleep pants. With my skin still hot from my shower, I threw a sheet around my waist and waited for sleep to take me.

But I wasn't surprised when the dawn came and sleep hadn't.

At eight, I picked up my phone and called Colt's. It rang a few times, before a groggy voice answered. "You don't fucking wait until nine, even when a guy is in the hospital?"

Relief flooded my system, and I grinned at my ceiling. "Hospital, huh? You still in there? You soft cock. I was ringing to make sure you were out of bed and ready for work."

Colt snorted on the other end. "That'd be right."

I sobered. "No seriously, man. How are you? It's real

fucking good to hear your voice 'cause I kinda thought you were dead for a little bit there last night."

Colt went quiet. "I don't remember much. But Lacey said Perry was here and that you got me out." He cleared his throat, but his voice was still thick with emotion when he spoke. "Thanks for that."

Guilt swamped me. Because the thing was, I hadn't done anything to save him. It hadn't been me who'd dragged him from Gen Pop and held pressure on his wound until Perry had got there. He had some random prisoner to thank for that, and I couldn't even remember the guy's name.

I couldn't even speak around the lump in my throat.

"Hey, man, I gotta go. My girl just got here, and I need my mouth to kiss her more than I need it to talk to you. Later, okay? I'll be hanging out here for a while they say, so I better see your sorry ass here soon. You can tell me everything I missed while I was floating off in unconscious land."

He hung up, and my phone rang again before I could even put it down. When I glanced at the screen, I canceled the call without answering it. I knew why the warden was calling. I was late for my shift, but I couldn't bring myself to care. I'd get there when I got there.

Despite that small defiance, I got out of bed and dressed in a clean but wrinkled uniform I pulled from the dryer and headed into work.

I never felt any joy driving this route, but I didn't normally dread it the way I did this time. The moment the prison gates rose, I wanted to turn around and drive in the other direction.

Subconsciously, I found myself searching the parking

lot for Mae's car, but that was stupid. Even on a normal day she wouldn't be here at this time. It was wishful thinking to hope she might have somehow known that I really needed to see her this morning and just somehow be here, waiting for me with coffee and a warm smile.

Instead, I got the warden glaring at me with a pile of paperwork. I took it from him, shifting through the papers, and then glanced up at him. "What's this?"

"Just got it through from the board. After last night's incident, they're bringing in a whole new team. I'm out."

My fingers clenched on the letter of dismissal. "What the hell do you mean you're out?"

"Fired, effective immediately. I've got today to clear out my office for the new guy who's already here doing God knows what. I recommended you but—"

I shook my head. I didn't want his job. I wasn't even sure I wanted my own. "Who is it?"

He grimaced. "Steven Tabor."

I'd heard of the man. His reputation preceded him. He was well-known in the system for being completely cutthroat, both in the way he ran his prisons and in the way he dealt with his employees.

"He stormed in here this morning with a team of twelve behind him. Fucking prick." The bitterness rolled off the warden in waves, but I didn't have much sympathy for the man. Fact was, we'd been understaffed for a long time. And he'd done nothing to fix the problem. Maybe some of that was out of his hands, I didn't know about the inner workings, but I did know that our lack of staff and resources and poor training was probably what had enabled last night's riot to happen in the first place.

People had died. It shouldn't have happened.

"Where is he?" I asked.

"He's set up shop in the schoolroom until my office is cleared out."

I nodded and slapped the older man on the shoulder. It was as much comfort as I could offer. I dragged my feet to my locker, spending too long staring at Mae's, before opening mine and dumping my personal belongings inside. Then I made my way to her classroom. Halfway there, though, orange cones blocked me off, a team of workmen already busy repairing the damage the fire had caused. It still reeked of smoke, the acrid smell burned into the back of my nose.

I'd stood right here less than twenty-four hours ago, with a wall of flame in front of me, and Mae on the other side.

"You can't go through this way, buddy," one of the workmen called to me. "Gotta go around."

I swiveled on my heel and retraced my steps to detour through other sections and come to Mae's classroom from the opposite direction. Her room was undamaged except for the smoke stench that clung to the walls, so the sprinklers must have come on not long after we were here last night. But when I stepped inside there was a large, dark stain on the floor that hadn't been there yesterday. I swallowed hard while my brain tried to run away with stories that weren't true. Whoever's blood that was, it didn't matter. Because Mae was out, safe and sound. She was at home right now, probably with Liam. Oddly, that thought elicited no jealousy from me. Just a sense of relief that she wasn't alone.

"Can I help you?"

I dragged my gaze away from the stain on the floor

and focused on the man behind Mae's desk. He wasn't all that much older than me. Mid-thirties perhaps, forty at most. He had the trim figure of someone who worked out a lot, and his hair was still a deep black, not even a fleck of gray at his temples. But there were lines etched into his forehead that spoke of too much time frowning, and a stressful job.

Definitely not one I wanted.

I stepped forward, offering him my hand, and he took it, shaking with a strong grip. "I'm Rowe Pritchard."

"Ah, Pritchard. They told me about you. Just in time. Let's go."

He pushed to his feet and strode out of the room, not waiting to see if I'd follow or not. I kept pace with him, falling into step at his side. His blue uniform contrasted with my brown one, his still sporting the emblem of the last prison he'd worked at.

He shot me an interested glance. "They tell me you were the last man standing in the riot last night?"

"I wasn't aware of that."

"I've fired most of the staff. Most of them ran off with their tails between their legs at the first sign of trouble. That might be how some men run their prisons, but it doesn't fly with me. My teams are the best of the best. Which is why you're still here. From what I've heard about you, I believe you're worthy of keeping your job."

I ground my molars to keep from saying anything and hoped the man couldn't hear it. He hadn't been here last night. He didn't know what it had been like. I didn't blame anyone for jumping ship when the damn thing was literally on fire and going down.

The guards here didn't owe the prison their lives.

But I held my tongue, because making an enemy of this man on his first day wouldn't be smart. "Thank you, sir."

He nodded curtly, leading the way through the halls like he already knew them back to front. He pushed open the doors to Gen Pop A so hard the creak splintered through the air.

I hesitated, still expecting the same scenes as last night. Chairs overturned. Men roaming around at will. Yells and hyped-up excitement echoing off the high-ceilinged roof enclosing the chaos.

But it was dead silent on the other side, because the prisoners were facedown on the floor, their hands held behind them with black zip ties.

I froze. The silence was uncanny. I'd never heard anything like it inside these four walls. There was always noise. The low hum of hundreds of men living and fighting for dominance in the small space never stopped.

But they weren't normally surrounded by men with guns trained on them.

"What's going on?" I asked quietly.

Tabor glanced over his shoulder at me, then smiled slowly. He raised his voice so it echoed around the silent room. "This is what happens to bad little boys who break the rules, isn't it, gentlemen?"

"Yes, Warden," the prisoners said as one.

What the hell?

"How long have they been like this?" I asked.

He shrugged. "A few hours, I guess. Enough time to practice the manners they'll need to survive with me in charge. Isn't that right?"

The room sounded off with an echoing, "Yes, Warden," once more.

I wasn't against them pulling the men into line, but leaving them on the floor for hours with their arms restricted didn't sit well with me. At my feet, an overweight man on his belly, the zip ties cutting into the flabby flesh of his wrists. The skin was red raw and the tips of his fingers turning purple. And yet he didn't make a noise because there were guns pointed at him.

This wasn't right.

I opened my mouth to protest, but Tabor clapped a hand on my shoulder. "Listen up, all you pieces of shit. I've just been informed two of you took a female employee hostage last night. And you don't know this about me yet, but there's nothing I hate more than scumbags like you, who think it's okay to lay hands on a woman." He drew his leg back and then slammed his boot into an inmate's side.

I widened my eyes as the man let out a howl of pain.

It didn't seem to affect Tabor at all, though. He went on speaking like it hadn't even happened. "Vincent Hanover and Heath Michaelson, on your feet."

There was movement to my right, and a sick feeling came over me watching Heath and Vincent struggle to stand. Nobody tried to help them. Vincent was up first, his dark hair flopping in his face, hiding his eyes. He looked younger than he had last night, but I wasn't stupid enough to think that just because he was quiet and unarmed now that he wasn't the same psychopath from the riot. Something had been unleashed in him, and I somehow doubted it could be put back in its cage entirely. At least not in the space of twenty-four hours.

Heath got up slower, his bigger frame making getting up without hands more difficult. He rose from the floor, and his gaze clashed with mine.

Fuck.

What was this?

"You were found in a solitary cell with both Officer Pritchard and your education officer, Miss Donovan. Not only that, but you're accused of having multiple weapons. Is that correct, Officer Pritchard?"

I swallowed hard because I suddenly knew where the man was going. Listing out a prisoner's indiscretions only led to one thing.

A stint in solitary.

Nobody in their right mind liked solitary. People weren't made to go for long stretches of time without other humans to talk to and connect with. It was a cruel, harsh punishment when so much had already been taken from you.

But what the hell was I supposed to say? I couldn't deny it. I knew Heath had been protecting Mae, but I couldn't say that here, without exposing their relationship to the entire room. If that got out, Mae would be in danger here. She'd be a target for any prisoner who had a beef with Heath.

It was the same reason I couldn't get involved with her.

And Vincent needed to be locked up. The darkness in him hovered like a black cloud, one that could burst and shoot lightning or stinging rain at any moment.

That couldn't happen in General Population.

Not when Heath was in here, too.

I wanted to groan out loud. There was no good option here.

"Yes, that's correct," I told Tabor.

Hurt flashed across Heath's eyes, punching through me. I could practically hear the accusations. That I hadn't stood up for him. That I was sending him to solitary because I wanted him out of the way.

I couldn't tell him he was wrong.

I couldn't say I was doing it because getting him away from Vincent, and from me, was the only way to keep him safe.

12

MAE

*L*iam's fingers traced over the curve of my hip. "What would happen if we never went back to work?"

We'd been holed up in my apartment for three days. Liam had called in sick, and the new warden had told me not to come in until the end of the week when he'd established full control of the prison once more.

I watched Liam draw idle patterns over my bare skin, goosebumps rising everywhere he touched me.

He'd been the very best sort of distraction. He was so easy to lose myself in, and we had, over and over again. We'd barely been dressed in days. Every time we'd considered going out, I pulled him back into bed and showed him why staying in was a better idea.

I reached between us and circled my fingers around the thick base of his cock. "We'd be well-satisfied. But probably broke. At some point they'd turn the electricity off." I stroked my fingers up his length.

He thrust his hips slowly toward me. "Who needs electricity anyway? I'll keep you warm."

Though the idea was inviting, we'd been doing this for days. Avoiding our real lives because they felt hard. "Liam."

"Mmm?"

I thought about addressing some of my problems, but in the end, I chickened out. It was easier to focus on Liam's. "What are we going to do about your mom?" The last time we'd seen Liam's mother, she'd been seeking help from a homeless shelter. She'd taken one look at Liam and bolted. We hadn't had any contact with her since.

He paused, opening his eyes. "Did you seriously just bring up my mom while your hand is around my dick?"

I couldn't help but smile. "Sorry. But my hand has been around your dick a lot lately. And that's starting to feel like avoidance. We have to talk about it sometime."

"We need to talk about your sister, and Heath and Rowe at some point, too."

I groaned, burying my face into the crook of his neck. "I've just remembered why we've had so much sex in the last three days."

He rolled away to lie on his back. "I don't see a solution for my mom problems right now. So let's put a pin in that one. But we can do something about your sister."

I sighed heavily. "I doubt Boston has had time to collect any leads from his tip-off line yet."

Liam's tone turned soft. "Actually, I think we're jumping the gun on that one. There's something else we should do first. I don't know if you want to do it alone or if you want me to be there, but I think you need to go through Jayela's room."

My heart rate picked up, and for the first time in days, it had nothing to do with Liam's naked body. The tremble started in my fingers and then worked its way across my whole body.

Liam noticed and immediately gathered me into his arms, holding me close, lessening the tremors. "Shit. I'm sorry. We don't have to. It was a dumb idea."

The thing was, it wasn't a dumb idea. He was right. It was something that needed doing. It was something I should have done a month ago, but I'd been too scared. Stepping into that room, despite having it professionally cleaned, would be like reliving the morning I found her. Even though her body was long taken away, I knew that the minute I walked in there, I'd see her again. I'd smell her perfume. I'd see her photos on the walls, and I'd have to remember it all. I'd have to remember the body-splitting agony of seeing her like that, and knowing that I'd been just down the hall when someone had taken her life. "I can't do it alone."

His fingers wrapped around mine, squeezing tight. "You don't have to. I'll be right there with you. Every step of the way. Always."

His voice was soft and reassuring, and I stared up at him.

There was something in his face, an expression that went beyond care for a friend he happened to get naked with.

Who was I kidding? He hadn't acted like a friend at all for the last three days. He'd been so much more, and I'd liked it. In fact, I'd loved it.

Being Liam Banks' girlfriend was a very appealing prospect. I'd never had anyone care for me the way he did. Not even Jayela. She had no maternal instincts and didn't deal well with sad.

"Liam, I..." I didn't know what I was going to say. But there were feelings welling up deep inside me that were hard to ignore.

Liam paused, waiting for me to finish, and his hopeful look nearly killed me. I wasn't even sure what to do with that. Did he want more? Did he want this to be a relationship? How the hell did that fit in with me kissing Rowe and Heath just a few nights ago?

The fact was, it didn't. Not until I'd sorted out my feelings. So I shut my mouth, pressing my lips together before I said something that would hurt him more than my silence would.

When it became clear I wasn't going to finish my thought, Liam went on like I hadn't spoken. He tossed my robe to me and swung his legs over the edge of the bed. He pulled up a pair of black running shorts, settling them low on his hips, ignoring the fact his erection still strained at the fabric. "Come on. Let's do this now. Before we think of a reason to put it off again. Rip off the Band-Aid and all that."

I got up, pushing my arms into the silky material of my robe and knotting it around my waist. He was right. I'd lose my nerve if we didn't do it now. I let him lead the way out of my bedroom and down the hall to Jayela's. He paused with his hand on the doorknob, glancing over his shoulder at me as he twisted it. "You okay?"

I nodded. "Let's just get it over and done with."

He gave me a short nod and then pushed the door open.

First thing that hit me was the smell. It wasn't right. It didn't smell like her. It reeked of harsh cleaning chemicals that hadn't been allowed to escape because of the closed window and locked door.

I tugged my robe sleeve down over my hand and then held it over my nose and mouth. Liam rushed for the window, and with his nose wrinkled, heaved it up. The cool morning breeze flowed in, taking away the worst of the smell instantly.

I dropped my hand. "Thanks. I should have thought to come in here and open the window and let some fresh air in. I just..."

Liam came back to my side and took my hand, lacing his fingers between mine. "It doesn't matter. We'll leave it open now to air it out. How do you feel?"

Everything. Sad that I couldn't smell her perfume. Anxious that her bed frame was bare, the mattress full of her blood incinerated. And yet there was a comfort in being around her things. I walked to her dresser and picked up a photo. It was of her and me and Tori. Jayela stood in the middle, her arm slung around both of us. Her smile was wide, a happiness radiating from the image. "I remember this day," I told Liam, handing him the framed print. "We went to Disneyland."

Liam gazed down at it and smiled. "You took Tori's son?"

I shook my head. "No. We went for Jayela's birthday. Just the three of us, grown adults. It had been Tori's idea. She insisted that Jayela would love it, and though I'd been a bit skeptical because Jayela was so straightlaced and serious most of the time, I'd been completely wrong. She loved it. I was a big chicken and didn't go on half the rides, but that worked out okay because I was happy to watch her and Tori go on everything." I smiled wistfully at him. "They started calling me the bag lady, because I would just stand in the crowd, holding their bags while they rode."

Liam chuckled. "I would have stood with you."

I tilted my head toward him. "Yeah? I would have picked you to be at the very front of the roller coaster line, with your hands up, smiling from ear to ear as you scream down hills and spin upside down."

Liam shuddered. "Hell no. I get motion sickness during car trips to the supermarket. Roller coasters are not my thing."

I smiled at that. It was nice to have something unexpected in common with him. He wandered around Jayela's tidy room, poking at the items on her shelves, though they were few and far between. "Your sister was a bit of a minimalist, huh?"

"She liked things neat and tidy. Orderly. Kind of the opposite to me."

"Your room isn't messy, though."

"No. But I like things. Clutter she called it. I'm sentimental in a way that she never was. If you look through my drawers, I've got every single hand-drawn card from my kids at school. I've got photos of my friends from high school, concert ticket stubs, and love letters from boys I dated in college. I don't throw anything out."

"I think that's nice."

I shot him a sidelong glance. "You don't. Your place is as minimalist as I've ever seen."

He shrugged. "I never really thought about it before, but it doesn't bring me any joy, you know? My grandparents' place was run by a staff. Everything had a place, and there was no room for anything that didn't serve a purpose. I guess I kinda forgot how to make a house feel like a home."

That broke my heart a little bit. "What was your mother's house like?"

He sucked in a sharp breath, and I knew I'd hit a nerve. "Sorry. You don't have to answer that."

He shook his head. "No. It's okay." He ran his finger along a shelf, making a line through the light layer of dust. "Her house was the complete opposite of my grandparents'. Tiny. The entire place could have fit in my grandparents' bedroom alone. But she worked hard to make it feel like a home. We had our drawings on the refrigerator. And I had a bedspread with Harry Potter on it that she'd found at a thrift store. Can you believe that? Somebody actually donated a perfectly good Harry Potter bed set."

I put a hand over my heart and gave an overexaggerated gasp. "The horror!"

He stared at me like I'd just grown an extra head. "If you tell me you're not a Harry Potter fan, this thing between us? It's done right now." He grinned. "Heath and Rowe are going to have to take you all on their own, because I don't need that sort of negativity."

I chuckled, then blinked in surprise at the sound. Who would have thought that I could laugh in this space ever again? But Liam did that for me. He was the perfect person to be here right now. "Actually, I love Harry Potter."

Liam fist pumped the air. "Yes! Our kids would totally be Ravenclaws. Don't you think?"

I went quiet at that and turned away, opening a drawer and hiding my uncomfortableness by searching through it. The idea of a couple of little kids who looked like Liam dressed in Ravenclaw cloaks was a dagger straight through my heart.

The top drawer was full of underwear. Most of it practical with only one or two sexier pieces shoved to the back. I closed the drawer quickly, feeling like I was invading my sister's personal space, and moved on to the drawers below it. T-shirts and shorts. Hoodies in another, all of them neatly folded and color coordinated.

I was about to shut the drawer, when something sticking out from beneath the pile of clothes caught my eye. I pulled it out, took one look at it, and dropped it onto the floor with a gasp.

Liam glanced over at me from a file of bills he was going through. "What? Did you find something?"

All I could do was stare at it, my hand over my mouth.

Liam stood and followed my line of sight to the floor. "Oh shit. Is that...?"

He stooped, retrieving the pregnancy test from the floor. "Mae. This is positive. Jayela didn't have a baby, right?"

All I could do was stare at the test, clutched between his fingers. Slowly, I shook my head. "No. She didn't."

"Okay," he said, thinking it over. "She wasn't pregnant at the time of her death. We know that from the autopsy results."

"You read them?"

He nodded. "As Heath's lawyer, I needed all the details. I'm sorry. I should have told you."

"No, no. It's fine."

"You obviously didn't know about this?"

"No. She never told me." I looked up at him. "Why wouldn't she have told me?"

But even as I asked the question, there was a part of me that already knew the answer.

Because she didn't think I could handle it.

"Dammit, Jayela. I am not as weak as you think I am," I mumbled. They were useless words now. Words she'd never hear.

Liam put his arm around my shoulders. "She didn't think you were weak."

"Then why wouldn't she have told me? I... I can't..."

"You can't have kids, right?" His voice was gentle. "I saw the look on your face when I mentioned kids earlier."

"I was diagnosed when I was a teenager. It would be a huge risk to me. I'd likely die, so it's not something I can even consider. But I've had a long time to make peace with it. I would have been happy for her."

"Of course you would have been. But she was your big sister. And maybe she was trying to spare you the heartache, especially if she knew she was going to..."

I blinked at him in surprise. "You think she terminated the pregnancy?"

He placed the pregnancy test back in the drawer where I'd found it. "I don't know. But it's a possibility."

My heart broke for my sister all over again. Because either way, whether she miscarried the pregnancy or terminated it of her own free will, that couldn't have been an easy thing to go through alone.

She'd done it alone. That broke my heart. But it took two people to make a baby.

"Liam," I said urgently. "If she was pregnant, that means she was seeing someone. Someone I didn't know about. Someone who could be a suspect in this case. What if he found out she terminated the pregnancy and that wasn't what he wanted? There's a motive there, isn't there? Something that could be used as reasonable doubt in Heath's case?"

Liam nodded slowly. "If we can find out who it is, then maybe."

13

MAE

*L*iam finally went back to work after a week of hovering over me at home. I was due back at the prison that night, but the day stretched out ahead of me, long and lonely without him. I practically pounced on my phone when it rang.

"Have you decided you don't really need a job?" I asked. "There's a position open between my legs." I grinned, staring out the window at the bustling street below.

There was a cough down the line. One that definitely didn't sound deep enough to be masculine. With wide eyes, I pulled the phone away from my ear and actually looked at the name on the display. I cringed. "Perry?"

"You were expecting somebody else, I assume?"

Embarrassment heated my cheeks. "I was. Sorry about that."

"No, no. I'm no prude, so that was amusing. Were you expecting Rowe by any chance?"

I choked a little. "Is that how you think I answer the phone when Rowe calls me?"

"I've no idea. I kind of thought that you two were together after the way he acted during the riot..."

I squeezed my eyes tight. I'd been trying really hard not to think about that night. What I'd done. What he'd done. Heath, Vincent, DeWitt. It had been easier to just live in Liamland. He seemed entirely uncomplicated by comparison.

"Ah, no. That's not how Rowe and I... We don't talk to each other like that. There's nothing going on."

"You don't lie well, Mae."

I sighed. I never had been able to lie. Jayela had always told me it was something she admired about me, but it seemed more of a character flaw than a positive trait sometimes.

Perry went on without waiting for me to respond. "Anyway. I actually didn't ring just to give you a hard time about you and Rowe making eyes at each other across your classroom. I just wanted to know if you've seen him."

I shook my head, even though there was no one around to see it. "No. Not since the night of the riot anyway."

Perry sighed. "I haven't either. I'm getting worried."

"Wait, are you not back at work either? I assumed they'd need you all last week. Your job is a bit more essential than mine is."

"That's what I'm trying to tell you. I've been here, but other than the morning after the riot, Rowe hasn't been. He's been totally MIA."

I sat up a little straighter. "Is he sick?"

"I don't know. I asked the new warden about it, and he seemed completely dismissive. Said Rowe just hadn't shown up, no phone call or anything. He's giving Rowe until his shift tonight to show, or he's out."

Worry trickled down my spine. "That's it? They're just going to fire him? He went through a pretty traumatic experience. He could be lying on the floor of his house in shock for all we know. They can't fire him for that."

"That's exactly what I said. But the warden said a week with no contact is more than enough grace period. I've been trying to call Rowe for two days, and he hasn't answered. Hence, me calling you."

"I sent him a message the day after, just to see if he was okay. But he never replied. Shit, Perry. What if he seriously is in shock on the floor of his bedroom or something? He could have been there for days."

"We could ring the police and ask for a welfare check."

I was already pulling on my shoes. "No. I'll go. Can you text me his address? It'll be on the employee database there somewhere, right?"

"That's probably supposed to be confidential, but I'm happy to break the rules right now, because I'm worried, too. He can be angry at us once we know he's okay."

I ran a brush through my hair but didn't stop to put makeup on. The trickle of worry became a flood. I couldn't imagine why Rowe wouldn't turn up for work without so much as a phone call unless he had no other choice. He was always so responsible and by the rules. Where the hell was he? My mind whirled with the possibilities of everything that might have gone wrong. What if he had smoke inhalation that hadn't been detected or something? Dammit!

By the time I got downstairs to my car, my phone had beeped with a message from Perry, giving me Rowe's address. I plugged it into my GPS system and headed into Saint View. I had to drive past the prison, and even though it had been a week, I found myself trying not to imagine what was going on inside. It would just drive me crazy, and I'd be back there tonight anyway, with it right in front of my face once more.

But first, I needed to find Rowe and drag his ass back to work with me. Because he wasn't getting fired.

I needed him there.

I found myself in a nicer part of Saint View. The sort of street where the houses were owned by a low- to mid-income families rather than the government. None of them were fancy or on large blocks of land, and most needed renovations the owners probably couldn't afford. But there wasn't the same state of disrepair that other parts of Saint View showed. The paths were clear of glass, and a little park I drove past had children swinging happily, their parents sitting on benches watching on. There wasn't the same sense of danger I'd felt walking down the main strip, and the streets where the Saint View Sinners hung out.

"Okay, fifty-three Saint Thomas Drive. Where are you?" I let the car creep along, checking the numbers on mailboxes, and eventually pulled up outside a small brown-sided house. I frowned and double-checked the house number against the message that Perry had sent me. It definitely said number fifty-three. But I instantly got the distinct impression that nobody lived there. I got out of the car slowly, closing the door and locking it behind me before walking over to the chain-link fence that ran around the front lawn. Weeds grew up through the mesh, and junk mail spilled out of the mailbox and onto the ground beside it. I bent and retrieved a brochure, pushing it back inside the mailbox while I stared at the house, debating whether to even bother going to knock on the door when it was so obviously uninhabited.

"Watch me, Grandma!"

A little boy ran around the yard of the house next door, his skinny legs sticking out beneath swim shorts that were too big for him. He sprinted beneath the sprinkler, giggling when it sprayed him directly in the face. "Grandma! It's hot today. You said you'd play with me. Get your bathing suit on."

An older woman, overweight and with heavy lines around her eyes, stepped through the screen door, letting it bang behind her. She slumped down heavily on the porch seat and sighed while she fanned her face with her hands. "Not today, sweetheart. Granny is too tired and old to do anything but sit here and try not to melt."

The little boy's shoulders slumped, but he didn't say anything.

Feeling like I was intruding on their conversation, I decided to try the front door since I was here. I lifted the latch on the gate, and it let out an obnoxious squeak.

The noise caught the little boy's attention. "Miss! Hey, Miss! Do you want to come in the sprinkler with me? It's really fun."

I grinned at him and opened my mouth to answer

him, but his grandmother cut me off with a stern warning. "Ripley. Don't speak to strangers."

I nodded politely to the woman and stepped away, respecting her wishes, even though the kid was really cute and looked so disappointed that I wasn't allowed to talk to him. I got the gate open and took one step inside before the woman called out to me. "Ain't nobody home, sweetheart. Whatever you're selling, there ain't nobody buying. So on with you now."

I paused. "Do you know the man who owns this house? Rowe Pritchard?"

Her eyes narrowed. "Who wants to know?"

"Oh, I'm sorry." I walked toward her and placed my hands on the top of the waist-high fence separating the two yards. "I'm Mae Donovan. I work with Rowe at the prison."

She stopped glaring at me but didn't make a move to get up off her seat. "He left."

Whoa, what? He'd just up and left? Without even a word? "Do you know where he went?"

The woman shrugged.

"Okay. Thanks for your time." I walked back out of the yard, closing the gate carefully behind me and slumped against my car. Ripley splashed joyfully in the cool water, and a few drops made their way onto my skin. The cool relief was short-lived, though, my worry for Rowe not helping with the muggy heat that had sweat beading on the back of my neck. I pulled out my phone, and called Liam, quickly filling him in on where I was. "Did he go to baseball practice this week?"

"No. Shit. I didn't even think anything of it, but after

the riot...I should have." He let out a long sigh. "I'm a shitty friend."

I knew the feeling. "We both are. Do you have any idea where he'd go?"

"No. I've never heard him talk about family or friends outside the team. I can call and ask the other guys if anyone has heard anything, but I'm the closest with him so I don't like the odds of them knowing any more than I do."

Worry gnawed at my insides. "What if he's in some sort of post-traumatic shock? I'm worried. And if he doesn't show for work tonight, that's it. He's out. The new warden isn't going to just let his absence slide any longer."

"Just come into the office. I'll take an early lunch break and we can brainstorm places he might have gone."

Without a better plan, I nodded. "I'll be there soon."

The old woman watched me from the porch, and I gave her a half smile before opening my car door once more.

"Wait," she called. She maneuvered herself slowly off the swing and clutched the railing as she made her way down the handful of steps at the front of her house. She pulled a phone from the pocket of her loose summer dress. "You're worried about him."

It wasn't a question, more of a statement of fact.

"Yes. Something happened at work recently, and he's been missing ever since. I just want to make sure he's okay."

"You try calling him?"

"Yes, but he's not answering mine or any of our other friends' calls."

The woman studied me, for what I didn't know, perhaps determining whether I could be trusted. Decision made, she pushed a number and held the phone out to me. "You and me both. Been worried about that boy for a long time now."

I glanced down at the phone, Rowe's name lit up on her screen. I took it from her weathered fingers, and she nodded at me in approval. "He'll answer a call from me."

I pressed it to my ear while it rang, my heart rate picking up.

"Norma? What's wrong? Is Ripley okay?" Rowe's voice was full of panic.

"Hey, no. It's me. It's Mae."

There was a confused silence, then, "What? Mae? How do you have Norma's phone? What's going on?"

"I'm at your house. Norma and Ripley are both fine. She let me use her phone since you aren't answering calls from mine."

He didn't say anything.

"Rowe, are you okay? Where are you? Can we talk?"

"I'm fine."

"I don't believe you. Tell me where you are. Wherever it is, I'll come to you."

"I told you, I'm fine."

"Until I see that with my own eyes, I don't believe you. So you can either tell me where you are, or I'll ring you every seven minutes from now until eternity. That'll get old real fast."

"I could just turn my phone off, you know."

I sighed. "Just tell me where you are."

"God, you're annoying. Two five two six Old South Road. It's off the Mountainside turnoff."

A little relief filled my body. He wasn't far away then. He hadn't completely packed up and left without a word.

He hung up without saying goodbye, and I handed the phone back to Norma. "Thank you."

"Don't thank me. Just go make sure he's okay. He's a good one, and he's been dealt a horrible hand in life. Tell him we miss him."

I smiled at her genuine fondness for Rowe, and promised I'd tell him. All while wondering exactly what he'd gone through to have the old woman's pity.

When Rowe said his place was off the Mountainside turnoff, he hadn't mentioned exactly how far out. Twenty minutes later, buildings had given way to gorgeous old trees that towered over my little car. I switched off the air-conditioning and wound the window down to let the fresh mountain air roll in. Finally, I found the turnoff, though Old South Road was barely more than a dirt track through the wilderness, wide enough only for one car. I prayed while I drove along that no one else would come up the other way because there wasn't room to pass. But there were no other cars in sight, and eventually, the road through the deep woods led to a clearing. I passed the mailbox on the way in and double-checked the number matched the one Rowe had given me, but I already knew it was right. Rowe's car was parked in front.

Everything was made from wood. The cabin. The steps. The porch swing that squeaked in the slight breeze that blew across the clearing. It was a welcome coolness, and I stood on the porch for a moment, letting it wash over me, taking away some of the clamminess of my skin. I wasn't sure that was because of the heat or because I knew I was about to see Rowe.

I knocked tentatively, and when nobody answered, harder. "Rowe?"

"Down here."

I glanced to my right and found him on the far side of the clearing, coming out of a small shed with two fishing rods in his hand. He glanced in my direction, and my breath caught. His bare chest glinted in the sunlight, like it was made just to kiss him. His skin was a deep brown that told me this wasn't the first time he'd walked around outside without his shirt on. His khaki-green shorts brushed his knee, and black flip-flops were the only thing protecting his feet from the uneven ground.

His gaze caught mine. "You just gonna stand there? Or you going to come fish?"

Without waiting for me, he disappeared into the woods behind the shed, and I hurried to catch up with him. Behind the shed, I found the path he'd taken and jogged along it, finding him again as I came around a curve.

That back...I willed myself to not stare at the muscles corded across his shoulders and the narrowing down to his hips and ass.

"You could take a photo, you know. It would last longer."

I scowled at his back, though part of me was relieved. This was the Rowe I knew. The one who gave me shit at every opportunity. It was familiar and safe, especially after what had happened between us last time we'd seen each other. That had been distinctly unlike us.

"Stand still then and I'll get my phone out. Jesus, once a model, always a model. Do you always need all cameras pointed at you?"

"I was never a model, Mae." He glanced back over his shoulder, and I thought for half a second I saw the curl of his upper lip.

I caught up with him and took in the fishing rods. "Is one of those for me?"

"I don't normally fish with two."

"You could just say yes."

"You could just tell me why you're here. I'm pretty sure you didn't just come to check out my ass."

"I came to make sure you were okay."

He fiddled with the handle on one of the rods, avoiding looking at me, and deftly changed the subject. "You saw Norma and Ripley?"

I blinked at the change of topic, but at least he was talking. "Yes."

"How were they?"

"Good. Ripley's a cutie. He was running around under a sprinkler. Probably getting a sunburn, but he was enjoying himself."

Rowe gave a genuine smile at that.

I wanted to make him smile more, and if telling him about his old neighbors, who he obviously cared about, made that happen then I'd talk about them all day. "Norma seemed well but tired. I think the heat was bothering her most of all. Does she mind Ripley a lot?"

"She has full-time custody of him."

"Wow. That must be difficult. I know exactly how

much energy kids that age have. It wouldn't be easy for a woman of her age to keep up with him. How old is he? Four?"

"And a half. He never lets you forget the half."

I smiled at that. "The kids at school are like that, too."

We reached the end of a path, and Rowe stepped down onto a small dock on the edge of the lake. He held his hand out to me, and I took it, his palm warm against mine. He helped me down and then passed me my fishing rod. "You know how to use one of these?"

I shook my head. "No. This is the first time I've ever held one in my life."

"Your dad never took you fishing?"

"My dad barely knew I was alive. He would've been just as likely to take me to the moon."

Rowe didn't offer me any sympathy, and I didn't expect any. It was what it was. I was hardly the first kid to grow up with a parent who actively avoided them at every opportunity.

Rowe dropped a tackle box at our feet and squatted beside it. "There's not much to it. Stick a bit of bait on your hook." He demonstrated by pulling a stinking bit of something through his hook. "Then you just cast it out." He drew the rod back over his shoulder and then flicked it forward gracefully, the line rolling out, the hook and sinker plopping into the smooth surface of the lake.

He offered me his fishing rod, but I shook my head. "I can do it."

I picked up a gross, slimy bit of bait and hooked it around the end of the fishing rod. I gave it a little wiggle, testing to make sure it would stay on, and smiled to myself when it did. I straightened and stood beside him, rather proud of myself. I flicked the rod back over my shoulder the same way he had and tried to cast it out. Absolutely nothing happened. The hook and line just wound itself around the rod, getting all tangled.

Rowe transferred his rod to his left hand and circled his right around me. "You've got this bit in the wrong position." He adjusted my line with one hand and then let his fingers cover mine.

I tried hard to pay attention. I swear I tried to force myself to listen to his coaching, but the man had his arm around me and his bare chest at my back. Before I knew it, he'd sent my line out into the lake, not far from where his had landed.

He stepped away, and I could finally concentrate again. "So what do we do now?"

"We fish."

He gazed down over the calm greenish-blue water. I did the same.

But the minutes dragged on, each one bringing us closer to the time we needed to be at work. "Where have you been?" I asked eventually. "Why haven't you been at the prison?"

He shrugged. "I needed a break. You're the one always saying I'd never take time off."

"Yeah, but normally when someone needs a break, they don't just go completely AWOL. Did you know the new warden is going to fire you if you don't turn up for work tonight? Perry called me this morning really worried because you just up and disappeared without a trace."

Rowe stared out over the lake, but his expression was

far from peaceful. "The new warden is an asshole," he bit out.

"So what? You don't like him so you're just going to quit?"

He shook his head. "No. It's not about him."

The unspoken words hung in the air between us, but he clearly wasn't going to say it without me pushing it. "It's because of me, then. Right? Because of what happened between us?"

He didn't say anything.

I tugged on my fishing line, feeling guilty. "Look. I'm sorry about the night of the riot. I shouldn't have kissed you. I was out of line. If you want to report me to HR or whatever, that's okay. I won't deny it."

He glared at me. "Do you really think that's what I want to do?"

"Then come back."

"I can't."

"Why?"

He shook his head hard, running his hand through his hair. The agitation poured off him in waves until he looked like a rat trapped in a cage, even though we were in one of the most open, beautiful places I'd ever seen.

He was holding back. Keeping something from me that he obviously needed to say but wouldn't.

"Seriously, Rowe. Why? I need you to come back. I don't trust anyone else."

His tenuous hold on himself snapped. "Dammit, Mae. Why say that? Why did you have to come out here at all? What we did that night? That was stupid and dangerous and reckless. Do you have any idea what could happen if the prisoners thought there was something between you and me? The reason for the nonfraternization policy is because if a prisoner has a beef with me, they could try to take it out on you as revenge. I've seen that happen with my own eyes. So whatever you're asking of me, I can't, Mae! Can't you see that?"

I threw my hands up in frustration. "I'm just trying to help you keep your job! That's it!"

He grabbed me by the tops of my arms. "Bullshit," he growled. "That's not it. That's never been all there is between us, and you know it."

I drowned in his eyes. They held me captive, while my heart slammed against my rib cage. "What are you saying, then? You do want something more?"

"I'm saying I want to break that goddamn nonfraternization policy every time I look at you. So don't fucking apologize for kissing me, when all I can think about is doing it again."

I blinked, heat rushing through me. Despite trying to forget the kiss between us for the better part of a week, it all came rushing back. The way he'd felt, his chest pressed to mine, his tongue in my mouth, and his erection nudging against my belly.

I wanted it, too.

There was no denying it. "And that's a bad thing because...? We aren't at work all the time, you know."

He stared at me. "Do you really need more reasons than your life being in danger every time you go into the classroom?"

He was being deliberately stubborn. A martyr, trying to ruin his own happiness without even giving us a chance. I refused to let him. "You're with me for every shift! So yeah, actually, Rowe, I do need more than that."

He glared at me. "Fucking hell, you're exasperating. How about because you're with Liam, then! Or Heath? I don't know. How about because you're fucking dangerous, Mae!"

He dropped the rod, and I threw down mine to glare back at him. What the hell? Of all the things I'd been called in my life, dangerous wasn't one of them. I was the cautious sister. The one who was safe and reliable and calm. "Dangerous how? I teach seven-year-olds, I don't believe in carrying a gun, and last I checked, I had no desire to maim or murder. I'm a freaking pussycat, Rowe." A fly buzzed around my face, and I swatted at it in irritation. I completely missed, and the fly happily continued his annoying dance around my head. "See? I'm not even a danger to insects."

Rowe paced up and down the dock, shaking his head. Then he covered his face with his hands, doubling over to suck in deep breaths of air.

I frowned at him. Shit. I'd pushed him too hard. Who the hell was I to tell him what he wanted or didn't want? I was way out of line here. All the fight went out of me as quickly as it had ignited. "Hey. Are you okay?" I reached out to touch his arm.

He flinched away so violently it was as if I'd scalded him with a hot iron.

I stepped back immediately, giving him some space.

But his head snapped up, and he turned huge dark eyes on me. They were so full of regret my heart broke instantly.

And when he dropped to the ground, I was sure it was his pain that pierced through me.

"Fuck. I'm sorry. I didn't mean..." He looked up at me again.

His anguish forced me to my knees as well. Everything in me ached to reach out and touch him, to pull him into my arms and protect him against whatever demons he was reliving.

"I can't do this," he whispered. "You'll break me, and I'm barely hanging on as it is."

I dared to stroke his arm, a featherlight touch that was just my fingertips, and this time, he let me.

Suddenly, it was like watching myself. The way I'd been right after Jayela's death, when I'd been so rocked to my core that even the tiniest of touches felt like being punched in the gut. Tears formed at the backs of my eyes, remembering that pain and hating that he knew it as well. "I'm broken, too," I whispered. "You think I don't know what it feels like to lose someone? Who did you lose? A parent?"

His brown eyes stared into mine. And it was the longest of times before he answered, "My wife."

14

ROWE

*M*ae threaded her fingers between mine and gently led me to the edge of the dock. She tugged me down to sit beside her, our legs dangling off the edge, inches above the sparkling water. "What was her name?" Mae asked quietly. She hadn't let go of my fingers, and now she squeezed them encouragingly.

I stared down at our linked hands, praying she wouldn't pull away. It was so fucking lonely out here. Without work to fill my time, the isolation began to feel less like an oasis and more like a prison itself.

"Rory. She grew up here, in Saint View. But I met her in Ohio. I was working in the prison there, and she was a nurse in the infirmary. Same job that Perry does."

I took a peek at Mae and watched the understanding dawn on her face. It was easy to see her putting the pieces together and realizing that I'd done this before. I'd had the workplace relationship, that clearly hadn't worked out well for anyone involved. Rory was gone, and I was left a broken shell.

"You fell in love with her," Mae prompted.

There wasn't any point in not spilling the entire story now, so I nodded. "Hard and fast. We got married six months later. It was complicated, though. When I met her, she'd just split up with her ex and was newly pregnant with his kid."

Mae raised both eyebrows. "That's a lot of pressure for a new relationship."

I shrugged. "That wasn't the hard part, to be honest. Everything about Rory and the baby were easy to love. But her ex held up a gas station a few months after they split and landed himself in the prison."

"With Rory working there?"

"She'd gone on maternity leave. It was only supposed to be temporary, until he went to trial and could be shipped off somewhere else, and because she wasn't working, it wasn't really a big deal. She planned our wedding, and her belly grew, and then the baby was born, and Zye was barely on our radar. I didn't wear my ring to work, so as far as I was aware, none of the other prisoners even knew Rory and I were involved." I glanced over at Mae and couldn't hide the hole inside me. "I was twenty-three and thought I had it all. Fuck, I *did* have it all... Until one of Rory's coworkers came down with mono, and they had nobody to cover her shifts. So they asked her to come back from maternity leave early."

In the middle of the lake, a fish jumped out of the water before plunging back in, sending a rolling ripple across the flat surface. I wished I could do the same. Dive beneath the surface and never come back up. It wasn't the first time I'd had that thought, but Mae's warm hand wrapped around mine stopped me from throwing myself off the end of the dock and trying it.

I cleared the hoarseness from my throat. "They swore up and down that Rory and Zye would never be in the same section at the same time. Both for her safety and because obviously, in the warden's mind, there was a risk she could try to slip him contraband if they were ever together. It wasn't ideal, but it's so hard to get staff at prisons, so they were desperate for her to come back. And we needed the money. We'd just bought a house, and there were things we needed for the baby... They promised she'd never so much as see him pass by her window."

Mae nudged her knee against mine. "What happened?"

"There was a riot."

Mae gasped. "Rowe..."

I shook my head, needing to finish it before I couldn't. "It was bad. By the time I got to her, he'd already beaten me to it." Agony ripped through me at the memory, and I slammed my eyes shut tight, trying to force it out. "It was years ago. But finding her there, on the infirmary floor, her eyes just staring at the ceiling, her body beaten and bloodied... I can't ever get it out of my head." I choked on the words, trying to fight the tidal wave, but as usual, it was completely pointless.

"Her ex killed her?"

"He's never been charged for it. There was no proof. They took out all the cameras, and of course there were no witnesses to come forward. But I know it was him. Rather than kill him and end up in jail myself, I picked up and left. I've been in Saint View ever since."

I glanced up at her sadly. "That's why you're dangerous, Mae. That's why I never wanted you working at the prison. I know the tragedies that can come from working inside those walls. I know how badly it can end, and how quickly. That day in Ohio, I kissed Rory goodbye, we both went to our separate sections, and an hour later she was dead. I never had a chance of getting to her, and the same damn thing happened all over again last week with you. The common link is me. I already care too fucking much about you."

"But I'm not her. I'm still here. I walked out of that riot uninjured because of you."

I didn't want to hear it. "You walked out because you got lucky. That may not happen twice."

She edged closer, until her side was fully against mine. "Hey. Look at me. I'm here. I'm not hurt. It wasn't because I was lucky. It's because you and Heath had my back. Not only did you get me out, you got Perry, Tori, and Colt out. You saved lives last week."

I shook my head.

She put her hand to the side of my face, drawing me in her direction. "I hate that you don't believe me. But it's true. I'm here. Look at me."

I didn't want to open my eyes, because I was scared of what I'd see in hers.

"Rowe. Look at me."

Slowly, I looked at her. I instantly knew it was a mistake. Because even though my brain swore and shouted at me to stop, my body was drawn to hers, and she was too close not to kiss. Before I could think about what I was doing, I pressed my lips to hers.

She pulled back. "Rowe... Are you sure this is what you want?"

But I had no idea what I wanted. It had been so long since I'd had a woman in my arms. So long since I'd been this close to someone wearing delicate perfume, and Mae's softness and gentleness called out to the place inside me that was so desperately broken. So I didn't answer and just kissed her again. I wrapped my arms around her, touching my palms to her back and opening my mouth to hers. She kissed me back, and when I slid my tongue into her mouth she moaned at the intrusion. I couldn't get enough of her. I hauled her closer, eliminating any remaining distance between us on the wooden pier. Her thigh pressed against mine, her arms around my neck, and fingers digging into my hair as we devoured each other. Weeks of pent-up frustration over not letting myself have this crashed down over me, escaping through my fingers that skated over every curve of her body, while my tongue danced with hers. I let my fingers roam from her back, down her sides, tracing over the indent of her waist and the flare of her hips. I clutched the fabric of her skirt, loving that she always wore them. The material was so thin, made for hot summers, and it was almost as good as tracing her body naked. With one hand at the back of her head, holding her mouth to mine, I used my other hand to feel her thigh, inching up the fabric as I went until it was up over her knee.

She moaned loudly when I slipped my hands beneath and touched the soft skin of her inner thigh.

I was so sick of being numb. That was how I'd existed for years now, never letting anything in, never letting anything touch the armor I'd built up around my heart after Rory had died. It had worked. Nothing could hurt me, but it was like walking around in a fog. Never feeling truly happy or sad. A constant flatline of being.

"Touch me," she murmured.

Fuck.

My brain screamed no. My brain screamed that I'd already gone too far in kissing her. Guilt reared its ugly head and whispered Rory's name. It whispered that I was bound to Rory forever.

I silenced the accusation. I'd loved Rory. I'd loved her with every ounce of my being, but I couldn't stay married to a ghost. It would destroy me. I knew, somewhere deep inside me, that I wasn't in love with Rory anymore. Too much time had passed. The guilt changed tack, reminding me that a relationship with me would only end in tragedy. But I needed this. One moment where I just got to give in, and then I promised the voice that I would shut it down.

If only I could just have this moment with her.

I pushed my fingers between her thighs, finding silky panties covering her center. She was already soaked through with arousal just from kissing. "Fuck, Mae," I groaned. "You're so fucking wet, and I haven't even touched you yet."

Her only response was to kiss me harder, her tongue plunging into my mouth, her knees falling apart. I pulled aside the fabric of her panties and stroked my fingers through the slickness I found waiting there. She gasped, moving away from my mouth, staring at me with big eyes.

Our gazes clashed and held until I touched her clit. Then her eyes rolled back, and she leaned back on her palms, her nipples straining at the fabric of her T-shirt. I really wanted to strip it off her and see her perfect tits, nipples straining up to the sky, but I didn't dare take my hand away from her pussy. Her breath had already changed to quick pants as I rubbed her clit, while my erection grew behind my shorts.

"I wish I could strip you naked," I whispered. "Fuck, Mae. I want to lay you out and taste every inch of your body. But I want to watch you come more."

She let out a tiny moan when I drove one finger up inside her. "Don't stop."

I pumped my finger in and out with no resistance, then quickly added a second. She dropped down onto her elbows, and I yanked her skirt up, so I could watch my fingers plunge in and out of her. I used my other hand to work her clit, building her higher and higher, until her moans became long and insistent, her legs trembled, and she clutched blindly for me.

"Rowe, I need to come. Please. Don't stop."

"No chance of that," I confirmed. "Your pussy tight around my fingers is the sweetest thing I've ever seen."

She groaned hard at the dirty words, and that was all it took to get her off. She shouted my name, and it echoed around us in the silence. Her internal walls clamped down on my fingers, and a fresh rush of arousal seeped from between her pretty pink lips. I worked her right until she begged me to stop, thrusting in and out slowly, wringing out every last drop of her orgasm.

She pushed my hand away, her entire body trembling with sensitivity. Then she lay back on the dock and stared up at me with a huge grin. I withdrew my fingers from her core and watched her while I sucked them.

She eyed me without saying anything, after-orgasm bliss glowing on her face. But as I lowered my fingers from my mouth, I began mentally shutting myself down. The walls came back up, the suit of armor strapped back on. I put her panties back into place and lowered her skirt so it hung around her ankles once more. I stood stiffly and moved away from her.

She sat up quickly and reached a hand out to me. "Hey, where you going?"

"I've got to go. It's time for me to go back to work."

She struggled to her feet, straightening her shirt as she went. "I'm glad. But, Rowe... This..." She waved a hand in the direction of the spot where I just made her scream my name. "Can we talk about this?"

I shook my head. "There's nothing to talk about. This was nothing. It won't happen again." I left her on the dock and went back to my cabin alone.

I'd made so many mistakes. Too many. But there was one mistake I wouldn't make again. I couldn't work with somebody I cared about. I knew that Mae was in love with Heath and I wouldn't ask her to give her job up. Not when it was the only way she'd get to see him regularly.

So the only alternative was that I give her up.

So when she called my name, I didn't look back. I just walked inside the cabin and closed the door.

15

MAE

*A*fter Rowe locked himself in his cabin and refused to speak to me, I'd come home in a huff, stomping around my apartment and slamming cupboard doors in frustration. I still tingled from his touch, and I couldn't stop replaying the feel of his fingers skating up my inner thighs and pressing up into me. I'd wanted to do more. I'd wanted to pin him to the ground, throw my leg over his waist, and ride him. He hadn't been able to hide his erection. It had been thick and hard behind his shorts when he'd walked away, and I bit my lip now, just thinking about how it would have felt to have him deep inside, rocking my hips against his, and watching him fall apart while I did.

But there was no space for him in my mind by the time I got to work that night. I was working on the women's side, and a guard met me at the entranceway. She introduced herself as Martina and handed me my new ID badge and access code.

"After last week's disaster on the men's side, the new warden has upped security," she explained.

"I guess that was to be expected." I took my card from her and clipped it to my shirt.

"Can you memorize that number, because we can't take it into the prison with us."

I stared at the six-digit number on the slip of paper, reciting it over in my head a few times before crumpling it into a ball and tossing it in the wastepaper basket. "Got it. Let's go."

I was itching to get inside. It had been too long since I'd seen the ladies I taught, and I wanted to get them back in a routine as quickly as possible.

As expected, my classroom was full and noisy when we walked in, but they stopped their conversations to cheer my name.

"Teach is back after taming the wild beasts in the prison riot of the century!"

"We thought you were dead for a bit there! Glad you aren't!"

I couldn't help but grin.

"I didn't finish my homework because I was real traumatized knowing you were over there and in danger."

I frowned in the direction of the woman who'd said that last one, and she gave me a sheepish grin that I couldn't help but laugh at. Martina took up a spot at the back of the room, watching like a hawk but not intruding in my handling of the class, which I appreciated. I clapped my hands together a couple of times and then waved for them all to take their seats. When they were mostly quiet, I took my place at the front of the room. "Okay. I know this place is bound to be buzzing with questions about what happened during the riot. You get three, then we're going to buckle down and get some work done. Deal?"

They all nodded, and hands immediately shot up in the air.

"Wow, okay, you all are nosy, huh?" I shook my head with a laugh. "At least you put your hands up. Gia, you're up."

"Did you see anyone get killed?"

DeWitt's dead, unseeing eyes flashed through my mind. I swallowed hard. "No," I lied. "Next question."

I gazed around the room at the waving hands, trying to decide who would ask the least intrusive questions. My gaze settled on Selina. I pointed at her. "Shoot."

She seemed ready to cry, her eyes red-rimmed and glassy. "Colt...I mean Officer McCaffery. Is he okay? We haven't been allowed phone calls this last week, and ..."

I smiled softly at her. "He was injured, yes. But he's fine. He's recuperating at home with his family...who are all well, too, so I'm told."

Martina looked at me quizzically, silently asking why I was giving out information about Colt's family. But Selina had confided in me that Colt was her son-in-law, partner of her niece, Lacey, though she'd raised Lacey and thought of her as her daughter. My heart went out to the older woman. It had to have been torturous, hearing about Colt going down and then not even being able to call and check in on her family. I made a mental note to ask someone when the prisoners would be getting privileges like phone calls back. Especially for the women, who hadn't even been involved in the riot, it seemed a particularly harsh punishment.

Selina's shoulders slumped in relief, and she nodded at me gratefully. I wanted to reach out and squeeze her hand, or even better, pull her into a hug, but I didn't.

"Right, last question, then we get on with some of our work, okay?"

I randomly picked a woman, Sasha, a tall, skinny blonde who was in desperate need of having her regrowth colored. The rest of the class groaned in disappointment over not having their questions answered, and Sasha stood and shushed them all. "Shut up, would youse? I got the best question anyway, the one you all too chickenshit to ask."

She spun back around to face me, a devilish grin on her face. "Is it true you were kissing someone in the middle of it?"

Shock punched through my gut.

Rowe pushing me up against the wall in solitary.

Heath sweeping me into his arms.

Both of them kissing me until none of us cared about the riot that raged around us.

"What a waste of a question," Martina stated dryly from the back of the room.

There were groans of agreement, and somebody threw a balled-up piece of paper in Sasha's direction. "As if, Sash."

But Sasha was insistent. "I swear, you guys. I heard it from a reliable source, who said he saw the teach and that Michaelson guy. You know the big beefcake dude? He's kinda new, but you guys can't have missed him, he so fine. Apparently, they were all over each other."

My mouth dried as I tried to find words. My gaze clashed with Selina's, and she spoke up over the din with a kind but knowing look in her eye, like she could see right inside my head. "That's not true, right, Miss Donovan? You're with Liam Banks, I believe?" She turned around and stared at the other women. "He's a lawyer. Very handsome and a perfect match for a teacher. She's not scumming around with prisoners, Sasha. You wasted your question."

I took the bone Selina had thrown me, though I had a feeling she knew exactly what had happened in that hallway with Heath. I didn't know how, maybe it was that she could truly just read me, but I was grateful for her help, whether it was intentional or not. "Selina is right. I'm with a very nice man, so no, there was no kissing in the middle of a riot." I tried to laugh it off, though I wasn't entirely sure how successful I was at sounding believable. "Who has time for making out in the middle of a riot anyway? I was too busy trying to avoid the fire and the men with weapons."

That did the trick. The class erupted into "Oh hell no!" and "Tell us about that!" Sasha's accusations were instantly forgotten.

I shook my head. "The deal was three questions then work. So let's do some math."

They groaned, but it was good-natured, and to their credit, they worked solidly for the next hour and a half. In fact, they were so well-behaved that Martina pulled a book from one of the shelves, sat back, and started reading. I hid a smile about that.

At nine, when my time was up, I dismissed the class. They all filed out while I packed up my things, but Sasha lingered behind. I glanced up when I realized she wasn't following the others.

She had her lips pulled into a worried line.

"Are you okay?" I asked her.

She shook her head. "I just wanted to say sorry about my comment earlier. It was really rude of me, and I don't want you to think badly of me because of it."

I shook my head quickly, reassuring her. "Of course I don't." Guilt nibbled away at my conscience. I hated that I'd lied to them, but there was no other way around it.

"I just want you to know how much this class means to me. You're a really great teacher. I wasn't much good at school. I could never follow what was going on, and so I just goofed off. And then I stopped turning up altogether. You're the first teacher who's ever explained things in a way I can understand."

I smiled at her softly. "Or maybe it's just that now you're ready to learn. Less distractions in here."

She nodded. "I've got a little girl at home. She's with my mom right now, but when I go home, I want to be better for her, you know? I want her to see that I tried even after I failed. You're giving me the opportunity to do that, so I just wanted to say thanks. And that I hope we're all good?"

I risked Martina telling me off and took Sasha's hand, squeezing it tightly. "Absolutely. Now go before you get in trouble. I'll see you next class. Do your homework!"

She grinned at me as she left the room. "I promise."

Martina didn't say anything about me touching a prisoner. We walked side by side out through the prison and back to the area that was open to the general public, where the offices and staff locker rooms were.

"You're really good with them," Martina commented as she let me out through the solid doors.

"Thank you."

"I've never seen a teacher like you in a place like this. But I hope you stick around."

"I appreciate that."

With a friendly clap on my shoulder, she disappeared back into the belly of the prison, leaving me to collect my things and see myself out.

I made my way into the locker room but stopped abruptly when Rowe was on the other side, talking to a guard I didn't recognize. My heart slammed against my chest, my pussy immediately clenching at the sight of him. But I was disappointingly empty. Though the other guard kept talking, Rowe's gaze tracked me across the room, watching intently as I collected my things from my locker. When the other guard left, leaving me and Rowe alone, I didn't say anything. I was still annoyed with him after the way he'd just locked himself in his cabin and refused to talk to me.

Every traitorous nerve ending in my body sparked to life when he stopped behind me, though. My mind ran away with fantasies of him pressing me hard against my locker and taking me from behind.

Even though I was angry at the man, I still wanted him.

Dammit.

"You didn't say hello," he murmured.

"Well, you didn't say goodbye. You just locked yourself in your room, like a moody teenager, so I guess we're even." I turned to leave, but he caught my wrist.

"Let go," I demanded, though it sounded weak even to my own ears.

"Mae...I..."

I whirled on him, yanking my arm from his grip, and jamming my hands on my hips. "You what? You're sorry for locking me out of your house after I kindly came to check you were actually alive? Next time I'll just leave you in your stupor and let you get fired."

"What happened between us...it can't happen again."

The weight of that statement crushed down on me. I didn't want to give him up when I'd only had such a tiny taste. There was something undeniable between us. A chemistry that drew me in and an attraction that made my knees weak. I wanted him. And I was pretty sure he wanted me.

"You're scared," I accused.

The anguish in his eyes flared. He stood so close to me that our breaths mingled. "Yes," he admitted. "You fucking terrify me."

I reached for his hand, but he flinched away, taking two big steps back. "I need this job."

"That didn't seem to matter this afternoon."

"But it does matter! I can't quit. And I won't ask you to. We don't work if we're working here!"

"Then just say it, Rowe! Say you don't want me. Because you're saying one thing and doing another." It was bold and brash and completely unlike me, but I just wanted him to admit it.

He groaned and slammed the heel of his hand against my locker. "Fuck, Mae. Are you serious? Of course I fucking do. I want you so bad it's killing me, but I can't. The danger is too real, and if I let myself fall for you, and then something happened to you, it would end me. I can't do it twice."

I took a step toward him. "Nothing is going to happen. I'm fine. We're both fine."

But he shook his head. "This job is all I know, and it's all I'm good at. You started working here to see Heath, and that reason hasn't changed."

"So that's it? I just get no say in it?"

He stared at me, challenging me to find another way around it. But he was right. I wasn't going to give up my job. It wasn't just for Heath, it was for the people here like Sasha and her daughter. I was making a change here. Making a difference that I'd never really felt teaching rich seven-year-olds how to read. While my old job was important, so was this one. Sasha had never had half the opportunities my first graders would have.

I wasn't sure when I'd made the decision to quit my elementary school job and make the prison my only job. I had a feeling it had been weeks before, but I just hadn't had the guts to say it. But tonight had cemented it. I belonged here, and even after we got Heath out, I didn't want to give this up.

I watched Rowe walk away. It broke my heart that finding my true calling in life meant giving up a man I could have fallen in love with.

16

MAE

I went straight to Liam's place after work.

He pounced on me the minute I walked inside the doors. "Is Rowe all right?"

I dumped my purse on his couch and pulled him down to sit beside me. "Honestly? I don't know. I mean, I got him to come back to work, but he's cut himself right off from me."

"What? Why? What happened?"

I let the softness of his cushions envelop me. I hadn't wanted to tell Liam in a text what was going on, so I'd just sent him one saying everything was fine and I'd talk to him tonight. "Things got hot between us when I went out to his cabin today, and now he's all freaked out about it."

Lust flared in Liam's eyes. "Hot how?"

I grinned at him. "Why do I get the impression you like hearing about what I'm doing with Heath and Rowe?"

He brushed the hair away from my neck and replaced it with a gentle kiss. "Did you come?"

Heat jolted straight between my legs. "Yes."

"That's what I like. I like knowing you were satisfied and well taken care of. I like knowing that other men want my girl as much as I want you."

"I like hearing you say I'm your girl," I whispered as he trailed his way down my neck, sucking the soft skin there and turning me on.

"Good, because I like saying it. Tell me what you did with Rowe."

God, I loved this side of him. It was hot and wild and mind-blowing.

"We were talking, sitting at the end of a little dock, overlooking the lake."

He kept kissing my neck but slowly reached down and unbuckled his belt.

My breath hitched, watching him.

"Keep talking, Mae. Every detail."

"He kissed me, and then he lifted my skirt and pressed his fingers between my thighs."

Liam sucked hard at the spot behind my ear, and I moaned, slipping my fingers into the elastic of my skirt and shoving it down over my hips. I raised my ass off the couch so I could drop the skirt to the floor. Liam's suit pants gaped open at the fly, and he did the same, pushing his pants to join my skirt.

"I was already wet for him," I admitted. "My panties soaked."

He groaned and grabbed a handful of my breast, squeezing my hard nipple through the fabric in a way that almost felt like a punishment. But if that was the case then I wanted to be bad again. So very fucking bad, just so he would do that some more.

"Take your shirt off," he demanded. "I want you naked."

I've never moved so quick. I ripped my shirt and bra off, tossing them somewhere behind the couch. I shivered as the cool air from the vents in the ceiling skated over my body, then stood to shimmy out of my panties.

"You're wet now," Liam accused. "I can see it between your thighs."

I nodded, breathless.

He stood, shedding the rest of his clothes until we stood naked before each other. My core ached at the sight of his erection, hard and proud, jutting from his groin, straining toward me. He palmed it, stroking his hand up and down.

"Get on the couch," he directed.

I did as I was told, lying back. He parted my thighs so he could kneel between them, and then worked his erection. "Did he fuck you? Did he take you here?" He reached down and pressed two fingers deep inside me.

I cried out at the welcome intrusion and at the pleasure shooting through me. I was so desperate for him to touch me.

"We didn't have sex," I moaned. "Just his fingers..."

Liam shook his head. "That must have fucking killed him. To have you there, so sweet and needy and then only use his hand." He drove his fingers in and out of my core while he pumped his dick.

"He was hard," I admitted between thrusts.

Liam groaned, and the thought that it turned him on only spurred me on harder. My orgasm built in my belly, the first beginnings dipping lower to my core, and sending my hips surging against Liam's hand. I rode his fingers in the same rhythm he worked his cock until we were both teetering on the edge.

"Liam," I moaned.

He slapped his fingers once against my pussy, a sharp jolt of pleasure that blew my mind and sent me barreling into my orgasm. I clenched down, yelling my pleasure, and then his dick was there, replacing his fingers and filling me so deliciously as I spasmed around him.

"Yes," I cried. "God, yes!"

He fucked me while I came, and then when he couldn't take it a minute more, he pulled out abruptly. "Spread your legs wide, Mae. I want to see your pussy while I come."

My heart slammed against my chest, and I did it because it was such a turn-on to be dominated by him like this. He fisted his glistening cock once more and came with a jerk. His cum spilled over my pussy and inner thighs, and he used his other hand to rub it in, working my clit and stimulating the entire area while he did it. Another orgasm built hard and fast, and he knew it was coming. His fingers brought me to the edge again, and I fell over it, screaming into a pillow so the down-stairs neighbors didn't hear.

It took me a long time to remove the pillow from my face and come back down to earth. But when I did, Liam stared at me with hazy, lust-filled eyes. "That was the hottest thing I've ever seen," he praised.

I was a sticky mess but I was right there with him. "I've never had sex like this," I admitted. "My exes were very...orderly."

Liam sniggered. "Orderly? What the hell does that mean in terms of sex?"

It really was laughable, how night and day having sex with Liam was compared to anyone else. "They just sort of rolled on top of me, stuck it in and out a few times, and then it was done. If I was lucky, they handed me a warm cloth to clean up with, but there was never anything...adventurous."

Liam kissed my mouth, pushing his tongue deep inside, which set off a whole new round of longing for him. But he pulled away then grabbed my hands, encouraging me to my feet. "They never came on you?"

My cheeks heated. "Ah, no. Not in the way you just did anyway. That felt...."

"Like being claimed?"

"A little bit."

"That okay with you?"

It was more than okay. It was amazing.

He guided me into the bathroom and turned the shower on, testing the temperature before ushering me inside. The water fell hot and fast on my back, and I reached for a sponge on a string, hanging from a tap. But he took it from me, lathering it up with soap, and then dropped to his knees before me. Slowly, he removed all traces of himself from my body, with gentle strokes. I rested my head back on my shoulders, letting the water spray over my face, while he tended to my most sensitive area.

When I was clean, he replaced the sponge with his tongue and licked his way between my legs. But it was slow, and gentle. Not a race to bring me to orgasm like it had been in the living room. I closed my eyes and just enjoyed the relaxing feeling.

"Mae..."

"Mmmm?" I ran my fingers through his hair, massaging his scalp.

"If you want to do more with Rowe..." He cleared his throat. "I mean, if you want to include Rowe in this...I'm down for that. The idea of him taking you while I watch..."

I looked down at him, his lips hovering at my pussy while he stared up at me.

"Are you serious?"

He nodded.

It was already so much that he wanted to hear about what I'd done with him. I couldn't imagine being intimate with someone while someone else watched and yet...heat flushed through me.

I wanted it, too. "Have you done that before? A threesome?"

He nodded. "Yes, but with two women. Never with another man...but that was just about getting off... With you, I just want to give you everything you've ever desired."

I went to assure him that he was what I desired, but he cut me off.

"No, I know you want me. I know there's feelings there. I don't want to stop what we're building. I want to enhance it. Make it bigger." He licked my clit, slowly massaging it with his tongue. "Do you know how good it would feel to have me lick you here, while his dick is inside you?"

"Oh," I moaned.

It didn't take him long to bring me to my third orgasm of the night. And even though we hadn't officially agreed to anything, there was an unspoken understanding that if the opportunity arose, we'd take it.

*L*iam's phone rang early the next morning, while we were still completely naked and spooning in his bed. He groaned at the ungodly hour but answered it anyway, mumbling about how he needed a new job, one that respected business hours.

But he sat up when he looked at the display and nudged me. "It's Boston." He answered it. "Hey, what's doing?"

I stretched sleepily, my body a delicious ache from last night's shenanigans. Liam tucked the phone between his ear and his shoulder and grabbed a pen and notepad from the bedside table, jotting something down in an illegible scrawl. He thanked Boston, then hung up.

I peered at the piece of paper, trying to make out what it said. "I thought only doctors had writing like that?"

"Hey, I can read it. That's all that matters."

"What did Boston want?"

"He's hit the ground running with this new protection company he's started. And they've had calls coming into the line he set up for info on Jayela's murder. A lot of them."

Nerves suddenly took flight in my belly. "It's only been a couple of days."

"I know. He said there was a lot of calls that he immediately dismissed as bogus, but one that came in last night caught his interest. They accused your father of knowing more than he's letting on."

I screwed up my face. "That seems unlikely. Jayela barely spoke to him. More than I do, because he doesn't actively despise her, but they weren't exactly going to father/daughter dinner dates."

"Are you sure about that? What if she was and she just didn't want to tell you because she knows how you feel about him?"

I frowned, not liking that idea at all. "That would be a pretty big secret to keep."

"Not as big as the pregnancy she didn't tell you about."

His words were like rubbing salt on an open wound.

He put a hand to my cheek and stroked his thumb across it. "I'm sorry. I didn't mean for that to hurt you. But we have to look into her pregnancy. Find out who the father was. It could help Heath's case."

"I know." Dealing with Rowe had been a welcome distraction, but at some point, I had to face that I didn't know my sister as well as I'd thought I had.

"If she was closer with your father than you thought she was, he might know something. We should at least go and ask him."

I groaned, flopping back into his bed. "Do we have to? What if I call all her friends this morning instead? Maybe she confided in one of them and we can avoid making contact with my sperm donor."

Liam chuckled. "Ouch. Things are that bad between the two of you, huh?"

"Worse."

He kissed me softly then got out of bed. "I've got to go to work, but try it. Call everyone. If nothing comes of it, we'll go see your dad on my lunch break. Together. Deal?"

"Ugh, fine."

I went back to sleep for an hour, so I didn't hear Liam leave, but when I woke up, it was a reasonable time to start calling people. Wrapped in one of Liam's too-big T-shirts, I wandered around his apartment, scrolling through my phone contacts. I didn't have the numbers for all of Jayela's friends, so some of them might have to be found on Facebook. But I had her high school best friend, and a woman from her gym who she was quite friendly with. Boston was her closest friend, but he obviously didn't know anything, or he would have said something by now. The only other person was Tori, and she was an easy place to start.

Tori didn't even say hello. "You better be calling to say that you're at my front door with cocktails."

"It's barely nine A.M."

"Not if you've been up all night with a screaming baby. It's totally five P.M. here."

"Is he okay?"

"He's fine. Just teething. But he's chewing an iced-up teething toy right now while I drink my fourth coffee, so tell me all about your exciting, single, no-cranky-babies life."

I grinned. "There's a lot of sex," I admitted.

She squealed in excitement, and after I filled her in on all the details, I steered the conversation back to my original reason for calling. "I need to ask you something about Jayela. Did you know she was pregnant?"

There was a stunned silence, and then, "No, she wasn't."

I bit my lip. "She was. Not when she died, that would have shown on the autopsy, but Liam and I found a pregnancy test in her drawer... We think she was seeing someone. But she never brought anyone home to meet me. Did she say anything to you?"

"No. Crap, I need to go, Mae. The baby is fussing again. Bye."

I blinked at the phone in my hand. I hadn't heard any noise from the baby. She must have been watching him on the monitor. I sighed and tried the two other friends that I had numbers for, but the high school friend hadn't heard from Jayela in years. The gym friend, whose name was Geri, answered on the second ring and immediately burst into tears.

I swallowed hard to keep from joining her.

"I'm sorry," she muttered eventually, pulling herself together enough to talk. "I just miss her."

"I do, too."

I filled her in on the pregnancy test, and she was as shocked as Tori had been. "I had no idea," she confirmed, and a piece of my heart sank. "She did stop coming to the gym on Wednesday and Thursday nights, though. I know she wasn't working because Boston was still there. I thought she was just being a slacker so I gave her a hard time and told her to get off the couch, but she said she had other things in her life besides work and the gym. I actually teased her about having a new man, but she insisted she didn't."

I slumped down on the couch after I ended the call with Geri. Then I shot Liam a message.

All I got was that Jayela gave up the gym on Wednesday

and Thursday nights. Sigh. Get your armor on. We're going to have to enter the lion's den. Time to go talk to my father.

17

LIAM

*A*t one, I told my receptionist to clear my afternoon because I might not be back. She grumbled when I explained I had something personal to do, but I ignored her. I had taken a lot of time off lately, between Mae and working on Heath's case, and my coworkers weren't used to me having something more than work in my life.

They were going to have to get used to it, though. Because if Mae needed me, I was going to be there.

She was waiting outside her building when I got there and hopped in right away.

"I would have walked up, you know?"

She shook her head, staring straight out the window. "No. The longer I stayed up there, the more I thought about just not going at all. I'd already thought up all the ways I could convince you not to go."

"Were they sexual?" I grinned, putting the car into drive and pulling out into the light, midday traffic.

"I was going to blow your mind."

I chuckled. "I could have resisted."

"You could have resisted lacy white lingerie and my vibrator?"

I snapped my head in her direction, my mouth dropping open. "Seriously?"

"As a heart attack. I had it on, and sex toys all freshly charged..."

I groaned.

"See why I had to come downstairs? You would have been way too easy to convince."

She wasn't wrong. "Now I'm going to have that vision of you in my head until I get to see it for real."

She patted me on the leg. "Don't worry. Ten minutes with my father will kill all good feelings. Lust for sure, but also joy, happiness, and hope."

She laughed, but it was weak. I reached across and squeezed her hand. "Sorry we have to do this."

"Me, too."

I drove us deep into Providence, taking us back toward my own apartment. "Want to trade shitty dad stories?"

She grinned. "Sure. Mine had a babysitter take me to my first day of school."

"Mine probably didn't even know I was old enough for school," I countered.

"Mine had our driver take me to the store to buy my first bra. He was an older man in his seventies. I've never seen someone so red."

I cringed. "That sounds bad."

She shrugged. "Probably would have been worse if my father had tried taking me himself. At least Winston had the sense to call his wife. She met us at the store and was so kind to me. She helped me pick out what I needed, and then the two of them took me to the movies." She smiled at the memory. "It was actually a pretty good day."

Her memory jogged one of mine loose. A day I hadn't thought about in years. "I went to a baseball camp not long after I started living with my grandparents. It was a real boy's boy sort of place, where baseball was life."

"Sounds right up your alley."

"It was. I loved it. Until father/son day. The parents were all supposed to come to the camp and spend the day doing coaching clinics with a big 'kids vs adults' game at the end."

She shot me a sympathetic smile. "That was a bit insensitive of them. There had to be a lot of kids whose parents couldn't make it."

"I was already a bit embarrassed, thinking that my grandfather would show up. He was so much older than the other kids' dads, and though he liked that I excelled at something, he wasn't into sports himself."

I took the turn into Mae's dad's street, and she pointed to a huge house on the left-hand side. The car coasted to a stop in the front, but she made no move to get out. She was waiting for me to finish my story.

"So the day comes, and the other kids are so excited to show off everything we've been learning for the last ten days. Then the dads start rolling up. The first two carpooled, and both of them got out wearing matching baseball shirts. I still remember how fresh and new they were. Not a spot of dirt on them, the white so bright against the dark blue of the sleeves and the word 'Dads' printed on the front in cursive. Their kids went tearing across the field to meet them. We were only about ten, still small enough to be picked up when hugged, and when one of the dads swung his kid around, his son's name was printed across the back of his shoulders. More and more families arrived, and the dads all had those shirts. All personalized with their kids' names."

"That's sweet. I can imagine how excited the kids would have been at that sort of attention. You must have been excited to see your grandfather with your name on his back?"

I clenched my fingers a little tighter around the steering wheel. "I might have been. If he'd showed."

Mae's mouth dropped open. "No. He just didn't turn up? What about your mom?"

I shook my head. "I don't think she even knew I was there. She would've wanted to, for sure. But the camp was only accessible by car. She didn't have one."

"It doesn't sound like your day ended with ice cream and movies," Mae said softly.

I smiled stiffly. "It was fine. They waited a long time for my grandfather to show, but eventually they had to start. One of the counselors threw the ball around with me while the other kids all got to hang out with their families."

She sighed and stared up at the house. "Well. You win. For now. But we're about to give my dad another chance, so don't get too attached to that first-place spot. You never know when dear old Lawrence will come through with a whole new way to suck."

*A*n older man opened the door to Mae's dad's house, but I immediately knew it wasn't her father when she threw her arms around him. The man smiled fondly at her embrace, patting her awkwardly on the back. "Miss Mae! What are you doing here? Your father didn't say he was expecting you."

She pulled back and took up my hand again. "He's not. But I need to talk to him anyway. Is he home?"

The man bit his lip nervously. "He is, but..."

"Yeah, I know. He won't want to see me. Tough luck." She moved past the butler, and he made no move to stop her.

"Hi," I greeted him, holding out my spare hand for him to shake. Mae had a death grip on the other one. "I'm Liam."

The old man gazed down at Mae's fingers wrapped around mine and smiled. "Winston. I'm Mr. Donovan's driver and butler. Lovely to meet you, Mr. Liam."

But there was no chance for further pleasantries with Mae pulling me through the house, speeding through one high-ceilinged room after the other. Each one was immaculate and decorated tastefully. A museum of a house, and not unlike my grandparents'.

"Father dearest, where are you?" Mae called. There was no answer.

Winston, trailing after us, cleared his throat uncomfortably. "He's upstairs."

Mae flashed him an appreciative smile. "Thank you, Winston."

She dragged me along the stairs, thundering up them at almost a run.

I tugged her hand. "Where's the fire?"

"I just need to get this over and done with. I hate this house."

She bypassed two closed doors and headed straight for the third, busting in like she was a cop on some police show.

The room revealed a solid mahogany desk, polished so perfectly it gleamed. But there was no father figure sitting on the chair behind it. Mae paused. "I thought for sure he'd be here. The only other place is his bedroom."

An uncomfortableness about bursting into her father's private room prickled at the back of my neck, but Mae seemed to have no such qualms, moving to the next door and throwing it open. "I hope you're dressed, old man."

I blinked in the sudden dimness. The only light that crept in was around the edges of heavy drapes. The room was clean, but an odd smell hung in the air.

Mae stopped abruptly. "Dad?"

"Mae?"

Mae's father struggled to sit up in his bed, striped flannel pajamas covering his chest. Mae stared, her eyes wide while the man pushed himself up on one elbow but then had to stop to rest for a moment.

On autopilot, I moved around her, grabbing a pillow from the other side of the bed, and putting it behind the man's back to support him.

He glanced up at me gratefully. "Thank you," he murmured. "I'm okay now."

I nodded and stepped back, taking up my spot beside his daughter.

Mae still hadn't moved.

Lawrence smoothed his palms over the royal-blue coverlet across his lap. Black circles marked the space beneath his eyes, and his cheeks were hollowed out, gaunt with poor health. "What brings you here?"

Mae ignored his question. "What's going on? Why are you in bed at one in the afternoon? You've never slept in a day in your life."

He pursed his lips together. "Things are different now. It's not as easy to stay awake during the day when your body is pumped full of chemo on a regular basis."

My heart sank for this man who was obviously unwell, and for Mae. She might not have been her father's biggest fan, but hearing he had cancer couldn't have been easy either. I brushed the back of my hand against hers, letting her know I was here for her.

She stared at him, her face completely blank of emotion. "Are you going to die?" Her question was so blunt, it was like being hit over the head with it. Even I felt the pain.

Her father didn't cringe away, though, the way I wanted to. "Aren't we all going to die at some point?"

"Don't give me your bullshit. You know what I meant."

He sighed. "Am I terminal? Yes."

"How long?"

"Six months? A year? They can't really say."

I took her hand this time and squeezed it. She squeezed back but then pulled away. I took a step behind her, knowing this was her fight but wanting her to know I had her back.

"Were you planning on telling me?"

"I tried."

"When?" The outburst of anger was the only real sign that this was affecting her at all.

"At your sister's funeral. I told you we needed to talk..."

She shook her head. "If that's true, you've got some seriously lousy timing."

"I know. I'm sorry—"

Mae held up one hand, her fingers trembling slightly. "The last thing I want from you is apologies."

"What do you want then? I didn't think this was just a social visit." Lawrence fiddled with the edge of the coverlet, his slim fingers absently tracing over the embroidered pattern.

"Do you know anything about Jayela's death?"

His brow furrowed in confusion. "Only what I read in the papers. I kept expecting the police to come and talk to me, but evidently you were listed as her next of kin, and then they arrested someone so quickly..."

"You were never questioned?" I piped up.

Lawrence turned his gaze on me. "No. I wasn't."

That was odd in a murder investigation. Immediate family were always the first ones interviewed, aside from witnesses. Just another way the cops had completely written this case off as soon as they'd decided it was Heath.

"They arrested the wrong man," Mae bit out. "The real killer is still out there somewhere."

Lawrence's mouth formed a soft 'O.'

He looked genuinely surprised to me, but Mae acted as if she didn't believe it for a second.

"An anonymous tip-off accused you of knowing more than you're letting on." She spat the words at him, like she was one-hundred-percent convinced of his guilt already. I put a reassuring hand on the small of her back, silently hoping it would act as a reminder to stay calm and just get the information we came for.

"What?" Lawrence suddenly looked sharper than he'd been the entire time we'd stood here. "Why would they say that? I don't know anything about her death."

As a lawyer, I had a pretty good bullshit meter. I could spot a lie a mile off. And though Mae clearly wasn't convinced, Lawrence didn't have the look of a man who was lying. Either he was a very good actor, or he was genuinely in shock.

"I believe you," I said softly.

Mae spun to stare at me, but I pulled away and sat on the foot of the bed. This visit wasn't going to do us any good if I didn't get her to actually listen to what her father had to say.

Lawrence's gaze darted between me and his daughter.

"I believe you," I said again. "But is there anything you can tell us? I know you and Mae are estranged, but did you have any contact with Jayela before she died?"

He focused his watery blue eyes on me. They were nothing like Mae's. She must have gotten hers from her mother. "We had dinner sometimes."

"Liar," Mae accused.

Lawrence's gaze snapped to his youngest daughter. "We did, Mae. I reached out to her after I first got my diagnosis."

"She knew you were sick?"

"Yes. I knew you wouldn't take my calls, but she would. I asked her to tell you, but she said she needed to find the right moment. I guess she never did."

"Guess not."

I tried to steer the conversation back to topics that would actually help us. "Did Jayela ever confide in you about a pregnancy?"

The man's eyes widened. "She was pregnant?"

I hadn't seen Jayela in a very long time, but I still felt like shit for betraying her privacy. I hoped if she was in some sort of Heaven or a ghost wandering around unseen, that she understood why I had to do it. "At some point, yes. We aren't sure when exactly."

"No, she never told me." His eyes turned sad. "That breaks my heart. I wish—"

Mae's eyes flashed with anger. "Oh, bullshit! Don't start with the regretful, 'could have been a grandpa' crap now. You were a shitty father and you would have been a shitty grandfather, too. Don't even pretend like you care."

The older man flinched. "I do care. I've been trying to tell you that—you and your sister—for a long time. I know I made mistakes with you both. But I was in pain—"

"You think I wasn't? You think it was easy growing up, knowing that every time you looked at me, you saw a murderer?"

I stared at Mae. Her fingers were balled into fists at her sides. "What?"

Tears rolled down her face.

Lawrence's voice was thick with pent-up emotion. "I never..."

But his protests were weak, and it was clear that Mae knew it, too. "You couldn't even look at me, Dad. It took me so long to work out that it was because of me that you never came home."

"What happened to your mother wasn't your fault."

"And yet, you made me feel like it was. How do you think it felt to be a ten-year-old kid whose father had never been present at even one of her birthdays? To know that any gift left for me had come from the household staff because they felt sorry for me?"

Lawrence sat a little straighter, staring his grown daughter down. "Do you love this man?"

Well, that had come out of left field. I stared down at my hands while I held my breath, not daring to look at Mae.

Mae spat back her answer. "That's none of your business. You don't get to know about my personal life."

But Lawrence wasn't dropping it that easily. "It doesn't matter. I can see the connection between you, even without your confirmation. It's in the way he supports you. I can see it just in how he looks at you."

I closed my eyes. *Fuck.* Was I that obvious that a complete stranger could see that I was falling for her?

Mae's gaze strayed to mine, but I turned away quickly.

"Now tell me how you'd feel if he was suddenly ripped away from you. How you'd feel if you walked into a hospital, with one little girl in your arms, and a heart full of excitement about having another. Only to have the woman you loved more than life itself taken from you."

Mae was shaking her head, but I could imagine it. I could see her and me, her belly swollen with my baby. And then I saw her never walking out of the hospital again. And even though it was just an image in my mind, it speared pain through my chest, hot and hard.

I wasn't just falling for Mae.

I was in love with her.

"I don't know how I'd feel, but I do know I wouldn't blame the defenseless baby who never got to know her mother."

The old man nodded. "You're right. I let grief blind me. That's something I'll go to my grave regretting."

Mae paced the length of the room in agitation, like she'd rather be anywhere but here.

Lawrence saw it, too. "I don't know anything about Jayela's death or her pregnancy."

"Was she seeing anyone that you knew of?"

He raised an eyebrow. "Well, yes, but I assumed you knew about that. The last time I saw her she couldn't stop smiling and when I asked who he was, she just grinned harder. She wouldn't give up any details, but there was no doubt in my mind that she was definitely in love."

Mae stopped pacing.

"When was this?" I asked. "What date?"

The man took his phone from the bedside table and poked at it a few times, presumably pulling up a calendar. He scrolled through it. "The fourteenth."

"That was a week before she died," Mae said.

Her father nodded sadly. "If I'd known it would be the last time I got to see her…"

He seemed genuinely distraught. I glanced up at Mae, and the hurt that flashed across her face was sharp and painful to watch. She spun on her heel and left the room without another word.

I smiled stiffly at the other man. "Thank you for your time. I uh…I really hope your treatment goes well."

I stood to leave, but he caught my arm.

"Be good to her," he implored. "I…I did a lot of things in this life that made me a bad man, and a worse father. I regret them all. She deserves a happy life. One with a man who adores her and would steal the moon if that's what made her happy. She deserves the happy life I robbed her of as a child." He paused to cough, the hacking noise sounding like it shredded his lungs. "I need to know she'll be taken care of."

A sudden image burst into my head. Me, Heath, and Rowe, the three of us surrounding Mae, protecting her smaller form from whatever came our way.

It filled me with a sense of right and peace I'd never experienced before.

It was with wholehearted confidence that I assured Mae's father that he didn't need to worry.

She'd be so very taken care of.

*M*ae was waiting by the car when I finally walked down the stairs of her childhood home, my mind whirling with more revelations than any one person could handle in the space of a single day.

We were both quiet when we got in the car, and for a while, I drove aimlessly, not wanting to be away from her, but not wanting to force her to talk either.

When she finally did speak, it wasn't the words I was expecting. "Well, that was a dead end."

I stopped at a light and glanced over at her in surprise. "He gave us a pretty big piece of information there. We know now that Jayela was definitely seeing someone, as close as one week before her death. That could be a game changer."

But she shook her head, her blonde hair falling

around her shoulders in silky waves. "The tip-off said my father was involved in her death."

"Maybe they just meant he had information."

"I just wonder if there was more to it than that. Most people don't know the extent of how bad our relationship is with him. He always put on a good front. So I don't know. I guess I just went there expecting more."

I steered the car over and picked up my phone. I scrolled through the messages until I found one from Boston.

"What's that?" Mae asked.

"That tip-off line isn't actually anonymous. People don't have to leave their names, but each call is recorded, and Boston is able to retrieve their name and address from a database."

"Is that legal?"

"Do you really want to know the answer?"

"No. You have the details of the tip-off?"

"Angela Erley, four fifty-one Grainer Drive, Saint View. Does that ring any bells for you?"

She shook her head. "No, but if you don't need to get right back to work, could we go check it out?"

I don't know how she didn't already realize that I'd do anything she asked. Her dad had seen right through me.

We arrived at the address and parked out front. It was in a part of Saint View that wasn't far from the prison. The house needed repairs to the roof, and a rusted pickup sat in the driveway on blocks, all four tires nowhere to be seen. "Do you think someone stole them?" Mae asked.

"Entirely possible. I remember it happening when I lived around here as a kid."

"That's insane."

"That's poverty."

She nodded sadly. "These people probably don't know anything about Jayela, do they? It's more likely they just wanted the reward and were hoping to get lucky by throwing a wild theory out there."

"Probably."

Her shoulders fell. "I don't think there's any point confronting them. Can we go work at the shelter this weekend? At least there I feel like I'm helping. It's too easy to forget how hard people have it around here. It's only minutes from my father's place and yet it's like a different world."

I put the car in gear and slowly pulled away, wishing there was something more I could do to bridge the divide as well.

18

ROWE

*A*gitation had plagued me from the moment I'd woken up. I'd slept badly, tossing and turning on my mattress on the floor, until I'd given up on sleep altogether. I'd found my fishing rod and wandered down the path to the lake as the sun peeked over the horizon, but sitting on the end of the dock with a line in the water hadn't brought me any peace.

There were two things I couldn't get out of my head. The first one being what Mae and I had done at this very spot. If I closed my eyes, I could still feel the wet warmth of her pussy clenching down on my fingers while she came.

My dick twitched. I'd pushed her away again, because I had to, but I'd hated every moment since. Seeing her at work was a special kind of torture I'd created for myself but one that I now had to live in, because the alternative —getting involved with her while she worked in the prison system—wasn't something I could handle.

I wouldn't lose anyone else I cared about.

But she wasn't the only source of my sleepless night. I hadn't seen Heath in a week since he'd been sent to solitary. He'd be out today. By the time I got to work, he'd be back in General Population, and I wouldn't be able to avoid talking to him any longer.

Thing was, I didn't even want to. I wanted to see him. I needed to explain.

That was why this beautiful lake, with the sun rising over it, did nothing for me. The turmoil inside me wasn't going away without facing it.

I got to work hours earlier than I was scheduled, impatient to make things right. The new warden looked up as I passed his office. "Pritchard."

I pushed down my annoyance at the interruption and backtracked a few steps. Heath wasn't going anywhere, and I was already on thin ice with the new guy after my disappearing act. "What's up, boss?"

"You're early. I'm not paying you for that, you know."

"Didn't ask you to. But I'm gonna work anyway."

"Good. I like your attitude. You had me worried for a bit there, when you disappeared without a word, but I'm not heartless. I know what it's like to need a moment after a riot. Been in too many of them myself."

I somehow couldn't imagine the drill-sergeant-like man feeling much of anything, but I could take his word for it.

"It's good you're here, though. I've just had word that we'll be getting some new prisoners and they're due in any moment."

I cringed. There was so little room, the prison already at capacity. Being overcapacity wasn't anything new, but it made things more difficult. But I'd almost expected it, seeing as we suddenly had so many new staff members. The powers that be loved nothing more than loading a prison up as far as they possibly could. "Yes, sir. I'll get things prepared. How many?"

"Twenty-three."

I gaped at him. "We don't have room for an extra twenty-three prisoners."

"I know. But there was a flood at another premises, and they've got men walking through knee-deep water, with damage to all the electricals and storm damage to the roofs."

"And we've got a fire damaged hall, workmen on site..."

Tabor raised an eyebrow, putting me back in my place.

"I'll sort something out," I mumbled, biting back my annoyance.

"That's more like it. On the bright side, these are guys from my last prison. I wasn't there long, just for crisis intervention like I'm doing here, but long enough to get to know the prisoners. I've already looked over the list, and I recognize most names. They shouldn't be any trouble. They respect me and they know how I run things. I don't anticipate any problems."

If those words weren't the kiss of death in a prison, I didn't know what was. But I held in my groan. Introducing that many men at once into an already established hierarchy was a recipe for disaster. When men came in one at a time they had to fit in with the others, taking up whichever spot they could eke out for themselves. When you dumped a whole group who already knew each other, it was like pitting one gang against another.

We already had enough problems with gangs in here. We didn't need another.

But of course, none of that was my call.

The warden dismissed me, and though I should have gone straight to the supply rooms, to find out if we even had enough mattresses for an extra twenty-three men, I didn't. I detoured past Gen Pop A, tapping my card and access number into the panel on the door.

The room was only half full, and Heath was nowhere in sight. I leaned on the wall beside the only guard in the room, greeting him with a handshake and small talk because I didn't want to make my interest in Heath obvious. But eventually I asked, "Did Michaelson get out of solitary this morning?"

"Last night. He's on work detail in the kitchen, though. Why?"

"Just something the warden asked me to follow up on," I lied vaguely.

I left and took the corridor to the cafeteria, my steps picking up pace the closer I got. I tried telling myself that was just because the weight of what I'd done, letting him do that time in solitary when it wasn't deserved, was heavy on my mind. But the rush of adrenaline when I saw Heath's broad back and the tattoos curling up his neck from beneath his prison jumpsuit said otherwise. The cafeteria itself was empty, nobody allowed in until the lunchtime rush, but two other prisoners worked diligently, preparing food, while a guard sat at a table, feet on top of it, scrolling through his phone, not paying any attention to the three prisoners whatsoever.

I ground my molars. "You can go," I told him. "Take your break. I'll cover."

He glanced up, scrambling to take his feet down, but then realized I wasn't anyone of importance. "I'm not due for another hour."

I shrugged. "I'd take it while you have the chance."

He nodded and put his phone away as he stood. He tapped his ID against the security panel and left me alone with the three prisoners. I wasn't going to waste a minute now that I had the opportunity. Getting a prisoner alone in this place was nearly impossible, and there was only one way I was going to be able to do it here. The two prisoners preparing food eyed me warily, but Heath ignored me completely. He dunked dishes into steaming, soapy water, the vicious way he scrubbed them the only real indicator that he'd even noticed I was there.

"Michaelson."

He only scrubbed harder. Tension radiated from his posture, his shoulders hunched over the sink that he was really too tall for.

I couldn't talk to him with the other two prisoners standing right there, listening to every word. I eyed a room off the side of the kitchen marked storage. "I need some supplies."

Heath pointed one soapy hand at the door. "Storage room right there. Knock yourself out." He still refused to look at me.

He was pissed. I couldn't blame him. He'd done a stint in solitary because I hadn't stood up for him.

"You'll get it for me," I bit out.

"Kinda busy, Officer Pritchard."

"I don't believe I asked."

He threw his scrub brush down with such force that dirty dishwater sprayed up and sloshed over the edges of the sink. He whirled on me, eyes flashing with anger. "Seriously?"

I stared him down, no give in my stance or my glare. Irritation rose inside me. I didn't want it to be this way, but I needed him to listen.

One of the other prisoners cleared his throat. "Um, Officer Pritchard? I can show you—"

I glared at him, and he dropped his gaze back to the soup he was stirring. "Or not," he muttered. "Sheesh."

Heath still glowered at me. I ignored him and gestured to the door, like I was sick of him wasting my time. He stormed over, yanked it open, and disappeared inside. I followed him, closing the door behind me.

He was on me the moment it latched, his chest pressed against mine, my back hitting the only exit. "Is this what you wanted?" he growled.

My automatic instinct was to deny it. But my dick springing to life behind my pants said otherwise. I twisted slightly so he wouldn't feel it and shoved him off me. "Fuck off, Heath."

He took two steps back, which is about as far away as he could get in the enclosed space. It was dimly lit by a weak lightbulb that cast a yellowish glow over his strong features and shoulders. "Why the hell am I in here with you, then?"

I folded my arms over my chest. "Because I wanted to explain..."

He gave a short, hard laugh. "Explain what? That you know very well I had nothing to do with that riot, and that all I did was watch out for Mae? You want to explain why you let me spend a week in solitary hell?"

That was exactly what I'd been wanting to do, but when he threw it in my face like that, an apology wasn't what came out. "What do you want from me? You're a prisoner, and I'm a guard! We aren't fucking friends, Heath."

"So you keep saying."

"Well, it's true!"

"How about you say some other truths, then? Since you're so big on honesty."

"What it is you think I want to say? Since you obviously have something in mind."

His gaze dipped to my groin. "How about you admit that Mae isn't the only one you want."

I let out a sharp breath.

He took a step forward. "How about you admit that you think about me, too. That you wouldn't stop me if I put my lips on yours right now."

I swallowed hard. I'd never really put a label on my sexuality but I wasn't scared of the possibility of being attracted to another man. That wasn't the problem here. Heath had that older, mountain man vibe that would appeal to anyone.

He stepped closer again, close enough that something in my gut tightened. He leaned in close enough that his lips brushed the stubble of my jaw. "I don't think you'd stop me at all. I think I could unbuckle your belt, drop to my knees, and suck your cock, and you wouldn't say a word except my name when you come."

Fuck. I closed my eyes, my dick so hard at the image

of fucking into Heath's mouth, hidden away back here, completely forbidden but the desire too great to conceal.

His lips trailed down my jawline, tantalizingly close to my mouth. "Yeah, that's what I thought. You think you hide it, but you want it so fucking bad I bet it keeps you awake at night." His hand brushed my thigh, and I didn't stop him. "Have you thought about me taking you? How that would feel?"

Precum wept from my tip, my cock aching for the things his words promised. I was so hard. So turned on. So desperate to come. I dropped my hand to my dick, rubbing it through my pants just to relieve a tiny bit of the tension. A groan escaped my lips, and I could feel more than see the grin on Heath's face.

"Good," he whispered.

Then he stepped back.

The space between us went suddenly cold, and I opened my eyes. Heath's expression was nothing short of a snarl. "Fuck you, Rowe." He shoved past me and pushed open the door. "Find your own supplies. And maybe find some balls while you're at it."

I locked myself in the employee bathroom, breathing too hard. Anger coursed through my body, but it all seemed to go straight to my dick, doing nothing to help the erection situation I couldn't seem to get under control. Fuck Heath. I wanted to put my hand down my pants and jerk myself until I came. It would be a poor substitute for the things Heath had promised, but it would relieve the burning ache to come.

Stubbornly, I wouldn't let myself do it. If I did, I knew I'd be thinking about him the entire time and I refused to give him that satisfaction.

Instead, I stood there, head pressed against the stall door, and thought about what I had to do next. Minute by minute, as I filled my head with thoughts of work, the erection slowly died.

The need for Heath didn't. But at least it wasn't physically obvious anymore.

"All available guards report to the intake area."

I sighed, getting myself together. I had a job to do, and I was doing it very averagely lately. That needed to stop. Mae, Heath... They had to stop being the things I got out of bed for. I needed to go back to training. Go back to seeing my friends. Fuck, maybe I needed to meet a woman. One I didn't work with. Or a man. Fuck if I knew what I was into these days. But somebody who had never stepped foot inside this prison.

I'd ask Liam to go to a baseball game with me on the weekend. That would be a start, at least.

Pleased with that decision, I washed my hands at the sink, lathering them with more soap than I actually needed, in the hopes of washing off the way I'd touched myself when Heath had been promising things in my ear. My cheeks flamed, knowing I'd let him make a fool of me.

Prick.

I hurried out of the bathroom, but instead of going to the intake area, I hurried back to the Gen Pop storage rooms to do the prep I should have been doing while I was in another closet with Heath. With jerky movements, I made a stack of the thin foam mattresses covered in plastic that each inmate was issued on arrival, piling them onto a cart to take to Gen Pop. Their uniforms would be issued in the intake area, but we also had small packs of basic supplies that each man was entitled to when they arrived. Toothbrush and paste. Deodorant. A bar of soap. A small notebook and pencil, along with a booklet with important information, including rules and times they were allowed to do certain things.

I was so busy putting those together I didn't notice the time slipping away.

I didn't notice the shadow that fell over me.

"Well, well, well. Fancy meeting you here, wife stealer."

I froze. Every muscle in my body stiffened to the point of pain, and memories crashed down over me like a baseball bat to the head.

The night Rory had died.

His voice in my ear.

Taunting me. Always taunting me. It was the same voice I'd heard in my nightmares ever since.

I didn't get a chance to turn around before I was slammed into a wall. The force took me by surprise, my cheekbone cracking off the cement, and the wind forced out of me so sharply my lungs screamed in agony.

But I didn't need to see him. I knew his voice, and I knew he wasn't alone.

Zye never did anything alone.

Except the night he'd killed his ex.

My wife.

Rory.

With the two big men on either side of me pulling back my arms, they spun me to face them, their weight holding me so I had no chance of moving. I couldn't get my mouth to work enough to utter a sound. Shock held my tongue hostage, while my mind filled with questions and accusations and beneath all that, anger.

Zye had always been a solid powerhouse of a man. He was too good-looking for the evil that lay beneath the surface, his smile too wide, teeth too white, and tattoos covering almost every inch of his skin. This was the man who had taken everything from me. My love, my life, any chance of a happy future. He'd taken it all because he was small and jealous and petty. He'd taken her life, just because he could. Because she dared to stand up to him and leave.

Because she chose me over him.

Zye laughed. "You aren't pleased to see me then, Rowe? That's rude. I was so excited to find out I was being transferred here. I was first on the list, did you know that? Compassionate reasons and all, with my son being here in Saint View."

My blood ran cold.

I lashed out, struggling in earnest with the men who held me, but that only earned me a punch to the gut. It spread fire through my midsection, but it didn't stop me. I struggled until I could look Rory's ex in the eye. "He's not yours. Never was. Never will be."

Zye's eyes were the lightest of blues. They were an abnormal color, one you normally didn't see on men as deeply olive as he was.

They were a color I'd only ever seen on one other person.

"Funny, I've got a birth certificate that says he is. Ripley might have your surname, Pritchard, but by blood, we both know very well he belongs to me." Zye chuckled and slapped my cheek. "You look positively green, my friend. And I haven't even told you the fun bit." He leaned in close. "I got a real good lawyer. He's getting me court-mandated visitation with my son. *My* son, Pritchard. You hear that?"

He stepped back and gave a nod to his friends as he left the room.

Typical fucking Zye. Never one to get his hands dirty himself. The two prisoners rained punches down on me, but I was too numb to feel any of them. What happened to me wasn't important.

The only thing that mattered was Ripley and keeping him the hell away from the man who had murdered his mother.

"What the fuck?" Heath's roar of anger cut through my haze, and I blinked through a swelling eye. He stormed the room, shoving the cart of mattresses out of the way, and throwing himself into the fight. "Rowe!" he shouted. "Rowe!" I knew I needed to fight back, or Zye's guys would think nothing of killing me right here and right now. Zye had been waiting for this opportunity for years. Two on two was at least a fair fight, if I could make my body obey.

But I couldn't. I was entirely locked up, lost in the horror of Ripley ever being near his biological father. Somewhere, in the back of my mind, I knew the day would come that Zye got out and went searching for his son. But I'd soothed those fears with the promise that Zye was in another state and that by the time he got out, Ripley would be old enough to know what sort of man his father was, and to stay the hell away from him.

He was only four and a half. Too young to know the

truth. If Zye was allowed a relationship with him, he'd poison him. Turn his sweet, innocent little heart into something dark and sinister like his father's. The thought made me ill.

There was another bellow, and suddenly the room was full of men. Guards' boots filled my vision, and the blows stopped, as Zye's guy was pulled away. I managed to lift my head from the floor long enough for my gaze to connect with Heath's. Tabor had his arms pinned behind his back, while he shoved restraints over his wrists.

Heath's accusations in the kitchen rang loud and clear through my head. "Tabor, no wait," I yelled. "Michaelson didn't do anything wrong. He was trying to help me."

But Tabor wasn't having it. He was already shoving Heath through the door, while other officers did the same with the other prisoners who'd attacked me. Tabor was particularly rough, though, putting his boot to the center of Heath's back and shoving him out of sight.

"Tabor! Stop!"

But the man shook his head, anger flashing in his eyes as his gaze rolled over me. His expression was that of a barely concealed sneer. "Get yourself to the infirmary and get a nurse to look you over."

"And Michaelson?"

"Will be dealt with in the same way the other prisoners caught attacking a guard will be dealt with. There's no special treatment here, Pritchard. I run a tight ship, and fighting won't be tolerated. These men will learn, and in the case of Michaelson, he'll learn the hard way if he has to. I run this place and I have a spotless record. Things are different around here now, and the sooner you all wake up and realize who's in charge, the better."

19

ROWE

The infirmary reeked of antiseptic. Perry frowned at me every time I flinched away from her cotton ball of death, but whatever the hell she was putting on my cuts stung worse than the injuries themselves. After she came at me for the fourth time, I waved her away. "Enough, enough. I'm fine."

She shoved her hands on her hips. "You're not fine at all. I think that gash on your forehead needs a stitch or two. And you need to get your ribs X-rayed."

"My ribs are fine." They weren't. They would be black and blue in the morning, but I wasn't getting X-rays or stitches.

The infirmary door banged open with such force it could have been a thunder crack. Perry flinched at the sound but then pointed in my direction. "Oh good, it's just you. Talk some sense into Rowe, would you? He's being a stubborn prick and needs to go to the emergency room."

Mae hurried over to my side and gasped when she

took in my face, her big eyes filling with tears. "What the hell happened? I heard you were in here, but nobody would say anything else."

God, she was a sight for sore eyes. It would have been all too easy to let her wrap her arms around me, press my face to her neck, and inhale the sweet scent of her.

But that would have made it all too easy to fall apart. She felt too safe, too warm. And right now, with Zye here, that was dangerous. She moved to touch me, and I flinched away.

The look of hurt and disappointment in her eyes cut me to the core. I needed to tell her everything. Not the half-truths I'd been holding her off with because the full truth was too hard for me to say aloud.

"Perry, can you give us a minute, please?"

She glanced between Mae and me, and when Mae nodded, Perry quietly left the room, closing us in alone. Mae reached for my hand again, but this time when I tried to move away, she wouldn't let me. Her warm fingers threaded through mine and held on tight. She stared up at me, waiting for me to talk.

"I didn't tell you the full story about Rory," I admitted. "But I need to now. For your own safety, you need to know everything."

She squeezed my fingers. "Okay. I'm listening."

"I told you Rory was pregnant when we met, right? By her ex."

Mae nodded.

"It never mattered to me that I wasn't the baby's biological father. I loved Rory, and the baby was just an extension of her. It was a no-brainer and felt completely natural to fall for the baby as hard and fast as I fell for her."

"Most men wouldn't have taken that on so easily, especially how young you were. You're a good man."

I shook my head sadly. "I don't deserve that."

Mae went to argue, but I cut her off, knowing she'd change her mind once she knew the whole story. "We got married three weeks before she went into labor." The memory was so soft and tender in my mind. Rory's belly swollen beneath a flowing white dress. Her complaining that her ankles were going to be huge in the wedding photos. But she'd never been more beautiful to me. I couldn't get enough of her.

"Was it a boy or a girl?" Mae prompted.

"A boy." I looked over at her, sitting on the bed beside me, her crazy-colored floral skirts a complete clash with the stark white sheets. "We called him Ripley."

Her eyes went wide. "What? The same Ripley..."

I nodded. "Yeah, the same Ripley you met the other day."

"But why isn't he with you?"

My heart cracked, with both guilt and pain. "This is why I don't deserve to be called a good man." I tried to laugh, but it came out more like a sob. I swallowed hard, forcing it down so I could talk. "He was so little when Rory died. And I was a complete and utter mess. So was Norma, understandably. She'd just lost her daughter. Her only child. I had no support in Ohio and a job I couldn't go to any longer because of what had happened. So I transferred here. The house next door to Norma's just happened to be available at the time, and it seemed like a sign, you know? To come back here, so Norma could help with Ripley. And at first, that's what it was." I stared at Mae, silently imploring her to understand the biggest failing of my life. "But God, it hurt so bad. Every day without her was a walking nightmare. I couldn't stop seeing her body...the way she'd died. It was so cruel and vicious, and every time I closed my eyes it replayed over and over in my head. I stopped sleeping. Ripley was so young. Too young to be away from his mother. I had no idea how to look after a baby without her. He cried all the time, and I convinced myself it was because he hated me. Or because he blamed me, for not protecting her. When Norma started taking him overnight so I could sleep, I let her. She needed him, too. She managed her grief by pouring love into him. While I did the opposite. I hid from him. Buried myself in work, knowing that he was better cared for by her."

Mae's hand stroked down my cheek. "I don't think that's true."

"I was a coward."

"It sounds like you had PTSD and needed help."

I nodded. "I know that now. But at the time, when Norma sat me down and told me she wanted full custody of Ripley, I agreed with her. I didn't feel fit to be his father, even though I desperately wanted to be." I fought back hot tears that pricked at the backs of my eyes. "I failed him so badly. I failed them both."

But Mae shook her head, her own tears spilling down her cheeks. "No. You didn't fail him at all. You did the right thing."

"I gave him up, Mae! How was that the right thing?"

"You gave him up because you recognized that you couldn't give him what he needed in that moment. That isn't cowardice. That's strength. It's the sign of a true father. You gave him what he needed, even when it hurt you to do it. I don't have kids..." She swallowed hard. "But if I were Rory, I would have wanted you to do exactly what you did. You didn't fail him, Rowe. You left him with a woman who loves him, while you sought help for yourself. Question is, what are you going to do about it now?"

I stared up at her. "What do you mean?"

She sighed. "Maybe I'm overstepping, but I saw Norma with him the other day. There's no doubt she loves him. That was clear in the way she watched him. But she's very elderly. She looked tired. You're well now. And you're his dad..."

I shook my head hard. "I'm not though, Mae! He has my surname, but it's Zye's name on the father section of his birth certificate. Rory had wanted to do the right thing. She was so honest, she couldn't lie on a legal document, even though I had wanted her to put my name on it. She said it wouldn't matter anyway, because if Zye ever wanted Ripley, he'd only have to get a DNA test to prove his paternity rights. So there was no point in lying."

"That doesn't make Ripley any less your son."

"Zye is trying to get visitation with him."

Mae's mouth dropped open. "From Ohio?"

I shook my head. "He's here. Transferred in this morning."

"What? How? Shouldn't he be in a super maximum?"

I nodded bitterly. "He was never convicted of Rory's murder, though. There was no proof it was him, though I know it was. He's alluded to it more times than I can count." I forced myself to put Mae's hand down. "He's dangerous and he has it out for me. Which makes anyone connected to me a target."

She blinked up at me. "So what? Even after this, I'm just supposed to stay away from you?"

"I'd prefer it if you weren't here at all."

She sighed. "You know I can't do that."

I nodded. It didn't matter that she was the only person I'd ever managed to tell the entire story to. "I know. So this really changes nothing." It only strengthened the resolve I'd tried to find the other day. "More than ever, Mae. Anyone connected to me is in danger. Zye will find a way to get back at me. I know that for a fact. Don't let it be through you."

20

HEATH

The four walls of the solitary cell were beginning to feel like old friends. The one Tabor shoved me into wasn't the same cell I'd just come out of, but it was fairly identical in layout. Narrow walls, a low bed frame for my mattress, and not a whole lot else. This one did have a window at least, though the thick glass was so scratched and dirty I could barely see through it.

Tabor stood in the doorway of the cell, staring me down. "You're making a habit of this."

He was a big guy, so we were eye height when I returned his gaze. "I was trying to help."

"You got a funny way of showing it. Seems to me like you just enjoy the fight."

I bit my tongue. In fact, it was the complete opposite. I knew how I looked. I was big and solid. I towered over most men, and even those who had the height rarely had the muscle to back it up. The tattoos and the deep voice all screamed *violent, thug, fighter.*

My own family had pushed those labels onto me. Even when I'd pushed back, telling them that wasn't who I was, they'd insisted they knew better.

I'd proved them right in one night.

But in the aftermath, in the weeks and months that followed, where guilt and remorse were so thick and the urge to end it all dominated my thoughts, I'd made a vow to never be that person again. To never lay hands on another man.

Until I'd heard Rowe's shout. Until I'd walked past that supply closet and seen them attacking him.

Then all I'd seen was red.

Tabor pulled the solid door shut. The tiny peep window matched the one to the outside world—grimy and scratched to the point it looked like frosted glass. I sighed, slumping down on the edge of the bed frame. I didn't even know how long I would be in here for, but it was going to feel like a lifetime without even being able to look out into the corridor. With completely enclosed, solid walls, the solitary cells were close to soundproof too, so I couldn't even talk to any other prisoners.

Not that I really wanted to. I wasn't big on chitchat.

Minutes turned into hours. At least I thought they did. Eventually, I was sure of it because the brightness from the window grew dimmer and turned a deep orange that told me the sun was sinking. I moved to stand by the window, uselessly rubbing at the grimy glass with the sleeve of my shirt and wishing I could watch the sun sink.

I closed my eyes and tried to feel the warmth of it on my face. I should have been out on an open road somewhere, wind at my back, and Mae's arms wrapped tight around my waist. Fuck. If I thought about it hard enough,

I could almost feel the press of her soft tits and the slide of her hands pressed to my stomach, slipping beneath my jacket and lower into my jeans.

I groaned. That was all I had in here. Daydreams of Mae.

And whatever the hell was happening with me and Rowe.

Who knew what the fuck was going on there, though.

The lights flickered on automatically as dusk turned into evening, and I wondered if Mae was downstairs somewhere, teaching her class in some makeshift room since hers was probably damaged by smoke.

I glanced up as the locks on my door disengaged and took up the usual stance at the back of the cell. By this point in time, I knew the drill. The guards would drop my food just inside the door but only as long as I stood well away while they did it.

When the door swung open, though, it was Rowe on the other side.

He stared at me, his arms full of things. Not only my meal, consisting of some sort of unappetizing slop, but my thin foam mattress, a change of clothes, and the book I'd been reading in my cubicle in Gen Pop.

I didn't move.

He avoided looking me in the eye and walked into the cell, closing the door behind him, before putting the pile of things down on my bed frame.

He shifted uncomfortably. "I, uh, searched around your cubicle for anything you might want, but the book was all I could find. If you want another one, though, or some paper and a pencil, I can get those for you—"

"Are you okay?" My voice, thick and hoarse, surprised even me. It wasn't what I'd planned to say. What I'd wanted to do was yell and tell him he'd thrown me under the fucking bus again. But the bruises around his face and the gash down the side of his cheekbone shoved all thoughts of anger right out of my head.

The thing was, he hadn't this time. He'd tried to stand up for me. I'd heard his pleas with the new warden.

"I'm fine." But he winced as he straightened.

Bullshit.

Before I knew what I was doing, I stormed the space between us, fisted my fingers in his shirt, and yanked it up. I bent over then recoiled at already purpling marks across his ribs. "Jesus, Rowe. You're not. You could have broken ribs. Did you get an X-ray?"

He shook his head but didn't say a word. When my fingertips ghosted over his injuries, he didn't stop me. I didn't press and prod at him the way a doctor would have. The idea of hurting him any further made me sick.

I straightened stiffly.

He didn't turn away. My fingers still gripped his shirt and, without thinking about it, I drew him closer.

For once, he didn't fight me. My heart pounded behind my rib cage, and something more sparked deep within me.

"I'm sorry," he murmured. "It's my fault you're in here. You shouldn't have got involved."

"You would have preferred I let them kill you?"

"Maybe." His gaze changed, the pain deep within him rising to the surface so quick it took me by surprise. He was so hard on the outside, but I knew what it was like to have a hard shell because the pain on the inside was so deep and raw it would kill you to expose it.

A fierce protectiveness rose in me, and before I knew what I was doing, my hand was at the back of his neck, my fingers pressed to the tendons so he couldn't look away. "No." I whispered. "You hear me? No. That's not an option."

Fuck, his pain was so raw. He was an open book, and staring into his eyes was like falling into a bottomless pit, one I knew all too well. "I'm not gonna let you fall," I whispered.

I pressed my lips to his, desperate to pull him back, desperate to save him like I wished someone had saved me, but all the while expecting him to push me away. I waited for it. The denial. The refusal. His hands against my chest as he shoved me then left.

It didn't come. There was only the grab of his fingers in my shirt and a murmured, "We shouldn't."

I didn't care.

My grip on him turned punishing, holding him in place, and proving to him that I wasn't going anywhere.

"You'll regret it," he whispered.

"I won't."

My lips found his, done with the excuses. I wanted this, and so did he. He hauled me closer, taking control of the kiss, and plunging his tongue into my mouth.

I groaned at his taste, and the feel of him, need curling within me. His fingers clung onto my biceps, the kiss owning my body, and sparking to life a part of me I'd ignored for too long.

But deep down, I knew this wouldn't last. And when he moved back, it wasn't unexpected. What was unexpected was the way he pressed his forehead to mine, his chest rising and falling with rapid breaths. "I can't keep doing this." His eyes flared. "The new inmate, Zye. Stay away from him."

"I can handle him."

Rowe shook his head. "Don't say that. Because I thought that once, too, and I was wrong. Shit. I need to go."

"Don't." The word fell from my lips before I could stop it.

But he pulled away, walking backward. At the last moment, he took a phone from his pocket. I stared at it like it was a bomb ready to go off. Rowe pushed it into my hand. "Here, take it. Mae...I think she needs to talk to you. And you probably need to talk to her."

I couldn't pass up the opportunity to talk to her. It had been weeks since the prison riot, and I hadn't been able to talk to her at all since then, and now, being in solitary, it could be anywhere from days to months before they gave me phone privileges again. But being caught with a phone in here was almost as bad as murdering another inmate. Phones were complete and utter contraband and came with hefty penalties if caught.

Rowe shoved it into my hand. "Put it under your plate cover when you're done eating, and I'll make sure I pick it up. You've got thirty minutes."

This could be some ploy to get me in more trouble than I was already in, and maybe if this had happened a week ago, I might have thought that true.

But after that kiss...a probably stupid part of me wanted to trust him.

An even bigger part wanted to hear Mae's voice.

I took the phone, not unaware of the intense spark that lit when our fingers touched.

Fuck. What the hell were we doing?

21

MAE

*L*iam played baseball in high school. I used to watch him from the stands as he pitched fastballs at the other team. A decade might have passed, but when Liam threw a pen across the room, it was like a missile flying through the air. It whizzed past me, colliding with the wall, before dropping to the carpet.

I raised one eyebrow at him. "Do I need to take the rest of the office supplies away from you? I'm a tad scared there's a stapler within arm's reach right now."

He flopped back in his seat, the chair spinning slightly on its wheels. He'd undone the top two buttons of his white business shirt, and his tie hung loose around his shoulders. His forehead was furrowed with frustration, and he rubbed his hands across his face. "I'm just sick of this. There's nothing to go on. Whoever your sister was dating, she obviously didn't want anybody to know, because she hid her tracks really damn well. I've never been so frustrated by a case in my life."

My heart sank. I got up and crossed to his side of the

desk, grabbing his hand and squeezing it tight. "Don't give up. I know it doesn't look good."

He sighed. "I'm not. It's just harder when you've got skin in the game. I hate seeing what Heath being in jail is doing to you, and to Rowe. I'm beginning to feel like it's my fault because I can't think of a way of getting him out."

I sat myself in his lap, then put my hands on either side of his face, tilting it up to look at me. "This isn't all on you. It's on all of us, and we will get him out. There's no doubt in my mind."

Some of his old humor crept back into his expression. "I know. I just really wanted you to sit on my lap and reassure me."

He was full of shit, we both knew it, but it was nice to laugh anyway. My phone rang, and I reached across the desk to pick it up. I flashed the screen at Liam with wide eyes.

"Rowe?"

But the grumbling tone that came down the line wasn't Rowe at all. "Try again."

"Heath?" I breathed.

Liam lifted me from his lap, and I frowned at him. He just kissed the top of my head then whispered, "I'm going to get a coffee. Take your moment with him."

I got up and wandered to the couch in Liam's office. It was on the fourth floor and had a nice view of the twinkling lights of the city. I stared out the floor-to-ceiling glass, almost hating that I had this beautiful view, while Heath was probably staring at a cinderblock wall. It wasn't fair. Liam and I had to work harder. We needed to get him out. There had to be something we were missing.

"Yeah. I'm here. I'm so glad it's you. How do you have Rowe's phone?"

"He sneaked it in. I can't talk long, he'll be back to pick it up soon."

"Liam and I are working hard on your case. We know that Jayela was seeing someone—"

"I know. You're doing whatever you can, you don't have to explain yourselves to me."

"But we do. It's taking so much longer than I would have hoped."

"I know how the system is. Nothing is ever quick or easy. You don't have the backing of the police, so that's going to slow you down again. I never expected you to get me out of here anytime soon, Mae. I'm grateful to have your help at all. I just wish I could see you." He sighed heavily. "I've missed your voice."

"I don't just miss your voice," I admitted. "That kiss..."

"I know. I felt it, too. And trust me, I'm going to do it again the minute I see you."

I grinned at the idea. "What if the next time you see me is in the middle of the hall, surrounded by guards?"

He chuckled. "Don't care. They're gonna get a show."

A sweet tingle spread out through my body. "You'll end up in solitary again."

"What's new? That seems to be my permanent address lately."

I sobered at that. "I hate the idea of you stuck in there again. But Rowe told me what you did for him... Thank you."

His voice turned gruff. "You don't have to thank me. I... Shit. I don't know, Mae. I knew getting in another fight would end badly, but I wasn't going to just walk past and ignore the fact there were two guys pounding the shit out of him."

"You care about him."

There was a long silence, then, "Yeah. I suppose I do. Fuck."

"He's not going to like that."

"He already told me as much."

"This new guy, Zye. He's got him rattled. They've got a long history together. A bad one. Rowe's convinced Zye has it out for him. And honestly? After hearing their story, I don't think he's overreacting."

"It's that bad?"

"Worse."

"Fuck. He needs you. I know you've got something going on with Liam..."

I flushed hot. "Liam cares about Rowe, too. We all do."

"Good. Don't let him push you away. I've been where he is, and it's dark. If you wallow there too long, it gets really hard to pull yourself out. I don't want to see that happen to him."

I smiled softly out over the dark night sky. This was why I'd always liked him. He cared about other people in a way most people didn't, always putting them ahead of himself. "You're a good man, you know?"

"Don't tell anyone. I've got a reputation to uphold in here." But there was a smile in his voice, like he was pleased with my opinion of him. I wasn't just blowing smoke, he really was one of the good ones.

And I wasn't letting him spend the rest of his life in jail for something he didn't do.

22

MAE

*R*owe grew more and more distant as the week progressed, quietly standing at the back of my classroom, with a vacant look in his eye that told me he was somewhere completely different in his head. Heath was still in solitary, and my skin crawled at the thought. Even Liam's usual sunshine-and-lollipops mood was dull. I barely saw him, as he threw himself back into Heath's case, working with a new determination that bordered on manic, some invisible clock counting down to a deadline he'd imposed on himself.

There was nothing I could do about Heath. But there was something I could do about Liam and Rowe. By the time Saturday rolled around, I was determined that this weekend would be one full of fun, instead of stress and worry and drama.

I double-checked the schedule, making sure Rowe wasn't working, then brainstormed a list of things that would make him smile. After twenty minutes of thinking about it, there was still only one thing on the list. I wasn't sure if I could pull it off, but if I could, it was guaranteed to bring him out of his funk. So I had to try.

I made a phone call, and when that worked out better than I'd expected, I drove my car out to Rowe's place in the woods, not long after dawn on Saturday morning.

I was still half asleep by the time I arrived, but like I suspected, Rowe was already up and moving around his yard when I pulled in. I put the car in park and got out, closing the door behind me, and leaning on it as we stared at each other across the clearing.

"Surprise," I said, cringing at the look on his face.

"What the hell are you doing here?"

"I thought you might want to have breakfast?" I gestured to the backseat of my car, full of shopping bags to make a feast. "I've got stuff to make pancakes."

"I hate pancakes."

My mouth dropped open. "Are you serious? Who hates pancakes? What's wrong with you?"

The tiniest smile flickered at the corner of his mouth. "They're too sweet. They're more like dessert than breakfast. And quit deflecting. What are you doing here? I told you, we aren't doing this. If anyone found out—"

Despite his protests, I grabbed the bags from the back seat and marched up to his house. "Yeah, yeah. I heard you. But I'm also choosing to not live my life in fear. I'm not gonna let you either. Zye is in prison. What we do on the outside, he never has to know about. And by the way, you probably shouldn't tell other people you hate pancakes either. They would judge you on that."

I flounced my way up the stairs, and let myself into his house, praying the entire time that he wouldn't stop me.

He didn't. He came in close behind me, the screen door banging closed. I held my breath, waiting for it. Waiting for him to kick me out and tell me never to come back. I could ignore him once, but if he continued to do it, what was I supposed to do? I couldn't make the man have a life.

I couldn't make him want to be with me.

I stopped one foot inside the door and stared around. I'd expected a cozy little cabin, a fireplace in one corner for the winter, even though it didn't really get that cold here, perhaps some overstuffed brown couches, and a thick rug on the floor.

Rowe's cabin was nothing like that.

It was almost completely bare. To my right was a large living area, but the only furniture it contained was a TV. It sat right on the floor, a camping chair the only other place to sit. To my left was the kitchen, which was equally bare. A few takeout Chinese containers still sitting on the counter, chopsticks discarded for the fork sticking out of the top. I moved toward the kitchen to put my bags down and caught sight of the bedroom just past the living area. A tumble of sheets and blankets sat messily on top of a mattress. No bed frame, just flat on the floor.

I'd expected a bachelor's pad, but this wasn't even that. Liam's place was a bachelor's pad. Rowe's place just broke my heart.

"Rowe..."

He moved stiffly past me, pulling open a kitchen cabinet and getting out a glass. He filled it with water from the refrigerator. He didn't offer me one and took a long sip before he said anything. "I'm not going to apologize. I didn't invite you here."

"Why would you owe me an apology?"

He sighed heavily. "It wasn't always like this, you know. This place, I mean. Rory and I bought it, not long after we got together. It was just a vacation house back then. Her mom used to drive her nuts, but she also loved her to pieces, so she wanted to visit a lot, but not actually stay at her mom's place." He smiled wistfully. "I still remember the day we bought it, and me and Rory and Norma standing out in front, with Norma loudly announcing, 'Thank God. Now I won't have to listen to the two of you in the middle of the night, thinking you're being quiet when really, you sound like an amateur porn movie.'"

I burst out laughing, and the smile spread across Rowe's face.

He shook his head at the memory. "Norma is something else. She doesn't beat around the bush."

"She sounds great."

"She is. Rory wasn't quite as blunt. Where Norma was never backward in coming forward, Rory was more patient. She had a big heart, and she was really well-suited to nursing. Especially at the prison. You need so much compassion to treat a prisoner who might have done unspeakable things in his past, and to do it without judgement. Rory never judged. Her and Norma were kind of yin and yang. Opposites in many ways, but they also just really clicked. There was a bond between them. True parent-child love."

Something panged deep inside me. A longing for that sort of relationship with a mother figure. "She was lucky to have her mom."

He nodded. "I was lucky to have her, too, for as long as I did."

"She still cares about you, you know? Norma, I mean."

He wandered around the kitchen, staring blankly, as if he was seeing the way it had been once before. "It used to be a home. But after she died, I couldn't stand looking at any of it. Everything reminded me of her, and all of it was agony. It was why I rented the place next to Norma's when I first came back to Saint View. This cabin had too much of Rory in it. It took me years to be able to walk in here at all. And then when I finally did, she was all I could see."

He focused his gaze on me. "I got rid of everything. Stripped it right back to the bare minimum. I don't even know if you're going to be able to find a frying pan. I haven't cooked in this kitchen in I don't even know how long."

"You just eat takeout every night?" I opened a few cupboards, searching for something to cook on, and coming up empty.

He shrugged. "Sometimes I go fishing and bake the fish over coals. I've got one of those barbecue plates that sits over the top of a fire."

I raised an eyebrow. "I also brought bacon and eggs. I have no idea how to start a fire, but I'm pretty sure I could make them on that."

He grabbed the bags from my hands. "You should have led with that. Come on, I'll go get it started."

I glanced at the clock on his oven as we passed and swallowed down the nerves that butterflied around my stomach. "Good. Because the second part of your surprise is coming soon."

"Erg, Mae. I hate surprises. What have you done, now?"

I wasn't sure about this surprise myself. Showing up here at the crack of dawn, with the things to make breakfast for him was one thing. But his other surprise was either going to be epic, and he'd look at me with grateful, happy eyes. Or it was going to go down as the biggest mistake ever, and he'd kick me out of his house and never speak to me again. In my mind, it was completely fifty-fifty. I had no idea which way it would go down.

Pushing those nerves aside, I followed him out into the yard and to a small firepit. Ash remains were still scattered around, and there were three thick logs that formed a semi-circle of seats a foot or two away from where Rowe started building up kindling. I watched him work, pretending I was going through the bags of supplies and organizing them, but really watching him from the corner of my eye. He worked diligently, quickly and quietly assembling a little pile of sticks. He was completely in his element out here in nature, to the point that I almost expected him to rub two sticks together in order to create a spark. But at the last moment, he pulled a lighter from his pocket and nursed a little flame until it caught and took hold.

"You've obviously done that a few times," I said.

"Even before we bought this place, I liked to go camping. My dad took me a lot when I was a kid." He stood to grab a few bigger pieces of wood to feed to the fire. His biceps popped beneath his thin T-shirt as he hefted the wood into his arms and brought it back to the pit. "It was something I really wanted to do with..." He forced a smile in my direction. "Never mind."

"With Ripley?"

He nodded. "Yeah. You kind of have all these daydreams, once you know you're going to be a father. I loved that kid from the moment I knew about him, you know? It was so easy to see myself taking him to school, and going camping, and sitting on the sidelines of his soccer games on Saturday mornings." He toed at the dirt in front of him so he didn't have to look in my direction. "None of that was mine to take. I wanted it to be, but without Rory..."

I walked over to his side and picked up his hand, squeezing it. "That's still yours to take. You needed help, and Norma was there to give it to you. But this... The way you've been going, doesn't need to be the way you carry on."

I squeezed my eyes shut tight as the rumble of a car engine came up the drive. Rowe turned toward the drive in curiosity. "That's weird. The only person who comes down here but me is the mail truck, and they don't come on Saturdays."

"Okay, this is kind of bad timing. Or maybe perfect timing?" That was probably wishful thinking. "But this is the other surprise I planned for you. Please don't be mad."

"Nothing good ever comes from somebody starting a sentence with, please don't be mad." He narrowed his eyes at me. "Pretty sure that's a guarantee the other person is going to be real mad, Mae. What have you done?"

Then his eyes widened, and I knew he recognized the car.

He recognized the small hand waving out the window of the back seat.

And the little boy voice that shouted, "Rowe! Rowe! Hello!"

Rowe's head snapped in my direction, and I gave him a weak smile. "Surprise?"

"We need to have a talk about your surprises." He glowered in my direction, but then he turned back to the car and the glower disappeared, disintegrating into a wide smile.

Something inside me relaxed. Because that smile was genuine, and it was directed at the boy who obviously owned Rowe's heart.

"Ripley!" Rowe yelled, waving as the car stopped. He jogged over and opened the back door, reaching in for a moment and unclipping Ripley from his seat belt, before pulling him out and up into his arms. "Hey, kiddo. Wow. Look at you. You've gotten so big. I don't even know if I can hold you anymore."

Ripley laughed, the delightful sound tinkling through the morning air, so sweet it was almost like birdsong. "Yes, you can." He rubbed Rowe's arm. "You've got big muscles."

I grinned, slowly walking over to join them. Rowe bent to kiss Norma's cheek as she circled the car. She glanced in my direction, and I held my hand out to her. She took it but then dragged me in for a hug. The embrace was a surprise, but I patted her soft back.

"Thank you for organizing this," she whispered in my ear. "I haven't seen Ripley this excited in a long time."

I squeezed her tighter. "Rowe needed it, too," I whispered back.

We stood together, smiling at Rowe listening in rapt attention to something Ripley was telling him.

He finally glanced over at us, and his smile turned into a frown. "Don't think I don't see the scheming looks on your faces right now. I'll deal with the two of you some other time. Little man and I have breakfast to cook." Then he glanced at Norma. "Is that okay? You are staying for a bit, right?"

His voice was full of hope I hadn't heard in his tone before.

"Actually," Norma said. "I've got an appointment at the salon this morning. I thought maybe I could leave him here for a few hours?"

Ripley let out a cheer of excitement. "Yes! Go, Grandma. Bye."

Norma chuckled. She patted her grandson's cheek and then focused on Rowe. "That good with you, too?"

"Say yes, Rowe!"

He hoisted the small boy higher on his hip and strode toward the firepit. "Of course. Leave him here as long as you like." There was such a soft tenderness to his voice that it was impossible to miss.

Norma smiled sadly in their direction, patted my arm, and then got back in her car. "I'll be back in a few hours," she called through the open window. "Be good, Ripley."

Rowe waved. "He's always good, aren't you, buddy?"

I watched her car crunch over the gravel drive, before turning back to Rowe. He put Ripley down and had him rifling through one of the shopping bags, pulling out bacon and eggs ready to cook over the fire. There was a new relaxed air about him. It suited him.

"Are you just going to sit over there all smug and smiling like the cat who ate the canary?"

"I'm not smiling at any such thing. I'm just sitting here, enjoying a quiet moment by an open fire, watching an attractive man make me breakfast with a very cute kid."

Ripley stopped and flashed the cutest toothy grin at that compliment. He really was adorable with his blond hair and gorgeous eyes.

Rowe was so good with him. He held his hands, helping him to place food over the fire, but always keeping him close and safe. And Ripley clearly loved being in his presence. He stared up at Rowe with huge eyes full of hero worship. It was clear there was a bond between them, even if they no longer lived together.

After breakfast, and when the campfire had been put out, I cleaned up while Rowe took Ripley to play baseball in the yard. I watched them through the kitchen window as I put leftovers in the refrigerator, with all the feels coursing through my body like a warm, fuzzy blanket. My ovaries went haywire, but I didn't try to reel them in. Watching a man teach a small child how to throw a ball was about as all-American as it got. I was never going to get to experience this with a man and child of my own, so I let myself revel in it, and let myself be happy I'd orchestrated this moment for Rowe. He shot glances in my direction every so often, but I looked away quickly each time, not wanting to give away how badly the scene was affecting me. My heart panged with every catch, with every pat on Ripley's head, with every squeal of delight from the little boy when he managed to catch the ball. Each one hurt, and yet each one was beautiful.

With the dishes done, I wandered back outside and over to the twosome. "Can I play, too?"

"I don't know, Ripley. What do you think? Should we let her play?"

"Yes!" Ripley ran over and jumped up and down excitedly at my feet, grabbing at my hand. He was a beautiful child. So friendly and outgoing.

I put my hand out to him and grasped his fingers in mine and let him drag me into the game. The hours ticked by, many more than how long it would take for Norma to just go to the hairdresser, but none of us minded. There was lots for us to do with a four-year-old who was full of energy. We hiked through the woods together and took him fishing, all of us cheering when he pulled in the tiniest of fish. The look of pure joy and excitement on his face had me whipping out my phone and snapping a pic of Ripley and Rowe, the two of them grinning ear to ear. Ripley began to slow down not long after that, and we took him back to the cabin and filled his belly with leftovers from breakfast.

In the middle of his meal, his eyes started doing the slow-blink thing, and Rowe glanced over at me. "He's tired."

"Norma had him up early to have him out here to us for breakfast. And he's had a big morning, full of running around." I tilted my head to one side, studying the sleepy little boy. "Want to have a nap, buddy?"

He shook his head. "I'm too big for naps."

But the kid was practically asleep in his chair.

Rowe grinned at me. "He is much too big for naps,

Mae. But how about we just go sit on the porch swing for a while? If we are really quiet, some animals might come into the yard. How does that sound?"

Ripley nodded sleepily. Rowe pushed back his chair, and we left the plates sitting on the table, more interested in being together than cleaning up this time. Rowe carried Ripley to the front of the house and sat with him on the swing. I sat on the other side of Ripley, but almost as soon as Rowe put him down, Ripley scrambled onto his lap. My heart swelled when Ripley put his head down on Rowe's chest, not even pretending to search for animals. It left only the tiniest of gaps between me and Rowe, which I couldn't help but close. He didn't stop me when I sidled over a few inches, so our legs pressed together. In fact, his arm twitched, like maybe he was thinking about putting it around me.

I wished he would.

But he didn't. Instead, he used that arm to rub soft circles on Ripley's back while the porch swing rocked gently. Within moments, Ripley's breathing changed, spacing out and becoming slow and steady, a sure sign he was asleep.

"I think he's out," Rowe said quietly, pressing his cheek to the top of Ripley's head. He didn't stop stroking the little boy's back, though.

I took a peek at Ripley's face, his long dark eyelashes fanning out over chubby cheeks. "Like a light."

Rowe pressed his lips to the top of Ripley's head. "Norma should be back soon."

"Have you had a good day?"

He glanced over me and then nodded. "The best. Thank you."

"You're welcome."

Questions bubbled up inside me, personal ones I had no right asking, but I really wanted to know the answer to anyway. "Why doesn't he call you Dad?"

Rowe let out a heavy sigh, one that felt laced with pain. It was on the tip of my tongue to take the question back, because I didn't want to hurt him. But at the same time, it seemed to me that Rowe had been bottling up a lot of things about Rory and Ripley for a really long time, and that nothing was going to get better for him until he talked about them.

"He used to. Dada was his first word, and he said it right to my face. But not long after that, everything happened, and then I wasn't really in his life enough for him to remember." He looked up at me, his face lined with pain. "I hate that I did that. Rory would have hated what I did. I should have kept him with me. But it was just so hard. I didn't know what I was doing without her, and I felt like I was always in a fog, never present, sometimes I didn't even hear him when he was crying until Norma came from next door to see what was going on. I wasn't fit to be his father, and so when I did see him, I encouraged him to call me Rowe instead. He was so little that the change was easy to make."

"And now?"

"Now I wish I could get a do-over. I wish I could do it all differently."

"For what it's worth," I said softly, "I think you did the right thing. You did what a parent is supposed to do. You sacrificed your own happiness for your child's. What he needed back then was someone who could give him a stable home and all the care he required. You couldn't give that when you were so deep in grief and guilt. But things are different now. You clearly love him, and he clearly loves you."

Rowe shook his head sharply. "No. Norma is the parent he knows. I would never try to take that away from him now."

"I understand. But maybe there is a place for you in his life." I brushed a lock of blond hair back from Ripley's forehead. He was completely dead to the world, his face relaxed in sleep, like Rowe's arms were exactly where he needed to be. "He clearly feels safe with you. And now maybe it's your turn to help Norma."

"Speak of the devil." Rowe nodded toward the drive.

Norma's car traveled slowly down the road and pulled to a stop in front of us. Rowe motioned for Norma to stay in the car, and he transferred Ripley to the back seat without waking him.

I went to Norma's window while Rowe strapped him in, and she whispered to me, "How did they go?"

I gave a her a triumphant thumbs-up, and the old woman's face creased into a wide smile.

Rowe closed the back door quietly and then joined me. He ducked down so he and Norma were eye height. "Thank you," he said sincerely. "I...uh... I needed that. He's a really good kid. You've done such a good job with him."

She glanced over at the back seat, smiling fondly at her grandson, and then turned back to her son-in-law. "I'm an old lady, Rowe. He's a lot for me. And a lot of the time I don't feel like I'm doing the right thing by him. He deserves the sort of parent who can run around with him and play. Someone who can get down on the floor. That's not me. I'm too old and fat."

Rowe shook his head. "You are not."

Norma waved him away like he was an annoying fly. "Get out of here with you. Don't blow smoke up my ass. I can keep a roof over his head, and food in his mouth, but don't you be a stranger, okay? He needs more than just his old granny."

"Okay," Rowe said quietly. "I hear you."

Norma nodded, satisfied by that response, and put the car back into drive. "We'll see you soon, okay?"

"Real soon," Rowe promised.

Norma's car disappeared down the drive, and Rowe sank onto the porch steps.

I sat beside him, nudging him with my knee. "Do you hate me?"

The silence hung in the air for so long that I began preparing myself for him to kick me out. He hadn't been able to yell at me for orchestrating this entire thing while Ripley and Norma were here, but now that we were alone again, all bets were off. He rested his elbows on his knees and stared down at the ground for so long that I started filling the silence with babble. "I'm sorry, okay? I just thought you needed something other than work. And Norma needed a break. She looks so tired. Did you see how rejuvenated she was by the time she got back? I really liked her haircut, too. It suited her, don't you think?"

Still nothing from Rowe.

I sighed heavily. "I'm sorry. Please talk to me. I can't stand the silence."

"Obviously," Rowe muttered.

I sighed. "Okay, well, I guess I'll just go. But I just want you to know that you did have a good time today. And that only happened because I meddled. So you can pretend like you're mad at me all you want, but I'm not sorry I did this. I am sorry I sprang it on you, but not that it happened."

I pushed to my feet and moved to walk away, but his hand shot out, fingers circling my wrist.

"Where you going?" His grip tightened.

"Home."

"Don't."

I turned back, and our gazes clashed. Slowly he got to his feet, never letting go of my arm. He towered over me, moving in so close I had to tilt my head back.

"Don't go," he said again.

Something crackled in the air between us.

"Okay."

He put his hand to the side of my face, his fingers at the back of my neck, and drew me closer. When his lips touched mine, they were soft and sweet, gentle and hesitant.

I wrapped my arms around his waist and kissed him back. There was a thank-you in his kiss, but it was more than that. He held me with a tenderness that hadn't ever been there between the two of us. It sparked to life now, wrapping its way around me, and burrowing deep inside, searching for my heart. It brought desire, and all the feelings I'd been shoving down all day. I opened my mouth, accepting his tongue, and deepening the kiss. I closed my eyes and fell into his touch, drowning in the sensation that he was letting me hold him, and connect with him. I could feel myself battling against the walls of his armor, each one sliding down a touch the longer we kissed.

"Nobody else would have organized this for me, you know that, right?" he mumbled against my lips.

"Somebody might have, if you ever let anybody in."

He shook his head, kissing me again. "You make me want to try."

He ran his hands down my sides to my hips, pressing his fingers in, and then in one swift motion, he picked me up, hoisting me into his arms almost as easily as he'd picked up Ripley. On autopilot, I wrapped my legs around his waist, my arms around his shoulders, and held on. He walked backward up the steps, never breaking our kiss, his tongue plunging inside my mouth and sending dizzying messages throughout my entire body. We passed through rooms in a blur, until we were on the floor of his bedroom, on his mess of a mattress, blankets strewn everywhere. He laid me down gently, and when he moved away, his lips were pink and swollen from our kiss, his eyes hazy.

"I've got a head full of questions and hesitations and regrets," he admitted.

My heart thumped. I didn't want him to pull away again. "It's just us. I know you've got ghosts, we both do. But right now, it's just you and me. What do you want?"

My fingers trembled, while I waited for the answer.

But he didn't hesitate. "You." He followed it up by leaning down and kissing me again, his body covering mine.

I wrapped my arms and legs around him once more, gasping when his erection pressed at my core. He didn't move away this time, he let me feel it. It was thick, and delicious, a perfect expression of the way he felt, right where I wanted him most.

"I want you," he murmured again. "Fuck, Mae. I've wanted you since the moment I saw you. You do my head in."

I chuckled, tugging his T-shirt. "I don't think that's a good thing."

"It's not. You keep me awake at night with wanting you."

I flushed hot at the thought of him lying here in this bed, thinking about me. "What do you think about us doing?"

Heat flared in his gaze. "You don't want to know."

That heat went straight to my nipples, my clit, my core. Because yes, I very much did want to know. "Tell me," I murmured.

He untucked my shirt, lifting it inch by inch and slowly dragging it up my belly, chasing it with warm kisses to my abdomen. This was normally the part of the deed where I got uncomfortable...especially in broad daylight like this. My stomach wasn't flat and toned like my sister's had been. I was soft and curvy. My tummy had rolls that had made me self-conscious in the past. They'd had me scrambling for sheets or turning off lights.

There was none of that with Rowe. He worshipped my skin, kissing his way so slowly toward my breasts that it was a sweet sort of agony. His palms touched over any spot his lips missed, quietly mapping out my body like he was committing it to memory. The indent of my waist. The curve of my hip. A tickle of his fingers up my ribs until he had my shirt up over my bra.

I'd been vain enough to wear a nice underwear set,

not so much because I'd hoped this was where the day would end, but because I'd wanted to feel pretty and desirable. He was so incredibly beautiful. Voices in my head tried to tell me that he was out of my league, but being with Liam had muffled them. Rowe didn't have to be here. Nobody was forcing him to touch me.

He did it because he wanted to.

Because he wanted me.

I let him drink in his fill of the lace covering my breasts before lifting again and undoing the clasp at the back. I watched his expression change as the lace fell away, leaving me topless.

"This," he groaned, taking two handfuls of my breasts. "I dreamed about your tits, but they weren't half as good as the real thing." He ducked his head, drawing one nipple into his mouth.

The hot rasp of his tongue over the very tip of me had my eyes rolling back. He drew my nipple between his teeth gently, licking and sucking it, while he worked the other into a stiff peak with his fingers.

His mouth alternated between my breasts, kissing the swells, and teasing me until arousal wet my panties.

"I wouldn't have picked you for a boob man."

He paused to grin at me. "No? What would you have picked me for?"

"Legs," I said without thinking about it. "I don't know why."

He sat back and ran his hands up my calves, taking my long skirt with him, until it settled around my belly, leaving my panties on display to him. "I'm more interested in what's between them."

Oh Jesus.

He cupped me there, finger pressing against my clit through the soaked fabric. He leaned down, so his mouth was right by my ear. "I've been thinking about your sweet pussy and how deep my fingers were inside you when you came."

My breath hitched as he nudged the fabric aside and slid one finger inside me.

"I've been thinking about how you would have felt wrapped around my cock."

My core clenched at the thought of his erection filling me. I pulsed around his finger and knew that if I let him keep that up, I'd come in seconds.

I batted his hand away and reached for his belt buckle. I undid it quickly, pulling it from the loops of his shorts and then undid the button on his fly. Tight black underwear beneath did nothing to conceal the bulge of his junk, and I was eager to see him. He let me strip the last of his clothes from his body, while he removed my panties and skirt, so we were both gloriously naked, late afternoon sun spilling in the windows of his tiny, isolated cabin.

No one would hear me scream out here.

Which was a good thing, because the glint in Rowe's eyes told me he wanted me screaming his name.

I reached for his cock before he could reach for me, circling my fingers around the base and stroking him in long, slow movements. Glistening precum beaded at his tip, and I smoothed it over with my thumb. Just like the rest of him, his dick was gorgeous. Big and thick, soft velvet over steel. The sort of dick that dildos were modeled from because it was so fucking symmetrical.

"Is anything about you not perfect?" I asked.

"Too much," he replied. His mouth turned down, as if he were suddenly reflecting on every part of him that wasn't saintly.

That wasn't what I wanted. I wanted him lost in pleasure, not thinking about his problems. I wanted him wrapped up in me. In us.

I got off my back and reversed our positions, pushing him down onto the bed and taking control. Surprise flared in his eyes, but he let me do it, his loud groan of approval all I needed for my self-consciousness to disappear. My boobs hung heavy, not high and perky like I wanted them to, but full and needy. There was nothing but desire in his eyes when he looked at them. And when I lowered my head and fit my mouth over his cock, his fingers fisting in my hair was all the encouragement I needed.

"Fuck, Mae. Your mouth..."

I grinned around his dick, bobbing and working my way down his length, taking as much of him as I could. I wanted to take him all. I wanted to blow his mind, but he was so damn big it was impossible. I worked his base with one hand, cupping his balls with the other. My lips and tongue ran up and down, taking him as deep as I could.

He let me go for a minute, his fingers clenching and releasing in my hair before he groaned loudly and sat up. He grabbed me by the hips, and I squealed around his dick as he dragged my ass around to his face.

"Rowe! What are you doing?!"

"Sit on my face, Mae. Get your damn knees apart and let me taste you."

"Ohhhh," I moaned. Just the idea of having him

between my thighs sent a new wave of arousal through me.

He swiveled some and got himself beneath me. I wanted his dick in my mouth, though, so I took him deep again and let him maneuver himself into a sixty-nine position, the anticipation of his mouth on my pussy so great my legs trembled.

His big shoulders pushed my knees wide, and I hovered over him, waiting for the touch of his mouth at my core.

"I said, sit on my face, Mae. Not hover over it." His arms hooked around my thighs and yanked me down.

I fought against him. "I don't want to suffocate you!"

"You can't ride my tongue if you're half a foot away from it." He pulled me down again, and this time, there was no arguing with him.

Oh Lord.

His mouth was pure heaven. He licked and sucked my clit, flicking at the little bud of nerves before making long, slow strokes with his tongue, right back to my entrance. My hips rocked like they had a mind of their own, and I took him deeper into my mouth, wanting to please him in the same way he was with me. I let his cock hit the back of my throat, and it only turned me on more.

But Rowe was better at this game than I was. His tongue plunged inside me, and his fingers guided my movements, building them up into a frenzy that had me on the edge of an orgasm. I had to abandon his dick. I couldn't focus with the pleasure he was eliciting from some place deep inside me. I sat up, grinding against his face.

"I'm so close," I moaned.

But I wanted to come on his dick. I wanted him to come with me. I wanted to see his face when he fell over the edge. I disentangled myself from his grip and crawled down his body, spinning around so I could see him while lining him up with my entrance.

His mouth was shiny pink, slick with my arousal, and he wiped it off on the back of his hand. He watched me intently but made no move to stop me when I nudged myself down on his erection. His eyes rolled back a little, but then he forced himself to focus on me. I sank down onto his cock, taking the full length of him inside me easily, despite how thick he was.

"Ride me," he whispered. "Don't fucking stop, Mae. I need this."

I knew. I needed it, too. He felt so good inside me, there was no way I was stopping this time until we both fell over the edge.

He seized my hips, helping things by thrusting up to meet each of my falls. He let me control the pace, but his punishing grasp at my sides was a constant reminder he was there, wanting this as much as I did, needing that release building inside both of us.

It spiraled up from the place we were joined, spreading out through my body, and leaving my breasts aching for his touch.

But mine was almost as good. I grabbed both tits, squeezing my nipples hard between two fingers, and rocking over him. His gaze turned molten, and he bit his lip, watching me ride him. "You've never looked more beautiful than you do right now, Mae. Riding my cock with your tits in your hands. I want to hear my name on your lips."

"Rowe," I moaned. "Fuck me. Please. I need to come."

He doubled his efforts. Slamming into my body from below me, each thrust of his hips powerful and strong. His fingers slid to the place we were joined and found my clit, working it furiously. As my orgasm barreled down the tunnel, I lost rhythm, giving myself over to him to control. He flipped me onto my back and drove home one last time.

My intense cry of pleasure echoed around the empty house, and probably across the clearing. I yelled his name while he yelled mine, both of us falling into our orgasms at the exact same time. A flood of desire coated the space between my thighs, mingling with his as he rode us both out, until neither of us could last a moment more.

Still dick deep inside me, he rolled us once more, so I was on top. I laid my head down on his chest, his erection fading inside me though neither of us did a thing to move. We both breathed so hard, our chests rising and falling, but fast, like we'd run a marathon and crossed the line together.

"What was that?" he murmured from beneath me. His words were sleepy and sated. "Who are you? What's my name?"

I giggled, stroking my fingers along the smooth skin of his muscled chest. "I don't know, but judging by the mess, it was good."

He pressed a kiss to my forehead. "So fucking good."

He glanced down my body and shifted his slightly. "No condom..."

The wetness between us was proof of that. "That was maybe not our smartest move."

"Are you...?"

"On the pill? No. But you don't need to worry about that."

"I know I'm clean. I have to have physicals for work, and that is part of it. I haven't been with anyone in years anyway."

I glanced at him. "You haven't?"

He shook his head. "No one ever compared to Rory..."

I swallowed hard, feeling like I was suddenly competing with her ghost.

But he tilted my chin up and stared deep in my eyes. "Hey. You made me realize it's not a competition. I don't compare you to her. You're you. You're different, and gorgeous, and I want you in a way I never wanted anyone else."

"Were you thinking about her?" I asked, almost not wanting to know the answer.

"Not for a second. All I could think about was you, and the way you feel, and the way you taste and the way that even though I know we shouldn't be doing this, I want to do it anyway. I've never not used a condom in my life, but I was so wrapped up in you, and how you make me feel, that I wanted to take you bare, and fuck the consequences."

His words sent a warm, rosy glow over me. They meant everything. I stored them away, locking them up in a secret part of me to relive later, when he inevitably pushed me away again.

Because I knew that once this bubble burst. Once we were back at work, with Zye's threat's fresh in his mind once more, that rejection would come.

But it wasn't coming tonight.

The only coming tonight would be from mind-blowing sex.

"I have another surprise for you," I confided.

"If it involves the use of my dick, you're going to have to give me a moment."

I grinned at him. "Actually, it involves a different sort of bat altogether."

MAE

I went back to my place to shower and change, and right on time, there was a knock on the door.

I'd dressed differently tonight than my usual style. Jeans that hugged my thighs, and sneakers I rarely wore, so they were blinding in their whiteness, barely a speck of dirt marking them.

Liam's eyes widened when I threw open the door, and he took in the baseball T-shirt. "Well, hello, sixteen-year-old Liam's wet dream."

"Sixteen-year-old Liam didn't just want me naked?"

He shook his head. "Hell no. That would have blown his mind. And his...other things...in about thirty seconds. But Mae in a baseball shirt...yes, please."

I grinned at him and did a little spin. "Not just any baseball shirt."

At the completion of my twirl, his eyes were wide, his mouth hanging open. He grabbed me by the arms, and without a word, very slowly turned me around again. He stared at my back for a long moment.

For so long, in fact, that worry trickled through me. "Is it too much?"

I dared a peek over my shoulder.

I didn't miss the way he swallowed hard, like he was forcing a lump in his throat down. "I don't know what to say."

My heart flooded with feeling. Some were just general good feelings that I'd made him happy. But so many of them were more than that. Some of them were big. Huge. And they came from somewhere suspiciously close to my heart. "Say you like it."

"You put my name on the back of your shirt."

"I did. After you told me that story about nobody turning up for you at your baseball camp, I thought you should know that at least one person is on your team. Do you like it?"

"Are you fucking kidding me? I love it."

He drew me in close and kissed me so softly it took me by surprise. He breathed me in, and I accepted his kiss and gave it back with everything I had. This man was so good. He was nothing like the arrogant prick I remembered from high school. That had all been fake, hiding the true man he'd grow into and sweet soul he'd always had. He was so incredibly selfless—spending hours on Heath's case, unpaid, and all because I'd asked him to. He gave up his time and money to work at the homeless shelter. And he'd given me the space to explore my feelings for him, as well as for Rowe and Heath without an ounce of judgment. He never demanded anything of me.

He just gave.

And for once, I wanted to give him something back.

"I love you," he whispered.

I pulled away, blinking in surprise.

I opened my mouth to speak, but he put his finger to my lips. "Don't. Don't say it back just so I don't feel like a dickhead, left hanging in the wind. I know you aren't there. We never even talked about this being anything more than casual, but this is me shooting my shot. And telling you I'm in. I don't know what that looks like, with Heath and Rowe, and I won't ask you to choose. I'm just telling you I want you, in whichever way you want me."

I tried to speak, but then Rowe was in the doorway behind him, hovering uncomfortably. "Did I interrupt something?"

I went to ask him for a minute, but Liam shook his head. "Nope. I've said what I needed to say." He grinned at me, any trace of self-consciousness over the massive bomb he'd just dropped completely gone, if he'd felt any at all. He brushed a kiss on my lips as he moved past me into my apartment and threw himself across my couch.

Rowe stared at me.

I stared at him. "Hey. You came. I wasn't sure if you would or not."

"I need to get out of the house more."

"And going to a baseball game with me is the highlight of his young life," Liam called from the couch.

Rowe rolled his eyes at him over my shoulder. "You're younger than me, dickhead."

"Never said I wasn't young, too." Liam twisted to grin over at us. "We've got time to kill if you guys want to hang out here for a bit first."

Rowe shrugged, noncommittal, but I suddenly got

nervous. Liam was already lying on the couch. I'd been naked with both of them in the last twenty-four hours, and after Liam saying he wanted to watch, all I could think about was combining the two experiences. Heat warmed through me pleasantly but brought with it a complete case of nerves.

"Let's just go. We can get drinks when we get there." I grabbed my purse from the back of a chair and made for the door.

Rowe blocked me in. "Why do you suddenly look like you're running away?"

"I'm not!" But it came out too squeaky to be believable.

Liam came over and leaned on the wall beside Rowe, studying me. He laughed and elbowed Rowe. "I told her I wanted to watch, and now she's freaking out."

Rowe glanced at his teammate. "Watch...as in..."

"You and her? Yep."

Rowe raised an eyebrow. "Kinky fuck."

"Like you can talk."

"Wait, what does that mean?" I interrupted, gaze darting between the two of them.

Liam slung an arm around my shoulders. "Ah, look. Sweet Little Miss Valedictorian. You show your pretty face again." He guided me out the door, and Rowe pulled it closed behind us. "So many things to teach you."

I glanced back over my shoulder at Rowe, but there was a heat in his eyes that gave me no reassurances.

The promises there lit me up from inside like a wildfire.

owe and Liam dominated the conversation on the way to the baseball stadium. Rowe insisted on driving, and Liam sat in the back seat between us, leaning forward, hands on the backs of our seats while Rowe filled him in on what was going on in the prison. Liam listened to every word carefully, even though he'd heard a lot of it from me, but I could practically see his lawyer brain storing away information for some point in the future when he might need it.

It gave me time to settle down and breathe through my nerves over this situation. And by the time we got to the baseball stadium, it felt a whole lot more like three friends out for a night of drinks and sports.

Until Rowe's hand landed on my thigh.

He drove through the parking lot with one hand, the other on my leg, burning a hole through my jeans and right into my skin. He massaged it absently like this wasn't the biggest deal ever. All the while, the two of them kept up their chatter like there was nothing weird about it at all.

At the stadium gate, we handed over our tickets, and I made straight for the drink line. Rowe and Liam followed after me, the three of us standing together and peering at the offerings on the board.

"Drinking to be social or drinking to get drunk?" Liam asked as we neared the head of the line.

"Just one or two for me," Rowe said. "Gotta drive."

Liam looked at me.

"Getting drunk." I grinned.

"Right back at ya."

"You two better not throw up in my car," Rowe grumbled.

"I make no promises," Liam ribbed him and stepped forward to order our drinks. He was so incredibly charming and handsome, flashing a smile at the female bartender whose fingers shook as she poured our beers. She darted little glances between him and Rowe, her thoughts so transparent they were practically a flashing sign above her head.

I couldn't blame her. They were a sight to see together. Rowe darker and more serious. Liam all flash and smiles and charm. She was a gorgeous woman, her long dark hair pulled back in a sleek ponytail, a black ribbed tank top clinging to her breasts. And yet I didn't feel any jealousy. Rowe stood so close behind me that it could not have been construed as simply friendly. And Liam's gaze continually sought me out, his smiles for me different to the ones he shared with anyone else.

Their attention filled me with a confidence I'd never had with my exes. They hadn't been half as attractive as Rowe and Liam. And yet everywhere we'd gone, I'd noticed their wandering eyes.

Liam handed me a beer, and we found our seats. It was still early, and the crowd around us thin. Liam set down the tray of drinks at his feet, careful not to knock them, and we gazed out over the empty field. Me sandwiched between the two of them.

Rowe reached across me to get his drink from Liam and frowned. "Hey, what's wrong? You went quiet."

I smiled and shook my head. "No, nothing. It's all good."

"Penny for your thoughts, then."

I shrugged. "I was actually just thinking about my ex."

Liam sat back in his chair, dramatically clutching his heart. "Damn, Mae. Here on a date with the two of us and you're thinking about your ex? Has he got a twelve-inch dick or something? I've got that covered, but I know Rowe can't compete."

Rowe flipped him the bird.

Liam sniggered, and I relaxed a little between them. "Actually, I was just thinking that the last time I came here was with my ex. He spent the entire time checking out other women."

"Fool."

"Dickhead."

They both inched closer to me, our legs brushing.

"Mae?" This voice was feminine and startled me after a day and evening full of Liam and Rowe's deeper tones.

I snapped my head up, almost guiltily like I'd been doing something wrong by having two men so close to me. "Tori!"

She and Will were picking their way down the stadium seating and had paused a few rows below us.

"Where are your seats?" I called.

Will checked their tickets again and then pointed over to his right. "Over there somewhere."

I pouted. "Come sit with us until it fills up."

They crab-walked along the row of seats, and I stood and reached across the chair in front of me to hug Tori. "You're extra short when I'm a step above you." I grinned at her.

"Shut up," she grumbled, but it was with a smile. She brought Liam in for a quick hug as well, and then turned to Rowe. "Fancy seeing you again."

"You look better when you're not petrified and covered in ash."

"Right back at ya."

He leaned down and hugged her.

She returned his embrace with a fierceness that spoke of shared trauma.

Will cleared his throat, and Tori drew back quickly. "Oh sorry, babe. I'm not just hugging random men, I swear. This is Rowe. He's the one who got me out of the prison in one piece."

Will's eyes widened, and he held a hand out to Rowe. "I'm glad I got the chance to meet you and say thank you. Tori said you were amazing."

The apples of Rowe's cheeks went pink. "She was amazing. Handled it like a pro. You coming back to the prison anytime soon?"

Tori went to answer, but Will cut her off with a laugh. "Not a chance. That night was enough excitement to last a lifetime. Wasn't it, sweetheart?"

Tori closed her mouth and nodded. "Absolutely."

I wasn't sure she really meant it. I knew that coming into the prison to help her priest with last rites and blessings had meant something to her, especially since she was struggling to find herself as a new mom. But I could also totally understand Will's perspective. It had almost been worse for Liam and Will on the outside. The lack of information had hit Liam hard, and it had to have been worse for Will. The bond between he and Tori was like no other I'd ever seen. They'd been together for so long, since they were kids, really. It must have been awful for him, waiting on the outside with their son, not knowing if she was going to make it out. I realized what a shitty friend I'd been in not reaching out to him, as well as Tori. I hugged him now and held him tight for a moment.

He patted my back and laughed in my ear. "This is different."

I didn't care. I just squeezed him until he gave in and squeezed me back. When we pulled apart, I gestured at Liam. "You know Liam, right? I think you've met before."

Liam nodded, and the two men shook hands. "Yeah, at the funeral."

"So what are you guys doing anyway?" I asked Tori. "Since when do you like baseball?"

"Since when do you?" she shot back, twinkle in her eyes as she darted looks at Liam and Rowe.

"I love baseball," I lied.

Liam snorted on a laugh and pointed out into the field. "Hey, Mae, if you're standing on that plate there, what position are you playing?"

I gazed at the plate blankly.

They all burst into laughter, and I couldn't help but grin. "Fine. I know nothing about baseball, but these two do, so they can teach me."

"Lucky you," Tori said with a knowing smile.

Lucky me indeed.

Will was the one who actually answered the question. "We decided to come into the city for a date night. Tori's mom has the baby, so we have a whole night to ourselves."

"Bow chicka bow wow." I grinned at him, laughing at the way his cheeks flushed pink.

Tori slapped my arm. "Stop embarrassing my poor husband. We honestly just really needed this night away. Will's been working late on Wednesday and Thursday nights, and he has tennis on Mondays, and I have church youth group on Fridays, so lately it feels like we're ships passing in the night." She picked up his hand and squeezed it. "We need some time to be adults."

I grinned at her. "Like I said, bow chicka bow wow."

She rolled her eyes. "You've been hanging out with Liam too long."

Movement to her right caught her attention, two people studying their tickets in confusion. "It's okay!" Tori called to them. "We're just leaving." She drew me in for a quick hug. "Liam *and* Rowe?" she hissed in my ear. "Seriously, my phone better be ringing first thing tomorrow morning because I already want *all* the details. All of them, Mae. This old married woman needs to live vicariously through whatever's going on here. Bow chicka bow wow to you, missy."

I laughed and shooed her away, waving to Will as he put his arm around his much shorter wife and led them to their seats.

I smiled fondly after them. Liam shoved his hands in his pockets, watching them walk away, too, but didn't say anything.

Rowe nudged me. "I heard all that by the way. Tori's whisper is about as delicate as a bull in a china shop."

I groaned in embarrassment. "She's jumping to conclusions."

"Is she?" he murmured. "I was kinda hoping you had plans..."

I sucked in a breath when our hands touched, but this wasn't the time or the place. The people in front of us had little kids who didn't need to hear about the distinctly adult things I was thinking about doing with Rowe and Liam.

But Rowe seemed intent on sitting too close, crowding me with his broad shoulders and delicious scent. He looked entirely too good in jeans and a T-shirt that hugged his muscles. The game started with the home team at bat, but Rowe seemed more interested in me than watching it.

"There's a bar near here," he murmured halfway through the game, when I was on my second beer. "We should go afterwards. There's a dance floor..."

"You dance?" I asked, twisting to face him. "That surprises me."

"Didn't I show you this afternoon that I've got rhythm?"

A lick of warmth curled through me. It was the first time he'd brought this afternoon up. "I almost thought you'd forgotten about that..."

"Liam distracted me with saying he wants to watch...I kinda can't stop thinking about that now."

The warmth turned into a fire. "You'd want to?"

"Depends on how you feel about it?"

I darted a glance at Liam, but he was intently watching the game, his baseball cap turned backward.

"I want to turn him on as much as he turns me on," I admitted to Rowe, the beer loosening my lips. "And I don't want there to be any secrets between any of us. There can't be."

He leaned in close, his lips brushing my ear. "The idea of fucking you with him watching gets me so hard."

He adjusted himself slightly on his seat, and I

chanced a glance at his lap, but he had it covered with a drink tray.

"We shouldn't be talking about this here," I whispered back.

"Why not?"

"Because I can't do anything about it."

Rowe took a long swallow of his beer. "Forget the bar. As soon as this game is finished..."

He didn't finish the thought, but it held the distinct note of promise.

It was an uncomfortably long wait for the final out, and I had no idea what the score was or who had won. I tried to look for Tori and Will, but the crowd swept them away and I gave up.

Liam was still quiet when we got back to the car, and I walked beside him, slipping my hand into his. "Hey, you okay?"

He glanced down at me distractedly. "What? Oh, yeah, fine."

"You don't look fine. You didn't enjoy the game?"

"No, it was fine. Good."

I frowned up at him. "Okay...but something is bothering you. Is it me?" Specifically, me and Rowe. Or me and the fact Liam had dropped an I love you which I hadn't said back.

He shook his head adamantly and brought my hand up to his lips. "Hey, no. It's not you at all. Not Rowe either. There's something sitting at the edge of my brain...you know when you feel like you've forgotten something?"

I nodded.

"I get that a lot when I'm working on cases and trying to put pieces together."

"Want to talk it out?"

We reached Rowe's car, and he hit the key fob, unlocking the doors.

"Nah, it's fine. Whatever it is, it'll come to me." He tried to let go of my hand, but I wouldn't let him. I slid into the back seat with him, letting Rowe sit in the front alone.

He eyed me in the rearview mirror. "What am I? Your chauffeur?"

I raised an eyebrow at him. "Hey, you got me on the way here. He gets me on the way home."

Liam's fingers moved to my thigh. "I get you on the way home?"

I blushed pink. "You know what I mean."

"I don't think I do, and I think I want to take advantage of that. Yo, driver? Does this car have one of those privacy partitions?"

Rowe glanced back at him. "You aren't the only one who likes to watch."

Liam burst into laughter and slapped his friend on the shoulder. "You perv."

"Like you can talk."

"You sure you won't crash us? If she's back here making all sorts of noises..."

Rowe snorted. "I don't have that much faith in your sexual skills to be honest."

I hid a smile at their ribbing.

"Oooh, a challenge."

Rowe put the key in the ignition and backed us out of the parking spot. "You talk the talk, Banks. But until I actually hear her moaning your name, that's all it is... You running your mouth. As usual. You're well-suited to being a lawyer, you know."

"You better not crash us."

"You better make her come before I come back there and do it myself."

"Oh, sweet baby Jesus," I whispered, pressing my thighs together.

Liam's fingers kneaded my thigh muscle pleasantly, inching toward my center. He brushed the seam that ran right between my legs. "You look good in jeans, you know? But I'm missing the easy access of your skirts right now."

"I'll never wear pants again," I joked.

Liam leaned over and pushed my hair aside, exposing the side of my neck and my ear. "Good. Because I like knowing I can take you anywhere, anytime."

My breath hitched at the growl in his voice and the thought of him wanting me like that. It was so different to what I was used to. Men who barely paid me attention, more interested in watching football than pinning me up against a wall in a public place, or taking me in the back seat of a car while their friend drove us home from a baseball game. Rowe's gaze met mine in the rearview mirror, and heat flared there. An intense desire focused entirely on me.

Liam's lips worshipped at my neck, kissing a trail toward my collarbone while he deftly undid the buttons on my shirt with one hand. But he paused before slipping his hand inside. "What are you thinking? I can practically see your mind whirring."

"Nothing," I assured him. "It's fine."

"It's never good when a woman says she's fine. Fine

does not mean fine," Rowe piped up from the front seat. "Talk."

I bit my lip, not wanting to sound like an attention-seeking idiot. But there was one question that burned in my mind. "You two could have anyone you want..."

"And who we want is you," Liam declared, twisting my chin to stare into my eyes. "Do you know how many women have seen anything in me other than my money and my job? Nobody has ever wanted to listen to my sob story about my family. Who else would have a T-shirt made with my name on the back? And the fact you don't even realize how stunningly beautiful you are is part of why I want you. It's part of why I love you."

A lump rose in my throat. Because I did see him. The man he was, and the boy he'd been. I saw his hurt and felt it on his behalf. He was selfless and kind, and the sort of man I'd spent years dreaming of, even when he'd been right there in front of my eyes. His gaze burned with need, and my core clenched around nothing, aching for him to be inside me. Liam was my male counterpart in so many ways, the two of us too similar to work and yet...we did.

He tried to kiss me, but I dodged his mouth, putting mine to his ear and letting my hair fall around us, giving us a tiny moment of privacy. "I love you, too," I whispered, only for him to hear. "You wouldn't let me say it before, but I do."

He pulled back, his eyes full of questions. "Are you sure? You don't have to—"

"But I do. Because you're so easy to love, Liam. And I couldn't stop it even if I wanted to."

His eyes went shiny, and I could only tell because the

streetlights outside flashed as we sped past. Rowe would have heard it, but I didn't care. Liam needed to know that he was worthy of love.

"Take your seat belt off," he said suddenly.

"What?"

"Take it off. I need to be inside you now."

Rowe let out a shuddering breath but didn't say a word. I glanced at Liam uncertainly. It had been one thing for them to talk about getting me off in the back seat. That could have been easily done, with Liam's fingers between my thighs, in the darkness, Rowe probably wouldn't have seen anything except my expression when I came.

But having sex with Liam on the back seat was entirely different.

Liam's lips brushed the shell of my ear. "Now, Mae." He reached across me, unclipping my seat belt.

I let him.

Cars flew by either side of us on the busy main road, but Liam didn't seem to care. His gaze ate me up hungrily as he nudged aside my already unbuttoned shirt, drawing it down my arms and immediately going for the clasp at the back of my bra. He put his lips to mine, kissing me deep and hungrily, his tongue plunging into my mouth and distracting me from the fact I was now topless in the back of a car for anyone to see. The darkness and the speed we were traveling provided some cover, but still. This was more public than I'd ever been before.

He cupped both my breasts as he kissed me, though, thumbs flicking over my nipples while he stole my breath with his lips.

"Fuck, Liam," Rowe bit out. "We're on the main road. You're serious about getting her naked?"

"As a fucking heart attack, brother. Enjoy."

From the corner of my eye, I saw Rowe shake his head. A moment later, the sound of his blinker clicked on, and we turned down a dark side street. We left the smooth surface of the road and bumped a long a track that took us into the woods near Rowe's place.

Though getting naked with Liam in public was exciting, I relaxed a tiny bit at the more cozy and intimate feel that spread through the car once we were in the privacy of the trees. "I feel like I'm fifteen and going to the lookout to make out."

Liam's fingers found the button on my jeans. "I want to do a whole lot more than make out." He lowered the zipper on my fly and pushed his hand inside my panties, cupping my mound. "And judging by how wet you are, you don't want me stopping at second base either."

I shook my head.

"Good girl," he whispered, rewarding me with one thick finger slipping up inside me.

"Oh," I moaned. I lifted my ass off the seat, and between the two of us, we got my jeans and panties low enough that I could toe them off. With my shoes and socks disappearing along with them, I was very naked in a dark car.

With two men.

Yes.

The thought startled me, but why shouldn't I have this? I would hardly be the first woman to have a threesome. But it would be my first threesome. And the thought sent unexpected arousal as well as a healthy dose of anticipation right through me. I thought I'd be drunk when this happened, and though Liam and I had both had a few, I was now incredibly sober.

Rowe steered the car over to the side of the track and turned the engine off. The silence settled around us, and though I concentrated on Liam's fingers deep inside me, I was well aware I now had Rowe's full attention, too.

Liam fumbled with his own pants, trying to keep up a rhythm between my legs while undoing his zipper with his free hand. I helped by lifting his T-shirt and running my hands all over his perfect abs.

"I can't wait any longer, baby," he murmured once we'd freed his erection. His cock was thick and hard, standing at full attention, just waiting to fill me. I didn't want to wait either.

"Get on my lap, Mae."

I swung a leg across his, ready to kiss him as I sank down on his cock, but he stopped me, darting a look around me at Rowe. "Turn around."

My eyes widened. There wasn't much room in the car for two grown adults, especially one of Liam's height. But a pulse pounded between my legs at the thought of having sex with him like this...my back to his chest...

Rowe would be able to see everything—my tits, my legs spread wide around Liam's, my clit, and Liam deep inside me. I couldn't help it. The moment I swiveled around my gaze met Rowe's, and a low moan fell from my lips.

"I'm not even inside you yet and you're moaning like you're going to come," Liam groaned. "Get on my dick, Mae. I need to feel you around me when you get there."

Rowe shifted on his seat, trying to hold my gaze in the

mirror, but then he squeezed his eyes shut tight. "Fuck it." He twisted around, watching me unashamedly, his gaze roaring over my naked body. The light was dim, but I didn't miss the way his gaze narrowed in between my widespread legs, and Liam's dick lined up at the opening to my pussy.

I sank down, taking Liam inside me in one, deep thrust. He shouted from behind me, yelling something about how tight I was. It was not the easiest position to get a good rhythm in, but I didn't want to move because the way Rowe's eyes ate me up had me more turned on than I'd ever been in my entire life. Arousal gushed from deep inside me, coating Liam's bare dick, and he found a rhythm, thrusting up to meet me. He wrapped one arm around me, finding my clit with his fingers and playing me like I was some sort of musical instrument that he'd had a lifetime of experience with. He knew how to work my body. We'd had enough sex that even though this position was new, and Rowe being here with us was different, it was still just me and Liam, his body fitting so perfectly with mine, just like it had for weeks now. He knew what I liked. He knew that rubbing my clit too fast didn't work for me so he rubbed it in slow, soft motions that were in time with the thrust of his dick inside me.

Rowe reached down, and though I couldn't see it because of the seat, the way he closed his eyes, relief filling his features, told me he was stroking himself.

I wanted to get him there faster. I rode Liam, taking him deep with every bump and grind over his lap, and I grabbed my breasts in a show for Rowe, squeezing my nipples tight while I battled the orgasm inside me.

Liam pinched my clit. "I want to feel you come, baby. I need to come with you."

"Yes," I moaned. "More."

I squeezed my nipples again, right as he pinched my clit. Rowe's hand moved faster on his dick, his attention trained on the place Liam and I were joined. Liam reared up from behind me, slamming himself into my pussy.

There was no holding on to my orgasm. I fell over the edge screaming in ecstasy, my core clenching down around Liam's thick length and setting off his orgasm as well. He shouted into the small space, his groans of pleasure spurring me on, taking everything he gave me, and grinding down on top of him to wring out every moment of my orgasm.

All while Rowe watched.

Liam finally slowed, his grip on my hips loosening. A thin coat of sweat covered my body, and Liam traced a lazy line down the center of my back, his fingers bumping along my spine until he got to the crack of my ass, and then back up again.

Rowe watched me, my nipples strained toward him. I had to wait a moment, until I was coherent enough to talk, but there was something I needed to know.

"Did you come?" I asked him.

He shook his head.

Heat bloomed between my thighs once more. And already feeling like some wanton sex goddess, my voice husky and raw from screaming out my orgasm, I asked Rowe something I probably never would have had the courage to say otherwise. "How do you want me?"

Liam groaned from beneath me, and Rowe's eyes

flared. But I wasn't taking it back. I needed him, and I had to know what he wanted.

"Get out of the car."

He got out of his side first and yanked his T-shirt off. I climbed off Liam's lap, not caring I was sticky with his cum and sweat. Neither guy gave a fuck, and neither did I. There'd be time for showers later, but right now, I needed to please Rowe the same way Liam had pleased me.

I opened the back door on the driver's side, where Rowe waited for me, surprised and grateful to find he'd dropped his T-shirt on the ground for me to stand on. The soft fabric covered grass and a few pebbles, but I barely noticed them dig into my feet, too focused on Rowe. I put a hand up to his face and brought it down to meet mine. The warm summer night air wrapped its way around my body as I kissed Rowe, completely naked, beneath the stars and the moon, and surrounded by nature. It called out to some inner goddess within me, I was sure. That was the only reason I could come up with for suddenly finding the confidence to be like this.

God, he was a good kisser. He wrapped his arms tight around my body and devoured my mouth until he was all I could think of. The rest of the world disappeared into his kiss, and that needy ache rose inside me once more. I slipped my hand between us, into his open jeans, finding him bare underneath, and a huge erection. I stroked my hand down his length, but he stopped me by grabbing my wrist. I looked up at him, a question in my eyes, and without breaking my gaze, he reached between my legs, swiping his fingers through Liam's cum and my arousal, mingled together inside me, and coated his fingers in it. With wide eyes, I watched him coat his dick, and then he replaced my hand. I now slid over his dick with ease, and he closed his eyes while I worked him to the edge.

"Fuck, that's hot," Liam said quietly from inside the car, and knowing he was watching only spurred me on. I moved my hand faster until Rowe groaned and spun me around, so I faced Liam once more. "Hold on to the car, Mae. Spread your legs, I want to fuck you from behind."

I did as I was told, putting my hands on the open doorframe, above where Liam sat on the edge of the seat. My gaze met his and then dropped to his lap. He was hard again.

But then Rowe was nudging at my pussy, while Liam inched forward and took hold of one of my tits bouncing in his face. He fit his mouth around my nipple, sucking and licking it while Rowe eased himself inside me. He held his position for a moment, letting me feel how big he was before he began a slow thrust.

It took me longer this time, already fully satisfied from Liam, and the orgasm built gradually, simmering away below the surface while Rowe sheathed himself inside me and Liam played with my breasts. But the longer we went, the greater the demand inside my body became. It was a building storm, ready to unleash as soon as the conditions were perfect.

"Her ass," Liam said to Rowe. "She likes it. Already found that out."

Heat spread across my entire body, from my toes on Rowe's T-shirt, right through to my scalp. I couldn't even look at Liam, though I didn't correct him.

Rowes fingers skated down my spine. "That true?"

I didn't say anything. The embarrassment was eating me up.

"Not gonna do it unless you say I can, Mae."

His fingers traced the very top of my ass. I craved the touch of him lower. I still remembered how it had felt to have Liam's fingers there, and though it was probably turning me pink to have it said out loud, I did want him there. His fingers at least. I wasn't sure this was the time or place for more than that.

"Yes," I whispered, giving him permission.

"Yes what?" he taunted. He pulled his cock from my pussy and teased it up between my ass cheeks.

I moaned loudly when it touched the place I really wanted him. "Yes! I want you there."

"One finger, Rowe," Liam warned. "No shoving your giant fucking dick in there. She isn't ready."

Rowe nudged his dick at my rear entrance, and I realized Liam was right. There was no way I could take him there.

He bent down and placed a kiss on my spine. "Hey, relax. I got you."

I knew he did. He pushed his dick inside my pussy once more, then swiped it across my asshole. He did it over and over, plunging deep in the front, then pressing to my ass until I was coated with cum and arousal and fully relaxed again.

He drove me wild with his gentle thrusts, building me back to where I'd been. Liam looked up past me to Rowe, and I had no idea what he'd communicated, but Liam nodded.

On the next, slow intrusion, Liam dropped to his knees on the ground between my legs and licked my clit. I yelled out, because at the same time, Rowe put the tip of his finger to my ass.

"Oh God!" I yelled, not caring if there was anyone around to hear me.

Liam licked me so luxuriously, while Rowe fucked me from behind, fingering my ass. I took his finger a little deeper with each thrust of his cock and each stroke of Liam's tongue, until he was fully inside me.

It was like nothing I'd ever felt. I wanted to come and yet never come so the feeling couldn't go away. They worked in perfect unison, driving my body up until I couldn't think straight. Pleasure curled within me, and the world could have exploded around us and I wouldn't have noticed because *everything* was exploding inside me. I came with a scream that would have been heard for miles. I yelled their names while my legs trembled, and Rowe hooked an arm around my middle to keep me from falling. He picked up the pace, pumping into my body as fast and hard as he could, my moans echoing out every time he slammed home. "Oh. Oh. Oh!"

He shouted when he came, my name on his lips in the still night air that deliciously wafted over our sweaty skin. He breathed hard in my ear, whispering my name. "You're amazing. You're so fucking beautiful. I've never seen anything like that."

I glowed under his praise and kissed Liam when he stood to join us. The three of us, naked in the moonlight, on the side of some road because they couldn't wait to get me home.

I'd never felt more beautiful. More wanted. More in love.

I kissed Liam deep, while knowing those same feelings I felt for him were building for Rowe as well.

24

MAE

*N*ot wanting to seem like a stage-five clinger, I didn't call or text Rowe or Liam after our post baseball game adventure. True to their natures, Liam called me the minute he woke up the next day, and we'd spent an hour on the phone, talking about everything and nothing, and ending in more *I love yous*.

There had been radio silence from Rowe.

But I was learning not to worry too much when he went quiet. I had so much more of him now to keep me going—his smoldering looks, and whispered words, and a firm belief he wanted me.

I smiled to myself as I got ready for work, Liam's I love you in my ear, and the knowledge that Rowe and I were scheduled on together tonight. When I arrived, he was leaning on the locker next to mine, scrolling through his phone. He looked too good in uniform, his shirt tucked neatly into the pants that sat low on his hips, belt buckle in place. You could just see the curve of his biceps below the hem of his shirtsleeve, and I delighted in the fact I'd gotten to see so much more than that. His uniform hid his ridged abs and defined pecs, and all the glory of his cock. I'd always suspected, but now I knew for certain everything he had going on.

"Hey," I said quietly, sidling up to him to open my locker. "How are you?"

He put his phone in his pocket, glancing toward the doorway where voices floated through. The locker room would be full soon, seeing as it was shift change. He took the chance to lean closer, and I didn't pull away. "That's a very formal greeting from someone who let me watch her ride another man's dick."

I flushed hot at the memory of grinding over Liam's lap while Rowe watched. "I haven't heard from you. I thought you might have forgotten."

He dropped his head, inhaling the scent of my hair. "You want to remind me with a repeat?"

Tingles shot between my legs, and arousal made me bold. "Yes."

His eyes flared, and he groaned softly. "Don't talk to me like that here. I've got an eight-hour shift before I can act on it. I can't walk around with a hard-on that entire time."

I giggled. "You started it."

He shook his head and straightened. "I know. I shouldn't have."

I nodded, trying to be serious. "Right. Professional at work. Are you sure you can be my chaperone, though? Maybe you should ask to switch positions with someone else?"

Though that was the last thing I wanted, I knew keeping our distance at work was important to him, and I wanted to respect that. But a rush of relief filled me when he shook his head. "No. It has to be me. I don't trust anyone else."

"Good, because neither do I."

He seemed pleased by that. "You want me?"

"In more ways than one."

He swiped his ID and punched in his access code, and the two of us walked down the empty corridors toward my classroom, deep inside the prison walls. My desk and things that had survived the fire all still smelled a little smoky. I didn't mind it too much, though. I was just happy to have a space for my students and to be getting back into our routine.

Two were noticeably absent, though.

"Rowe?" I asked.

There were noises from behind the Gen Pop doors, but nobody wandered the corridors except for the occasional inmate on cleaning detail. The new warden had this place locked down tighter than I'd ever seen it. The only time they were allowed out of Gen Pop was for their one hour of exercise, and for a lucky handful who were assigned work detail. Rowe eyed one mopping the floor in the slowest possible way, and stepped closer to me, but didn't make comment on the man's sloppy work ethic.

"Mmm?" he replied, distraction in his tone.

"Where's Vincent?"

"Psych ward, last I heard. Might have been moved to solitary by now."

"Oh."

"That bothers you?"

I shrugged. "I know he's a bit...much."

"A bit much? He killed DeWitt right in front of you."

"He was trying to protect me."

"He slit his throat, Mae. Then held you hostage for the rest of the riot."

I shoved my hands into the pockets of my skirt, thinking about the way Vincent's big dark eyes intelligently took in every detail of his surroundings. He wasn't always the man who wanted to maim and kill. "It wasn't exactly like that. He thought we were escaping together."

Deep lines formed between Rowe's eyebrows. "He's completely unhinged."

I did know that. But I also remembered the young man who had sat so diligently in my classes and tried to better himself. "If I gave you some worksheets for him, do you think you could give them to him for me?"

Rowe looked doubtful. "He probably isn't allowed pencils if he's still in psych. Stabbing opportunity."

I blanched but tried to hide it. You'd think I'd be used to that sort of talk by now. "If he's been moved to solitary, though?"

Rowe's expression softened, a little of the tenseness in his posture melting away. "If he's been moved to solitary, I'll get him the paperwork. Give it to me at the end of class."

"Thank you. One more question. Have you talked to Heath lately?"

"No."

Worry pumped through me. But I didn't want to put that on Rowe. He had his own problems to deal with in here, what with Zye and the new warden.

But Rowe saw through that. "You miss him."

There was no point lying about it. "I haven't seen him since the riot. It's been weeks. I'm worried."

"I'll sort something out."

Hope flared inside me. "Really?"

He opened the door to my classroom and ushered me inside, shutting the door behind him. It was new, replaced by the work crews who had repaired things after the fire. This one was solid, no window to see out of. "Yeah, really. I hate seeing you sad."

"I'm not sad, just concerned about how he's coping. This is all taking a lot longer than I thought it would." Absently, I reached for the spot where my neck met my shoulders and dug my fingers in, trying to ease the tension.

He followed me over to my desk. "You're sad about it, too. I can tell whenever you're thinking about him. Your shoulders hunch, and you get this frown line right between your eyes."

"Great, thanks. I'll add Botox to my to-do list." I laughed, but I knew he was right. The muscle in my neck was like a solid brick, so tight my fingers kneading into it barely took the edge off. "I think I'll get a massage while I'm at it."

He glanced at the closed door, and then the clock on the wall, before he moved behind me, pushing my hands aside. "Stop, you're doing it wrong."

I rolled my eyes. "How would you know? Were you a masseur in a past life?"

"No, but my hands are stronger and bigger than yours."

His fingers brushed the sore spot, but I pulled away. "Don't. Not here."

"You're in pain."

"I'm respecting your rules."

His big hand clamped down on my shoulder, pinning me between him and the desk. "I can't sit at the back of your class, knowing you're hurting, and that I could have fixed it with a sixty-second rub."

I opened my mouth to argue again, but then his fingers were kneading the aching muscle, and all protests flew right out of my mouth. "I should make a joke about you and sixty-second rubs but that feels too good to complain."

I let my head loll to one side, giving him better access, and my eyes drifted closed as his touch took away some of the stress.

He inched closer while he worked, until his body was pressed tightly to my back, the edge of the desk digging into my thighs. "Dammit, Mae. Stop."

I dragged one eye open. "Stop what?"

"You're making tiny noises that sound like you're verging on an orgasm."

I hadn't even noticed. "That's hardly my fault. You're the one in control here."

He groaned, dropping one hand to my hip and then sliding it around to cup my ass cheek. "You're killing me. All I can think about is pulling this skirt up and bending you over the desk."

My nipples went hard, beading inside my bra, aroused at the thought of him inside me, while anyone could walk in. "Would it be so bad if you did?"

"It would if we got caught."

"So be quick."

He squeezed my ass hard, and for a moment, I thought he might actually do it. But he pulled away and moved to take a seat on the other side of the room. "Temptress."

"Tease."

"Later?"

"You better."

He grinned as he sat. But then he stood right back up and retrieved something from his back pocket. "Oh, that reminds me. I got you something. It just jabbed me in the ass when I sat down."

He walked back over and handed me a phone in a metallic pink case. My eyes widened. "You got me a phone? What on earth for?" Phones were expensive, and the prison didn't exactly pay big money. Rowe couldn't be spending that sort of money on me, especially when I didn't even need a new phone. There was nothing wrong with the one I had.

But he shook his head. "It's not a phone. They call it a personal protection stun gun. Sort of like a police Taser but disguised as a phone."

My eyes widened, and I took it from him, turning it over in my hands. "It looks exactly like my cell phone."

"That's the point. It's got a safety here, so you can't accidentally zap yourself, but I don't want you in here unarmed. This is enough that you can't seriously hurt anyone, but you can get away if something were to happen again."

I switched the safety off and gave the button an experimental push. I jumped when an electric current crackled to life. "If the warden found out…"

"Yeah, he'd probably be pissed, but fuck him. He wasn't here that night. I got one for Perry, too. And if Tori comes back, I'll get her one as well."

"We aren't even allowed to bring our phones into work." But my protests were weak, and a new wave of like for Rowe came over me.

"A minor slap on the wrist if you're caught. Better than one of the prisoners getting you alone again."

I grinned, waving it in his direction, though I'd slipped the safety back on. "Should I try it out on you?"

"I already did."

My eyes had to be as big as dinner plates. "What?"

He laughed ruefully. "They were twenty dollars from a personal security company. They had great reviews, but I didn't really think they'd work. So I tested it."

"On who?!"

He cringed, rubbing at his thigh absently as if he still felt the current coursing through his muscle. "Myself. Tased myself right in the leg for you, Donovan. I hope you appreciate that."

I burst out laughing. "You didn't?"

"I wish I were lying because it's not an experience I wish to repeat. But the point is, it works. And it's enough to drop a grown man long enough for you to run. So take it and use it."

My heart swelled, not just at the fact he wanted me to be safe, but that he'd also thought of Perry and Tori. I grinned at him.

"What?" he scowled.

"You're a pineapple."

"What on earth? Is that a compliment or an insult?"

I wanted to reach up and kiss him, but I didn't. Because he was right. We couldn't be doing anything here where anyone could walk in. "Spiky and rough on the outside. Sweet on the inside. That's you to a T, Rowe."

He let out a humph of annoyance and went to his seat at the back of the room, but not before I saw the tiniest flash of a pleased smile.

---

*Z*ye joined my class that night. I knew it was him the moment he walked in the doors, because of the way his piercing blue eyes sought out Rowe. They were the exact same color as Ripley's which was disconcerting, because the intent behind them was not the same sweet, four-year-old innocence.

Whatever lurked behind Zye's eyes was dark and sinister. His lip curled in disgust when he saw Rowe sitting in the back. He deliberately took up the seat right beside him, slinging Rowe a fake smile. "Good evening, Officer Pritchard. I see your bruises have healed since last week. That's real good. Glad to see you're keeping yourself out of trouble."

Rowe threw him a cool glance, but to his credit, he didn't take Zye's bait.

But my hackles rose. I knew what this man had done. Both to Rowe and to Rory. I didn't want him in my class. There was nothing I could do about that, I didn't get to dictate which inmates showed up to learn. But I didn't want him near Rowe.

"Zye, right? You can sit over here in the front row. You'll need help catching up to where the others are at."

His gaze ran lazily over me. "Near you? No problem, sweet thing." He got up and strolled to the front of the class, swagger in his step.

Rowe growled. "Show some respect. Call her that again and you're out."

I shot Rowe a warning glare. He wasn't helping by jumping to my defense. By now, I could handle these men. Zye calling me sweet thing was the least of my problems.

I got on with the class, and Zye didn't interrupt again, though Rowe had his gaze pinned on him the entire time. At one point I wondered if Rowe was even remembering to breathe, he was so hyperfocused on Zye. But I played my part, making sure I didn't focus on Rowe much. I didn't want to give Zye any extra ammunition against him. My finger itched over the Taser in the pocket of my skirt, but Zye seemed to be on his best behavior. If I hadn't known what he was capable of, he wouldn't have been on my radar at all.

I dismissed the class on time and waited for them to empty out before I went over to where Rowe still sat, fingers wrapped around the edge of the desk so tightly they'd turned white.

I slowly peeled each one back. "Hey. It's done."

"For tonight. What about tomorrow? The day after? How long until something happens?"

"You're going to drive yourself insane thinking like that."

"What other choice do I have?"

I didn't know. It was too much to ask him to just forget what had happened the last time Zye had been in his prison. I didn't know what the answer was. "Walk me out?"

Rowe pushed his chair back. "Yeah, of course. Let's go."

It grew quieter as we moved away from the inmate housing areas and toward the front of the prison. Rowe sighed heavily. "I wish I could put my arm around you."

I wanted that, too, and it sucked we couldn't have it here. "Come over after your shift finishes, okay? No matter what time it is. I'll wait up."

"I finish at four A.M."

I grinned. "Fine. I'll go to sleep and get up early. But either way, come over afterwards. I don't even care if you just want to sleep. I just want to be around you."

His fingers brushed mine in an unspoken yes.

I punched in my code to get us out and grabbed my purse from my locker. Rowe walked me all the way to the front, but the moment we opened the doors, a figure stepped out of the shadows.

I jumped back, a squeal ripping from my chest.

Liam put his hands up in a calming gesture. "Hey, hey. It's me."

My heart pounded behind my rib cage. "Jesus, Liam. I could have Tased you."

Rowe frowned. "You didn't even go for the Taser. We need to work on that."

I rolled my eyes. "You literally just gave it to me. Cut me some slack. He took me by surprise."

"That's kind of the point," Rowe muttered.

I shot him a glare, but then Liam was taking my hand, and it filtered through that it was odd that Liam was outside the prison at nine at night. He had done this once before, though. "You here to take me on a date again?"

He bit his lip and shook his head slowly.

Rowe stiffened beside me. It took me another second

to realize Liam wasn't smiling. My heart sank. "What's wrong?"

He squeezed my fingers. "It's your dad. They've been trying to call you. He's taken a turn for the worse, but he's saying he has information about Jayela's murder that he'll only tell you."

"What?" My bottom lip trembled.

"We need to hurry. They don't think he's going to make it through the night."

25

MAE

*D*espite the warm summer night, a chill washed over me while we drove to my father's house, Liam behind the wheel and Rowe in the back seat.

"You didn't have to come," I said to Rowe again. "The warden—"

"The warden can get fucked if he has a problem with me leaving early." He reached forward and squeezed my shoulder. "You need me. I'm here. Got it?"

I nodded. I was grateful for both of their presences.

I'd never thought about my father dying. Even after we'd visited him and saw how sick he was, I hadn't let myself consider that he was close to the end. It hit me now like a freight train. I'd never had a mother. My sister was gone. And even though my father and I were estranged, there was something in knowing that I wasn't the only one.

If he died, it would just be me.

Liam's hand landed on the back of my neck, a warm and reassuring presence like he could read my mind and knew I needed it. His thumb stroked the spot behind my ear as he drove with one hand, and a little of the tension eased out of me.

His touch said I wasn't alone.

But if my father had information on Jayela's murderer, I needed to know what it was. "Hurry."

Liam put his foot down, taking each turn to my father's house in Providence faster than he should have. I gripped the seat to keep from bumping into the window but didn't say anything.

I don't know what I'd expected, but my father's house was dark and quiet, the only light coming from a single bulb in the entranceway. I didn't bother knocking. I opened the door and immediately ran up the stairs, taking them two at a time, both guys hot on my heels behind me.

I threw open my father's bedroom door and stopped in the doorway. Two men looked over at me, Winston, his aged face solemn. The other man was vaguely familiar, but it took me a moment to place him. "Dr Harrison?"

"Are you his daughter?"

He obviously didn't remember me from the handful of times I'd been sick as a child. I didn't bother commenting on that. I'd found my own doctor the moment I was old enough to so my father wouldn't have any access to my health records, so I hadn't seen this doctor in over a decade. "Yes."

The older man nodded solemnly. "I'm very sorry."

Shock punched through me. "What? What do you mean?" I stormed to my father's side, the two old men moving back to make way for me.

Lawrence's eyes were closed, a peaceful expression on

his pale face. He seemed as if I could simply reach down and shake his shoulder, and his eyes would fly open with surprise. I'd done that a few times as a kid, gotten yelled at, and never done it again.

But those times his cheeks had been rosy pink with life. His chest rose and fell in the steady breath of sleep.

There was none of that now. He was deathly still. There was no need for anyone to tell me. "I'm too late."

The doctor made a tutting sound in the back of his throat and put his hand on my arm. "He tried to hang on. But his body was too weak. You only missed him by about ten minutes. I really am very sorry."

I shrugged off his touch. If I'd been a good daughter, perhaps I would have cried. But my eyes were dry, and a roaring anger strangled the place where any sympathy might have lived. "Fuck you," I whispered.

The doctor gasped and stepped back. "Excuse me?"

"She didn't mean you," Liam assured him quietly. Even still, the doctor huffed his way out of the room.

I barely noticed. I couldn't stop the hate from pouring out of me, even though my father wasn't alive to hear it, it needed to be said. "You were never there. Never around to help with homework, or go to our concerts, or drive us to school. You never made us dinner, or any meal for that matter. You barely knew I was alive, and you know what? Most of the time I was glad for that. Because when you did look at me, your thoughts were written all over your face. That I took the only person you ever loved. But that's bullshit, Dad. I was a baby. I can't help that she died, but you punished me every day of my life for it. And now you're punishing me again in your death. You're the most selfish person I've ever met. Why didn't you tell me?

You could have told me everything you knew the last time I came to see you. But instead you wait for some deathbed confession?" My voice grew shriller and louder the longer I let the truth spill from my lips. "You went to your grave, withholding information about your daughter's murderer. I hope you're proud of yourself. I hope you know what you've done and what you've taken from me. I hope you're burning in Hell!"

I stopped short of spitting on the man's body, though God, a big part of me wanted to. But I'd said all there was to say. I spun on my heel and stormed from the room. Rowe and Liam backed me up, the three of us thundering down the stairs for the door.

"Mae," Rowe said.

I shook my head. I couldn't talk until I was out of his house and away from all the horrors it hid from the world with its fancy façade.

I was almost at Liam's car when Winston's voice stopped me. "Please don't go. I need to talk to you."

I stopped and glanced over my shoulder at him, standing on my father's front step. "I can't right now, Winston. I'll call you tomorrow to organize his funeral. But not tonight. I can't."

He rushed down the steps and along the path to stop me from getting inside the car. "No. It needs to be tonight." He stared at me with big, dark eyes, full of wisdom and the knowledge that came with working for a man for thirty years. "I'm privy to all your father's secrets. There is something you need to know."

*T*he antique clock in my father's sitting room read almost eleven, but Winston still placed a tray of tea and cookies on the low-lying table. He fussed around the three of us, making sure we had all the sugar and milk we wanted, before he sat gingerly on the edge of the couch. The three of us stared at him, all of us silent, waiting for him to speak.

He sighed. "I don't know if this is what he was going to tell you. Your father... He had many ghosts. Many secrets. But there isn't much I didn't know about him. It's easy to overhear things when you've spent a lifetime blending in with the furniture." He ran a hand over the pristine couch fondly. "I worked for him my entire adult life. I'm not sure what I'll do now."

"You've always been good to me," I assured him. "We'll work something out for you. I promise."

He smiled, and his eyes crinkled at the corners.

"Did my father kill Jayela?" It was the worry that had plagued the back of my mind since Liam had picked me up from the prison. The one I couldn't comprehend. There was no love lost between me and my father, but he had cared about Jayela, at least a little bit. I couldn't imagine him killing her, and yet, what else had I been summoned to hear? You only drop bombs like that on your deathbed.

But Winston's mouth formed an 'O' of surprise. "No. No, he would never. He wasn't a good father to you girls. But he never wished you any harm."

I breathed out a sigh of relief. That was something at least. "Then why? What did he want to tell me?"

Winston bit his lip.

I took the older man's hand and pressed my fingers to his palm. "Please, Winston. I need to know."

"I know. It's just that I believe this will hurt you. And you've already suffered so much. It seems unkind to add to that burden."

Liam picked up my hand and laced his fingers between mine. "She's tough. You can tell her."

I nodded in agreement. "Please."

Winston straightened his shoulders. "After your mother died, your father was never the same. Before that, he'd been a doting father. The sort of dad who chased Jayela around the backyard, her squeals of joy ringing out across the neighborhood." He smiled fondly at the memory. But I couldn't imagine it. The idea of my father ever being happy, was a completely foreign concept.

"We were all devastated when we lost your mother. But no one more than him. He grieved hard, and for a year, we struggled to get him out of bed each day. But life rolls on and, and eventually, so did he. He met a woman at a grief support group."

I frowned at that. "He dated someone?"

Winston shook his head, though. "I'm not sure I'd call it that. But he found comfort in her, yes."

I read between the lines. He'd had casual sex with someone. A fuck buddy.

"What has this got to do with Jayela's murder, though?"

"Your father's...dalliance...with this woman went on for many, many years. And to my knowledge, she had several children during that time."

My eyes went wide. "Are you saying what I think you're saying? My father has other children?"

Winston nodded. "Though they aren't children anymore. They're only a little younger than you are."

"Do you know who they are?"

"I know their faces. I watched them grow up every time I dropped your father at their house. He never told me their names."

Rowe put an arm around my shoulders, while Liam squeezed my hand reassuringly. The two of them pressed in on me, their presence warm and comforting at my sides. I drew from their strength, because God knew I didn't have any of my own in that moment. "Is this why he was never around when I was a kid? He was too busy with his other family?"

Winston gave me a sad look. "I think there was just too much sadness surrounding this house for him."

"Yeah, well, there was too much sadness in this house for me and Jayela, too. We didn't get to go make a new family elsewhere, did we?" The words, bitter and sharp on my tongue, weren't directed at Winston, but at the man whose body was lying upstairs in his bed.

"How long did this go on for? Was he still seeing her? Where is she now? If their relationship went on for years, it should be her here by his side, not me."

Winston shook his head. "Things turned bad between them several years ago. There was an almighty row one night. They were so loud I heard them from where I sat in the car, waiting for him out front."

"What about?" Liam asked. Then he cringed at me. "Sorry. Lawyer. I like to know all the details. Tell me to shut up if you want."

"No, it's fine. I need to know, too."

Winston twisted the teacup in his fingers. "It was

about money. They always fought about money. She lives in Saint View, in one of the government-owned houses. It's very small, and she had many children there. Your father..."

"Did nothing to support her?"

He screwed up his face. "I don't think he ever truly believed the children were his, and she couldn't afford a paternity test. She kept taking him back into her house, but they fought about other men, and child support, and how you and your sister lived in luxury while her children had holes in their shoes."

My anger for my father only grew. "They were his kids, though, weren't they? You believed that to be true?"

"Yes. One of them...she looks just like your sister."

I blanched at the idea. I'd always known Jayela was more like our father than I was. But it hurt to know there was some other sister out there who was more like Jayela than me.

"Just recently, I found some letters...they were addressed to your father, but I always opened his mail so I wasn't intruding on his privacy, I swear."

"Of course not."

"They were threats. Demands for money. For years of owed child support and pain and suffering."

"He ignored them?"

Winston nodded. "But after you were here last, your father said he didn't think the Michaelson fellow had done it."

"He didn't."

Winston smiled. "That might be the only thing you and your father ever agreed on."

That brought me no joy. "Who did he think did it

then?"

Winston's voice dropped an octave. "He accused his mistress."

But that didn't make any sense. "What motive would she have? As far as I know, Jayela never even met the woman."

"She knew he was sick. On his death, his money all becomes yours. Without you and Jayela in the picture, that money would go to your father's other biological children. All she'd have to do is prove his paternity."

My mouth fell open. "And he never thought to tell me any of this?"

"He convinced himself that because you were still fine, he'd been wrong. But his mistress showed up here early this morning...they argued again, and then he told me to get you over here."

"She made a threat against Mae?" Rowe growled.

"I believe so."

"Can you give us her name?"

"Angela Erley. She has a place on Grainer Drive in Saint View."

"Why does that sound familiar?" I asked.

"We were there the other day," Liam answered. "The address from the tip-off line."

I blinked. "The one that accused my father of having something to do with Jayela's death?"

"That's the one."

"What the hell?"

Liam's phone rang, and he grabbed it from his pocket to glance at the screen. His mouth twisted into a line. "Sorry, It's work. I need to take this."

"This late?" I asked.

"Anything before midnight is fair game when you're a lawyer." He opened the front door and closed it quietly behind him.

Rowe was still putting pieces together. "But why would she call and point the finger at your father? If she murdered Jayela, then that would only draw more suspicion in her direction."

"It's supposed to be an anonymous tip-off line."

"Or maybe she hated your father so much she was trying to frame him for a murder she committed?" Rowe's forehead furrowed in confusion.

Winston paled at that suggestion, and he put his teacup down with trembling fingers. "That would be the height of pure evil. Your father...he wasn't always a good man, but nobody deserves that."

Despite my feelings for my dad, I was inclined to agree. I didn't want to see anyone in prison for a murder they didn't commit. Heath was already living that injustice. I just wanted to know the truth.

Liam walked back into the room, and the three of us looked over at him. The interruption was a welcome distraction from all the murder speculation. But Liam's expression was stony.

I stood, my heart plummeting. "What is it? Who was on the phone? Is everything okay?" My hand hovered over my mouth as a horrible thought popped into my mind. "Oh God, is it your mom?"

But he shook his head, and relief coursed through me.

But it was short-lived, as Liam delivered his news. "Heath's case has been escalated. He goes before a judge in two days."

26

MAE

"Somebody needs to tell Heath," I murmured.

Rowe got to his feet. "I'll go."

I shook my head. "It should be me. I need it to be me."

Rowe frowned. "He's in solitary. He can't have visitors. He can't even make a phone call. You'll see him in two days when he's free."

But something deep inside told me it may not be that easy. And the look on Liam's face confirmed it. "Is that what's going to happen?" I asked him.

His mouth drew into a grim line. "I'm not going to lie. We don't have half the information we need. I'm going to the office now. I've got to organize witness prep, evidence examination, counter-arguments…I want to chase up Jayela's medical records and this mistress of your father's. Something still isn't sitting right with me about this whole thing. There's something we're missing, I'm sure of it. I'll probably be there for the next two days straight, but I'll get my whole team on this. I'll do everything I can to get him out, Mae. I promise."

He took me by the arms and kissed my forehead. But I felt the worry in his embrace. I knew that this was all happening too quickly. Two days' notice wasn't enough, and we all knew it. I was sure that had been a deliberate move. Everything felt stacked against us.

Liam drove us back to the prison, dropping us in the parking lot by our cars and then disappearing into the night in the direction of his office.

I stared after him. "He's going to work all night, isn't he?"

Rowe put his arm around my shoulders. "He'll be fine. He's got a couch in his office. He'll get some sleep when he can."

I buried my face in Rowe's chest. "This is all going to shit." The case. My father's death. The fact I hadn't even seen Heath in weeks.

Rowe just wrapped his arms around my waist and held me.

"I need to see him," I said again. I turned pleading eyes up at Rowe.

He gazed down at me, indecision flickering in his expression. "Mae..."

"Just look the other way," I told him. "Just this once. I've got a swipe card and access code. The warden isn't here, and we all know the night staff are probably sleeping in the breakroom. Nobody has to know."

He groaned. "Your access isn't going to get you into solitary. You're going to need mine."

I held my breath.

Rowe sighed. "Jesus. You could talk your way into Fort Knox with those puppy eyes." He cleared his throat. "*I'm* going to solitary to tell Heath about his case. If you happen to slip in the door behind me, and I don't see it, then so be it. Okay?"

I grinned and pushed up onto my toes to kiss his lips. He pulled away, grabbing my hand, and leading me through the prison doors. Butterflies rioted around my belly, nerves and excitement crashing together and quickening my breath. I hadn't seen Heath in so long, and the anticipation of seeing him again now was killing me. I didn't know whether this news of his trial date was truly a good thing, though part of me wanted to believe that in two days' time, he could be on the outside. With me. With us.

That was what I needed to focus on tonight. There was no place for doubt in my mind. Even if it was there, flickering away in the background, I couldn't let Heath see it.

The prison was quieter than I'd ever heard it. We passed to the Gen Pop areas, and the normal noise from behind the doors was completely absent. I found myself walking quieter, practically tiptoeing around the place despite the fact I had an ID tag hanging around my neck and could probably fairly easily explain why I was here to a random night guard we might stumble across. Rowe led the way to solitary, punching in his code and opening the door to the main walkway. Rowe was no-nonsense once we were on the inside. He strode to the far end, ignoring any prisoner who woke up and questioned what we were doing there in the middle of the night. He unlocked Heath's cell and let us in, quickly closing the door and checking it was locked.

"What the hell?" Heath's voice was thick with sleep. He sat up on his narrow mattress and blinked at us in the darkness. His gaze landed on Rowe first but then quickly slid to me standing slightly behind him. His eyes were wide in the dim light from the window. "Mae? Are you okay? What's going on?"

I pushed past Rowe, closing the few steps between me and Heath and throwing my arms around him. He grunted in surprise at the force of my hug, but his arms wrapped around me quickly, engulfing me in his warm, safe embrace. I breathed in the scent of his skin and reveled in the strength of his touch. His lips pressed to the top of my head, and I could feel the silent conversation he had with Rowe, but I was too lost in Heath to pay attention to it.

It was Rowe who spoke first. "Your case has been moved up. You've got two days."

Heath's entire body stiffened, but then he let out a slow breath. "This is a good thing, right?"

Rowe didn't answer.

I told Heath all I had. "Liam is already at the office working on it. But yes. This has got to be a good thing. We're going to get you out." I tried to force conviction into my tone, but my voice wobbled at the end.

Heath paused. "We still have nothing?"

I shook my head hard. "Not nothing."

"Not much," Rowe muttered.

I glared at him.

Heath tilted my chin away from Rowe. "He's only speaking the truth. I've got faith in Liam. If he can't get me out, nobody can."

"We found a pregnancy test in Jayela's room," I said to him. "It was positive, so we know she was seeing someone. That puts another suspect in the lineup."

"A recent pregnancy test?" Heath asked.

My brow furrowed. "Liam is working on getting a hold of her medical records to confirm, but…"

Heath's expression showed everything I needed to know.

My stomach sank. "It was your baby, wasn't it?"

He scrubbed his hand through his hair with a sigh. "I don't know. Maybe she got pregnant twice, and the test you found is recent, but there was a pregnancy, years ago when we were together."

I swallowed down the lump in my throat as tears pricked the backs of my eyes. Hurt welled up inside me again. Heath and I had been friends back then, and yet neither he nor Jayela had told me what they were going through. "You could have told me."

"Mae…" He reached out and stroked his hand down my arm. "You know why she didn't want to. It wasn't my place."

I nodded, brushing away the tears. "I hate that she felt like she had to do it alone. I would have supported her."

He wrapped an arm around me. "She knew that. I would have as well. But she didn't want that."

"Is it what you wanted as well?"

He shook his head sadly. "No. I wanted the baby. I wanted a family, even though I knew things weren't really right with me and Jayela. I would have loved that baby so hard, no matter what happened between me and her."

"Me, too," I sniffed. Being an aunt was as close as I was ever going to get to being a mother. But now that chance was gone, too.

"It was her choice."

I nodded. "Of course."

"I'm sorry." He clutched me tighter. "This probably makes the case against me worse."

I shook my head, dragging myself out of the past and into the present. "It's ancient history. Like you said, maybe there was a more recent pregnancy..." But even as I said it, I knew it was unlikely. My sister wasn't perfect. She might have made a mistake once, but she wasn't the type to do it repetitively. Terminating her pregnancy would have eaten her up inside which was exactly why I felt so bad I hadn't been there to support her. I already knew there'd be no record of a recent pregnancy when Liam received her medical files. And we needed to keep Heath's spirits up. "This doesn't change anything," I assured him. "The court will see this wasn't you. We have other options."

"Okay." Heath's fingers stroked down the side of my face. "I can't believe you're here."

Our gazes locked and held. His expression said everything I was thinking.

"I don't want to think about this anymore. I just want to enjoy whatever time we have together tonight," he murmured.

Just like it always did, my entire body lit up under his attention, my heart pounding triple time as I took in his gorgeous face. His hair was tousled with sleep, and the stubble across his jawline had thickened into a short beard since he'd been in solitary. It suited him so well, only serving to make him look a few years older and more rugged. Every part of me wanted to kiss him. It had been weeks since his lips had pressed against mine, and yet they tingled now in anticipation, wanting him.

Rowe cleared his throat. "I'm gonna give you guys a minute."

He moved toward the door, but Heath shot out a hand, blocking his way. "Don't."

Heat flared in Rowe's eyes. I glanced between the two men, taking in their expressions and the way they looked at each other. I'd always known there was something between the two of them, something that simmered away just below the surface.

Heath's voice was deep when he spoke. "It'll draw attention. You hanging around outside my cell. Better you stay here."

Rowe's gaze met his. "That the only reason you want me to stay?"

I sucked in a breath, something changing in the air around us.

"No."

I wanted to question what was going on between the two of them, but then Heath was tilting my head up and dropping his mouth to mine. All rational thought flew right out of my head. He kissed me deep, his tongue plunging into my mouth, and owning the kiss I'd been dreaming of for weeks. He pulled away and glanced over my shoulder at Rowe. "You going to report me for that?"

I watched Rowe carefully. But there was nothing but desire in his eyes. "No. She needs it. She's had a shit night."

"That the only reason you're letting me do it? For her?"

"You gonna keep asking me questions? Or are you going to kiss her?"

Heath held Rowe's glare until the very last second and

then he lowered his head once more. He only closed his eyes when his mouth touched mine again. This time, he dug his fingers into my hips and hoisted me up into his arms. On autopilot, I wrapped my legs around him and held on, taking his kiss and feeling it way down to my toes. He walked me to his bed and sat with me on his lap. His palms stroked up and down my back as he kissed me, each movement pulling me closer, until our chests touched and I sat right up over his dick.

The kiss was hot, sensual, and so full of feeling it was easy to lose myself in and forget that we were inside a tiny prison cell. In the darkness, I could pretend we were anywhere and that it was just him and me, no barriers between us.

But the longer Heath and I kissed, the more it became apparent that Rowe was no barrier. We kissed long enough for Heath to grow hard beneath me, and for his hands to switch from my back to my front, squeezing my breasts. Unconsciously, I rocked my hips over his.

He groaned beneath me. "Fuck, I want you," he whispered, like Rowe wasn't even in the room.

I melted into his touch, moaning quietly when he tweaked my nipples. "I want you, too."

He glanced over at Rowe, defiance in his eyes. Slowly, he dug his fingers into my T-shirt and inched it up, exposing my belly.

When neither Rowe nor I stopped him, he pulled it over my head. His gaze dropped to my cleavage, and he pressed kisses all over the swell of my breasts while he undid the strap at my back.

A voice deep inside me questioned whether I was really going to let him do this in the middle of a prison.

But I was surrounded by two men who I felt incredibly safe with, and the tiny cell provided a false sense of privacy. One that I was willing to take, because the questions in my mind shouted louder.

If Liam can't get him off, what happens then? Will he be transferred to another prison? Will he be left in solitary? Somewhere deep inside me, the worst one rose, rearing its ugly head. *What if he never gets out? What if this is the only chance you get?*

I squeezed my eyes shut tight. I didn't want to give that question any sort of strength by truly considering it, because the answers were terrifying. I had to put my faith in Liam. But tonight, I needed Heath to put his body on mine. I needed to remind myself that he was here, and that he belonged with me, and that somehow, no matter what, we'd get to be together.

I looked over at Rowe, begging him with my eyes to understand. He walked over and kissed my mouth. "I know you need him."

"I need you, too."

Heath groaned below me.

Rowe's gaze raked over him, hot and needy. "We have time. He doesn't." He lowered his mouth to my ear, and I closed my eyes as his lips brushed the sensitive spot on my neck. "Give him what he needs. There'll be time for us later."

Rowe stepped back and quietly let himself out of the cell. This time, Heath didn't try to stop him. He flipped me onto his mattress, tearing my skirt and panties down in one quick swipe. Heat pooled between my legs, needy and wet. He fisted the back of his shirt with one hand and yanked it over his head. Then his pants came down, exposing his thick erection.

Heath's gaze devoured me, sweeping my body so thoroughly it was like a physical caress. And then he was on top of me, erection pressing between my legs, his body covering me like a blanket. His weight was delicious, my nipples beaded and rubbing over the thin dusting of coarse hair across his chest.

"I can't be gentle with you," he groaned into the crook of my neck. "God, I want to be. I want to be alone with you, in some romantic room, on a bed with silk sheets and soft music playing in the background. I want to take my time with you, and lick between your legs, and taste you, and worship every inch of you. But I can't do that here, Mae. Everything about this place is fast and dirty, including me."

Something about those last few words sank deep into my soul. There was a desperation to them that rocked me to my core. We needed to get him out before this place ate away at him any more than it already had. Before it turned him into a man I didn't recognize. I grasped his face between my hands and forced him to look at me. "I know who you are. You're good, right down to your very soul. You just have to hang on to it."

He shook his head sadly. "I don't think I believe that anymore."

But I knew it in the way he held himself back, waiting for my permission. His dick was right there at my entrance. He could have taken me at any moment, but he didn't. He waited.

"Take me," I begged.

It was all the permission he needed. His dick pushed

inside my core, and though I braced myself for the intrusion, I needn't have worried. My body welcomed him home, accepting his girth despite the lack of foreplay. Seated deep inside me, he moaned and rolled his hips, coating himself in my arousal while he kissed me. His hips moved slowly at first, proving he could be gentle, but each one picked up speed, until he was thrusting into me with abandon. His gaze raked over me, each roll of his hips hitting that spot inside me that lit me up, his pubic bone nudging my clit every time he sank down.

"You're so beautiful," he murmured. "I've thought about this so much." His breaths came in pants, and his arms shook from holding himself over me. "Fuck, Mae. I need to come so bad. It's been so long."

I pulled him down on top of me, and he braced himself on his forearms, closing the distance between us. "It's okay. Let go."

The torture was plain in his eyes. He was on the edge and ready to fall into it. It didn't matter to me that I hadn't come. I didn't need the orgasm. I just needed the connection. The moment with him, and the touch of his skin on mine. I needed to imprint it all in my head in case that tiny voice of doubt inside me was right, and this was the end.

But Heath wasn't having it. Despite the hunger in his eyes, he pushed one hand between us, finding my clit.

"Oh!" I cried, pleasure zinging through me. I tried to rock my hips against his, desperate for more.

He pinned me to the bed. "Hold still. If you move, this will all be over, and I'm not ready to give you up yet."

He held me down, his dick deep inside me, stretching me so perfectly while his fingers worked the bundle of nerves between my thighs. He built gradually, until he was working my clit so perfectly it was like he'd done this a thousand times. Slowly, he let me move again, and I worked myself up and down his length, taking him in rhythmic slides while my body sang out in pleasure.

He alternated between kissing me deeply and staring at me like he wasn't sure I was really here. I couldn't get enough of him. As the orgasm built inside me, I wasn't sure I was ready for it. Because coming meant this would end. This would stop. I'd have to leave again.

"It's not fair," I whispered.

He pressed his forehead to mine. "I know."

His lips met mine, soft and sweet, muffling my cries when my orgasm took hold. It spiraled through me, lighting up my core, but then headed straight for my heart.

I stifled tears that threatened to build. He didn't need that. He didn't need my worries or my feelings on top of his own. He came with a quiet groan, his face pressed into my neck, his cock deep inside me. His body trembled, and I held him close, whispering into his ear, promising him a future I had no right to offer when so many things were out of my hands.

27

ROWE

*I*t took everything in me to stand in the corridor, leaning on the door to Heath's cell, and not turn around and stare through the tiny window. I told myself it was so scratched and dirty that I wouldn't have seen anything, especially since the interior of the cell was so dim.

But my heart pounded with the knowledge of what was going on inside. Sneaking a woman in here for a prisoner went against every fiber of my moral being, and yet, it didn't.

I wanted this for her. And for him. I didn't know when I'd jumped onto their bandwagon, with full faith that Heath was innocent, but here I was. Knowing it with everything I had inside me.

He didn't belong in this prison cell any more than I did.

So I'd looked the other way when I saw the need in Mae's eyes and the longing in Heath's. I pushed down the fact that what they were doing in there had me so achingly hard I could barely think straight for wanting to join them.

Muffled snores from the other cells broke the silence, and somewhere else in the prison, somebody dropped something, the clatter ringing out across the wing. I glanced at the phone I wasn't allowed to have in here and lit up the time. It was after one o'clock. But the noise had reminded me that not everyone in the prison was sleeping. There were other guards, and work crews who mopped the floors in the common areas after lights out when there was nobody around to slip on the wet floors.

I'd given Mae and Heath as much time as I could. It was time to go.

I unlocked the door and slipped inside.

The scent of sex hung heavy in the air. Heath's big body covered Mae's smaller, very naked frame. He made no move to get off her, no move to cover them up. He gazed over at me, challenge in his eyes from his sweet spot, buried deep inside Mae's pussy. My dick kicked.

I wanted to go over there and touch them. Let them touch me.

"Rowe," Mae whispered. Her tits were so full, her dark nipples pointing up at Heath, just begging for his mouth.

My gaze dropped to Heath's bare ass, her legs wrapped around him. He fit so perfectly between her thighs, it was almost beautiful.

My gaze collided with Heath's. Something passed between the two of us. Something so full of raw masculine energy it was practically a lion's roar in my ear, a demand to do something, a demand to take what I wanted.

Heath pulled out of Mae's sweet slit, his dick still mostly hard and coated in their arousal. He stalked across the room to stand in front of me, the electricity between us sparking so bright that if harnessed, it could have lit up a room.

Heath stared at me. "You keep looking at us like that and I'm going to get down on my knees."

Jesus fuck. I needed to say no. It wasn't right. I knew Heath shouldn't be in here, that he deserved to walk free, but it wasn't my call to make. I could probably be charged with something myself just for allowing Mae to be in here. And letting Heath do what his eyes promised would definitely be breaching a code of ethics. I was a guard. He was a prisoner. Though I knew plenty of guards who weren't above taking what they could get, I never had. I'd never had any desire to.

Until now.

Heath slowly lowered himself to the floor. He stared up at me and reached for my belt.

I wrapped my fingers around Heath's wrist.

"You want it," Heath growled. "You stop me, but you've thought about this. Probably more than this, am I right?"

I had no idea what it was about him. Every time he was near me, something inside me yearned to get closer. I had the same urge every time I was with Mae. I didn't know if it was the clear connection between the two of them that drew me in. I wanted Mae in a way that was familiar and safe. I wanted to be in her company constantly, and listen to her sweet, melodic voice and worship her curves all night long. Something inside me wanted to protect her and cherish her and give her the world. Heath provided a danger I'd never known I'd wanted until I met him. A darker, rawer lust that screamed out to some part of me that wanted to be owned by him, taken hard, slammed against a wall.

Mae's breath hitched. It was loud in the silence of the tiny room, and both of us glanced over at her.

She watched us with burning eyes.

"That turn you on?" I asked.

"Yes," she admitted.

Breath hissed out of Heath's lungs, and I knew what he was feeling. I wanted her turned on. I wanted her watching this, with her hand between her thighs.

I wanted them both.

My fingers fell away from Heath's wrist. I slumped against the door and let him undo my belt. My erection raged behind my pants, desperate to break free and find relief in Heath's mouth.

I closed my eyes for half a second, letting him yank down my pants and underwear. It was too much to look at him, even though I was desperate to. But I was so fucking turned on I was sure I'd embarrass myself if I did.

Instead, I watched Mae. God, she was like some goddess, pale light spilling in from the window behind her as she sat up to watch, her breasts bare, light glinting off her soft blonde curls. She'd dragged Heath's thin blanket over her legs, but her tits were enough.

Her tits and Heath's hand around my cock. He gave it a few quick strokes before he paused.

I gazed down at him.

With his eyes pinned on me, he opened his mouth and wrapped it around the head of my dick.

I bit down on my lip at the feel of his hot, wet mouth,

and fought the urge to thrust deep inside him. His mouth was amazing. I had no idea if he'd done this before but if he hadn't, he didn't hesitate. His head bobbed over my erection, taking in more of me with every pass, his lips and tongue working together in unison. One hand wrapped around my base, the other found my balls, and I let out a groan.

Mae let out a tiny moan of her own, one hand disappearing beneath the blanket, the other grabbing her boob, nipple squeezed tight between her fingers.

Fuck me. The two of them were trying to kill me.

I threw my arm over my mouth to muffle the noise of my moans and gripped the doorframe with my other, holding myself back, trying to keep still.

Heath pulled off, and I stared down at him. My dick bobbed by his mouth, both of them wet and shiny.

"Stop fucking holding back," he growled at me.

"I'm not."

"Then grab my head and fuck my mouth like you want to." There was a challenge in his eyes. A clear, 'I can take whatever you've got, so give it to me.'

My gaze strayed to Mae, her fingers working furiously beneath the blanket, her mouth open slightly, her fat bottom lip pouty and her eyes hooded with desire.

I wanted to fuck his mouth. I wanted to watch her fall apart while I did it. I grasped the back of Heath's head and pushed my cock deep inside his mouth once more. It hit the back of his throat, and he made an encouraging noise which spurred me on to do it again. He gripped the back of my thighs, holding me tight, and I put the same sort of pressure on the back of his head, showing him exactly how fast to go, exactly how I liked it.

God, it felt good. My orgasm rose from deep inside me, pleasure rocketing around my body and culminating in the clenching of my balls. "Fuck, I'm going to come," I moaned. I let go of Heath's head, giving him the chance to move away, but he didn't. He rammed himself around me, harder and faster, sucking the tip, working my length, gripping my balls in a way that was so tight it was almost punishing but felt all too good.

Mae threw her head back as her own orgasm took hold of her, and that was the most perfect way to come. Watching Mae's face contort with pleasure and desire and release, her tits pointed to the ceiling, with Heath's wet mouth around my dick.

I came in shuddering spurts, spilling into the back of his throat harder than I'd maybe ever come before. Everything about this was wrong and yet it was so fucking right. I pumped in and out of his mouth a few times, letting him lick every drop of cum from my tip before withdrawing from his mouth.

He was still naked. His body made for sin. And something deep inside me wanted more. I should have stopped, shouldn't have let myself go there. And yet I reached for his hardening cock, wanting to give him more than he'd given me.

He let me for a second. His erection impressively thick in my hand. But then he grabbed me roughly and put his lips on mine. He tasted of my cum, and I didn't care. It was a fucking turn-on, the way he'd taken everything I had to give. "Not tonight," he murmured, inching away. "You two have already been in here too long. Someone is going to notice. You need to go."

He pulled from my grasp, and I went to argue but I

knew he was right. We had to have been in here an hour. If anyone checked the logs, I was going to have a hard time explaining that.

The three of us dressed quickly, then stood there, staring at each other.

"Two days," Mae said quietly.

"Two days," Heath and I agreed in unison.

A slow smile spread over Mae's face, and it was contagious.

We were going to get him out.

Two days was nothing.

---

*M*ae and I hurried down the hallway like two naughty schoolkids, my fingers threaded through hers because I couldn't stand not touching her. I squeezed her fingers. "I love knowing these were inside you just a minute ago. Fuck, that was hot."

She let out a breath, her smile wide and her cheeks flushed with the aftereffects of two orgasms. "I can't believe we just did that."

I couldn't either. "Me neither."

She reached up and smoothed back my hair. "Reckless looks good on you."

I couldn't help myself. I was so keyed up, so high on her and Heath and what we'd done that I swept her into my arms and stole a kiss. She was grinning hard beneath my lips, and we pulled away, hurrying around the corner.

"Well, this is cozy."

I let go of Mae's hand as quick as if it had been set on fire.

But Zye's eagle eyes didn't miss it. He dropped his mop into a bucket of dirty water and leaned on it, and I cursed the warden for his obvious favoritism of the new prisoners. The overnight cleaning should have been done by minimum security inmates about to be released. Not someone like Zye.

His gaze bounced between me and Mae but landed on me. "Just coming from solitary? Not much else up that way. Had yourself a little gang bang, huh? Good for you, Pritchard. Never knew you batted for both teams, but it just widens the playing field, doesn't it?"

My mind whirled. I had no idea whether he really knew what had gone down or if he was just throwing accusations out there and hoping something stuck. Either way, I wasn't going to confirm or deny anything. "Mind your business and get back to work." With stiff, jerky movements, I walked around him.

I was an idiot. I'd let myself get caught up, and now the one thing I hadn't wanted to happen was happening. I couldn't even look at Mae. I couldn't give Zye another ounce of ammunition.

He moved fast.

Lightning fast for a man of his size, he had Mae up against a wall, hand around her throat.

She didn't even have time to scream before he cut off her oxygen.

I lunged for her, but he was quicker. "Stay where you are, or I press a little harder. You don't come back from a crushed windpipe, do you, Officer Pritchard?

Rory's body, pale on the floor, her lips blue danced in

front of my eyes. The coroner's report, death by strangulation, whispered in the back of my memory.

I'd known it was him all along. But there'd never been any proof, no witnesses, no working cameras, nobody to stand up for Rory and say they knew she'd died at the hands of her ex.

Nobody 'til now.

I lunged at Zye again, blind with rage.

Until Mae made a choking noise that stopped me dead in my tracks. Zye's fingers dug into her neck, pressing into the tender flesh I'd had my lips on not all that long ago. I froze, a million emotions crashing down over me all at once.

I couldn't lose another woman at the hands of this man. "Zye, please," I croaked out around my terror. "Let her go."

His grin widened as Mae slapped fruitlessly at his hands. He glanced over at me. "You took a woman from me, perhaps I take one from you."

"I never took Rory from you. She left of her own free will."

"Bullshit!" he roared. "She was mine, her and the kid. You think you get to play happy family with my blood?" His grin turned evil, the true depth of his depravity showing itself. "Nah, bro. He's mine, just like she was—"

The zapping noise of electricity crackled, and Zye's entire body lurched away from Mae. He howled, clutching his neck as he doubled over in pain.

It was all Mae needed. That one second to get the upper hand. But anger flared in her eyes, and she followed up her first attack with a second round of electrocution, right to Zye's face this time, the phone stun gun I'd given her clutched tight in her hand.

Zye dropped to the floor, yelping in pain.

Mae's eyes were wild as she pinned him down with the weapon, not letting her finger off the trigger.

It took me a second to launch into action, because dammit, it was tempting to let her do that to him all night long. But I forced myself to grab her arm. "Mae."

She flinched but then realized it was me.

"Let him go."

The Taser had no sign of losing battery anytime soon, and though I was sure the electric pulse wasn't enough to kill a man, Zye writhed on the floor in a way that made me not want to push our luck.

She backed off, stumbling, but I was there to catch her. Racking coughs wheezed from her chest and throat as she rubbed at her neck, the stun gun held out between her and Zye. I wrapped my arm around her middle and hauled her back, supporting her weight when her feet didn't move as quick as mine did. We rounded the corner toward the exit, and her arm finally dropped, though her fingers still gripped the phone like it was a lifeline. Her body went limp against mine, coughs taking hold of her body.

"It's okay I got you," I assured her, hurrying to the exit.

The doors were in sight when Zye's evil laugh echoed back through the silent corridors. "Nicely played, Rowe. 'Til next time."

28

LIAM

I'd never been more grateful for the fact my office bathroom had showers and that I kept several suits hanging in a cupboard there. Normally my coworkers and I used the showers after running to work or on our lunch breaks, and I often got changed there so I was completely fresh before court.

But I hadn't left the office in close to forty-eight hours. Because despite my assurances to Mae that we would get Heath out tomorrow morning, I still had no idea how we were going to do it.

The fact that Jayela's baby had been Heath's only strengthened the case against him.

That was a disaster of epic proportions. Mae's father's deathbed claims, while concerning, hadn't revealed anything of use when I'd had an intern dig into his mistress' life. Sure, she was very likely owed a small fortune in child support if her children really were Mae's half siblings, but she had an iron-tight alibi for the night of Jayela's murder. I'd appealed to the police multiple times and got nothing but radio silence in return. Boston's call line had produced nothing else of interest, and all of it felt like a hard dead end.

I needed to give the court something. Some sort of reasonable doubt, and yet the evidence continued to mount against Heath, until I was so buried by it, it felt impossible to dig myself out of.

I stepped out of the shower, wrapped a towel around my waist, and swiped a hand across the fogged-up mirror. Even after a shower, I looked like shit. Stubble coated my jaw, and dark circles had appeared beneath my eyes. I hadn't slept more than an hour or two since I'd left Mae and Rowe at the prison.

All I could see was the complete and utter devastation on Mae's face if I couldn't do the one thing I'd promised her and set Heath free.

I'd lose her. The one woman I'd let myself fall for. The one woman who actually made me feel something.

She wouldn't just come right out and say it. There'd be no, "You didn't get him out, we're over." But it would come between us. Of that, I was sure. How could she look at me every day, knowing that the man she loved was behind bars because I'd fucked up his trial? Sure, she said she loved me, too, but I wasn't sure I believed it. When she'd looked in my eyes, smiled up at me, and told me she loved me, I felt it right to my core. It lit me up like a beacon on a dark night. But the minute she'd walked away, doubt plagued me.

I was never good enough. Not for my father to stick around. Not for my grandfather to be proud of. Not to make full partner at the firm. Not for my mother to forgive me. Not for Mae. Losing this trial was just going to prove it once again.

"Get your shit together, Banks," I murmured to my reflection.

I dressed in front of the window, high enough up to know that nobody could see in. The sun rose over the horizon, splashing pinks and yellow across the rapidly lightening sky. I buttoned my shirt, breathing deep in an attempt to calm my nerves. I needed to get down to the prison. I wanted to be there to check Heath had a suit and that he got transported to the court on time.

Nothing could go wrong. Not one thing.

I closed my eyes as the morning sun bathed me in its glow. "I'm missing something."

It was the thought I couldn't shake.

The empty room didn't provide any answers, but it was there again, that feeling I'd had off and on for a while now. That I had the answers to unraveling the puzzle, but I couldn't make the pieces fit. I kept trying to shove them together, but nothing worked. Snatches of conversation, bits of information from the police, and pieces of evidence all floated around my mind in a whirlwind, messing up my puzzle and never letting me finish it.

I was still standing at the window when my assistant knocked on the door and stuck her head in. "Liam? It's time to go."

I wasn't ready. I needed more time.

But the only one who was going to get that was Heath.

Time behind bars.

29

MAE

I'd been to the local courthouse a few times. I'd sat in the back row and watched my sister take the stand to give evidence about a number of cases she'd worked on. But those times I'd sat alone, not caring about the lawyers, or the judge, or the person on trial.

When I walked through the doors on the morning of Heath's trial it was with an army of support behind me. Rowe. Tori and Will. Perry. Boston and his new girlfriend, Eve. And Liam, already standing behind a desk at the front of the room. He didn't look my way as we entered, and I tried to catch his attention, but he steadfastly stared at the empty judge's seat, in some sort of trance.

I took a seat just behind him but didn't want to call out to him for fear of making it obvious to the entire room how I felt about him. My heart panged watching him up there, pride that he was mine thickening around my heart even through my nerves.

I sat squished between Rowe and Tori, clutching their

hands, my fingernails likely leaving little half-moon shapes in their skin, but neither complained. Will sat at Tori's other side in a crisp gray suit, and the room slowly filled as the clock hands crept closer to nine. There were some teacher friends from my old school who waved tentatively in my direction as they took their seats. I tried to smile back, grateful for their support despite the fact I'd basically ghosted them since everything had happened. Boston sat in the row behind us, his hand heavy on my shoulder, but also incredibly comforting. I knew he was probably having a hard time, too. He'd quit his job on the force but now he was surrounded by his old colleagues, who had shown up for Jayela.

That should have made me proud and grateful. That she'd had so many people who cared about her and was so well-respected that they'd allowed so many of her colleagues to attend today. And yet I was sure they all believed Heath guilty. There was anger and judgement in the eyes of every person in uniform, and all of it directed at Heath.

Nerves rose up my throat, still tender from Zye's hands around my neck. I rubbed at the marks I'd covered with makeup. We hadn't told Liam what had happened with Zye. We hadn't seen him in days, and I hadn't wanted to tell him on the phone when telling him things like Heath and Jayela's pregnancy was more important. I was fine anyway, there was no need to distract him.

Rowe frowned at my hand absently rubbing at my neck. "Are you okay? Are you still sore?"

I gave him my best reassuring smile. "I'm fine. I'm just nervous."

"Me, too. But Liam has this. Have you ever seen him in court?"

I shook my head, grateful for the distraction. "No, have you?"

"He took a case for one of the guys on the team last year. Just a misdemeanor thing, not really a big deal, but Liam was a shark. Got the case thrown out in about fifteen minutes, tops." Rowe grinned at the memory, then put his arm around my shoulders and pulled me to his side. "He's the best man for the job. You did good, Mae. You know that right? Everything you've done for your sister, and for Heath, is above and beyond. You're a little bit incredible."

I didn't know about all that, but it was nice to hear him say it. I couldn't resist ribbing him, though. "Are you complimenting me, Rowe Pritchard? I thought you hated me?"

He rolled his eyes. "Don't get too used to it. But for the record, nobody could hate you, Mae. Least of all me."

Words bubbled up on my tongue, but they didn't have a place here. Then the doors at the front of the room were opening, and in unison, the judge took his place, while Heath was led into the court, cuffs around his wrists, but a smart, expensive suit fitted perfectly to his big body. Liam had to have bought him that.

His gaze sought mine the moment he entered the room, and I sucked in a breath. He was so incredibly handsome, freshly showered with his hair neatly combed. His tattoos were still visible at his neck but only if you were looking for them the way I was. His gaze flicked to Rowe for a moment but quickly came back to me, and held there until he sat. Liam leaned in close to whisper something in his ear.

Then the judge took up her gavel, banged it once on the table, and called the court to order.

30

LIAM

*T*his wasn't going well.

That was clear to me from the very moment the judge peered down her nose at Heath, and then over at the room full of police uniforms. They all had the right to be here, but their presence certainly didn't help our case. It only drew attention to the fact that the victim of this murder had been a well-loved police-woman. And that the other members of the force wanted to see Heath behind bars at any cost.

I sighed.

Mae took the stand, and my heart had swelled with pride at the way she calmly stated the facts and perfectly laid out the events of that night, keeping to the points my associate had coached her on. But that was about all that had gone in our favor. Johnson, the cop who'd beaten Heath's confession out of him, had only stirred up anger in the room. His falsified details of Heath's arrest drew cries of outrage from the audience and jury alike, until the judge had shouted for order. I'd tried to spin every statement made by each witness only for the opposition to throw them back in my face, each argument getting stronger and stronger until Heath quietly said, "Well, this is a shitshow, huh?"

I couldn't lie to him.

So I didn't reply.

But that was an answer in itself. Heath nodded, almost to himself, his shoulders slumping in defeat.

I couldn't even tell him not to give up until it was called, like I would have for any other client. I wanted to, but I just didn't feel it in my heart.

We were going to lose.

Heath. Me. All of us.

For the first time all day, while the opposition prattled on, I turned around to look at Mae.

Her eyes were huge. Big and brown, and full of hope. A hope that was about to be crushed beneath the judge's gavel because I'd fucked the whole thing up and failed Mae completely. Rowe had his arm around her, his eyes full of questions I couldn't answer. On her other side, Tori and Will watched the proceedings quietly.

Will let go of Tori's hand for a moment and pulled a tissue from a small pack in his pocket. The movement caught my eye.

Something slotted into place inside my head.

The phone call with Jayela's friend, Geri. She'd said Jayela had stopped going to the gym on Wednesdays and Thursdays.

The baseball game where Tori had explained that she and Will never got to see each other anymore because he'd started working on Wednesday and Thursday nights.

At this stage, I needed a miracle, and perhaps one had appeared.

Will put his tissues away and picked up his wife's hand again. She smiled up at him, her other hand clutched tightly around Mae's.

I rifled through the file of papers on the desk in front of me, searching for Jayela's credit card records. I'd had my assistant go through them and highlight anything of interest. My heart thumped as I ran my finger down the list, flicking back through pages, and months of Jayela's spending. I fired off a rapid message to my assistant and waited impatiently for her to get back to me, praying that my hunch was correct.

A theory formed in my mind, the feeling familiar and welcome. This was what I did. It was what made me good at my job. When people asked me how I did it later, I wouldn't be able to tell them, but that jigsaw puzzle suddenly came together in a blinding flash of light.

But I didn't like the picture it painted. If I said it out loud, and I was wrong, it could very well be the worst mistake I'd ever made.

It would hurt people.

Heath shifted next to me, his eyes downcast.

It would hurt him if I didn't say it. I needed something. Anything.

I pushed my personal feelings for Mae aside and got slowly to my feet. "Your Honor? He's not on the witness list, but I need to call up William Dudgeon."

"What the hell, Liam?" Tori hissed.

I could practically feel Mae's questions even though I wouldn't turn around to face them.

"Seriously, Mr. Banks?" The judge glared at me.

"Yes, Your Honor. It's important."

"Approach the bench."

The prosecutor and I both stood and walked to the judge, but I barely heard the lecture she gave me and the argument that ensued with the opposition. I watched Mae from the corner of my eye as she leaned across Tori to Will and hissed, "Do you know what's going on?"

Will's eyes were huge, and he shook his head in confusion. "No idea at all."

"Why would he call you up?"

Will appeared to be thinking it over for a minute, but the bafflement on his face never changed. Eventually, he shrugged. "I've honestly got no idea."

"Looks like we're about to find out," Rowe said when the judge called for the chatter to cease and banged her gavel again.

I jumped, dragging myself back into the game. It took me half a second to realize she'd agreed to have Will take the stand.

I went back to my seat, avoiding all eye contact with Mae, and bent my head close to Heath's.

"What the hell, man?" he asked.

"Just trust me."

"I do, but I don't see how this is going to help."

"William Dudgeon, take the stand."

For a moment I didn't think Tori would let go of her husband's hand, but Will disentangled himself from her clutches and squeezed past Mae and Rowe to the little wooden gate that separated the audience from the lawyers, jury, and judge. He waited for a clerk to unlock it for him and then took up the witness seat at the front of the room.

"He's nervous," I murmured.

Heath shrugged. "Wouldn't you be if you'd just been randomly called up in a murder case?"

He had a point.

"You called this witness, Mr. Banks. Do you plan on actually questioning him?" the judge asked, annoyance dripping from her tone.

Shit. That wasn't good. I flashed her my most charming smile and stood to button my suit jacket.

The glare she gave me told me she'd seen one too many of my smiles for them to still have an effect on her.

I focused on my witness. "William, you're married to Tori Dudgeon. Correct?"

"Yes."

"Tori was close with Jayela Donovan, wasn't she?"

Will fidgeted with his tie, straightening it, even though it already hung dead center down his chest. "Sure. She's closer with Jayela's sister, Mae, but Jayela and Tori had developed a friendship, too."

"That's how you met Jayela? Through your wife?"

"Yes."

"Did you know her well?"

Will shook his head. "No, I didn't, I'm afraid. We have a young son, so when Tori socialized with Jayela and Mae, she mostly went alone."

I nodded thoughtfully, slowly making my way closer to where he sat. "Your wife said recently that the two of you were like ships in the night."

As subtly as I could, I wiped my sweaty palms on my pants. I knew what I was going to say next wouldn't go down well, but I'd gone down the rabbit hole now, and there was no stopping it. *Shit.* This was insane and reckless. I hadn't thought this through well at all, and my personal involvement was clouding my judgment. I'd gotten desperate. That was never a good thing in a courtroom and a position I wasn't used to. But I had to say it now. An entire courtroom was waiting on me to spit it out. "Everything all right at home?"

Will's eyebrows furrowed together. "I don't see what that has to do with any—"

"Please just answer the question."

William pressed his lips together then said, "Everything is fine."

I raised an eyebrow, playing the part of cocky, confident lawyer, even though I didn't feel it. "You love your wife?"

"Of course."

"How come you're never at home then?"

"I work a lot."

"Ah yes. The old nine-to-five. It had turned into a bit more than that, though, according to your wife. It seems you were working nights, too. Specifically Wednesday and Thursday nights."

"So?"

The judge sighed. "Do you have a question, Mr. Banks? My patience grows weary. How about you get to the point?"

I nodded. "Jayela Donovan was a creature of habit. We've already established that during this trial. She went to work, the gym, and then home again, rarely breaking that routine. She'd had the same friends for years, dependable friendships that were rock solid and a career she loved. But a few months before she died, she quit going to the gym two nights a week. Wednesday and

Thursday. And yet she still left the apartment she shared with her sister at those times. I didn't notice it at first, because the listings on her card are always different. But every Wednesday and Thursday, there's payments all in similar amounts... The amount of an average hotel room. She wasn't where she said she'd be, and her credit card records prove it."

"Okay, but what has that got to do with me?" Will asked.

"You weren't where you said you were either, were you?"

William turned pale. His eye twitched.

Something inside me crowed. I was grasping at straws, but he was hiding something. And I was damn determined that it was coming out, right here, right now.

"I checked with your workplace. They didn't extend your hours, did they?"

Will rubbed a hand across the back of his neck. "No, but—"

"But you weren't at home with your loving wife and son either, were you? You told her you were at work, but you lied. What else are you lying about, Mr. Dudgeon?"

"Nothing! I mean, I—"

"Your Honor, Jayela Donovan's father admitted he knew she was in a relationship, but Jayela had not ever introduced this person to her sister or her friend. She'd kept her affair quiet, a secret for months, meeting at hotels. Why? She'd never done that before. She introduced my client to her family after their second date."

"Wait, what are you saying?" Will stood up in the witness box, his fingers gripped around the banister.

"That Jayela and I... Liam! I go to church every Sunday. And I love my wife more than anything. I'd never!"

I stared the man in the eye and tried to see past his floundering.

I didn't believe his 'man of God, I love my family' bullshit. The accusation sat hot on my tongue, not enough proof for a court, but a soul-deep belief that this man was a liar.

If I was wrong, it would be a huge crater on my career and relationship.

But if I was right, an innocent man wouldn't spend the rest of his life sitting in a jail cell.

I glanced over at Mae. Her mouth was wide open in shock, gaze clouded with confusion and hurt. She clutched Tori's hand. Tori looked like she wanted to launch herself across the room and rip my throat out.

She very well might when she heard what I had to say.

"The way Jayela Donovan died is consistent with crimes of passion. That's why Heath Michaelson has been on trial all along." I sucked in a deep breath. "I allege that William and Jayela were having an affair. And I believe he killed Jayela Donovan."

31

HEATH

*A*fter the uproar of noise in the court, the quiet of the little room Liam and I waited in was comforting. In solitary, there would be entire days where I barely heard a noise, and I'd been there for weeks. After that, being around so many other people was jarring.

Liam paced the tiny room, the loop of his tie pulled slack and his top button undone. He jumped a mile when his phone rang, and the blood drained from his face as he listened to whoever was on the other end. He hung up without saying goodbye.

"Liam. What?"

He shook his head. "The jury has come back too quickly."

"They're back already? That's bad?"

"It's either really good or really bad. It means the case was cut-and-dried for them and they all agreed quickly." He redid his tie and studied me with a critical eye. "Come on, we don't want to keep them waiting."

I was suddenly sure I was going to be sick. My entire

future rested in the hands of this jury, and one word from them would determine which way it went. I couldn't look at anyone as we entered the court. I could feel Mae and Rowe's gazes heavy on my back but I couldn't meet them. Liam didn't turn that way either, and I knew why. He'd put everything on the line for me. Come up with an alternative that seemed crazy but had to prove the cops had not done their job in investigating this case properly. His accusation had to show that I wasn't the only viable suspect, just the easy way out.

I paused before we got to the courtroom door. "Thanks, Liam."

He glanced over at me. "Don't thank me yet."

"Worst-case scenario, they realize there's other suspects and I sit in jail a few more months until I get a retrial. Right? Not saying I don't want to be walking out of here a free man today, but if I have to, I can do a few more months. My solitary cell has become like a second home." I tried to laugh, but neither of us were feeling it.

Liam pushed open the door for me, waiting for me to walk through ahead of him. "Come on, let's get this over with, huh?"

The judge entered the court a moment after we did, staring me down with her sharp gaze.

An uncomfortable prickling feeling came over me, an acute awareness that this entire room was staring at me, waiting for this jury to seal my fate. I smoothed a crease on my suit pants as discreetly as I could while the jury filed back in.

"Has the jury reached a decision?" the judge asked unnecessarily since we wouldn't be back here if they hadn't.

A man in his fifties perhaps, tall and slim, rose from his seat. "We have, Your Honor."

The judge nodded at him to go ahead.

"On the charge of murder in the first degree, we the jury, find the defendant, Heath Michaelson...guilty."

The noise of the courtroom consumed me once more, echoing off the walls, bellowing around the space, wrapping itself around my limbs until it felt like rope tying me up so tight it cut off the circulation.

I couldn't breathe. The noise and the weight of the jury's decision sucked the air from the room, leaving me empty.

I should have known.

I didn't deserve anything more.

The jury saw me for who I really was, even if they were wrong about me murdering Jayela.

"Heath." Liam's hand came down on my shoulder.

But I shook him off.

Behind me a woman's cries cut through the din, and I was sure it was Mae, but I couldn't look at her. I only prayed Rowe would hold her and comfort her because I couldn't.

The judge banged her gavel and demanded order in her court. "While sentencing may normally take place another day, I see no reason to drag this debacle out any further. The jury have made their decision." She glared at me, the hate in her eyes no longer masked by professionalism. "I have no sympathy for a man who lays hands on a woman. And even less when that woman was a member of our police force. The way you killed her in cold blood, in the middle of the night, while the woman slept, is the height of cowardice." Her eyes flashed with all the things she didn't say.

You scum of the earth.

You pathetic excuse for a man.

They kept coming, and I felt each one like a physical blow.

"I sentence you to death row. And I want it expedited. I don't want you sitting in a prison cell, clogging up the system when men like you don't deserve it."

"Your Honor!" Liam bellowed. "This isn't right! This is a huge miscarriage of justice!"

Her hold on her professionalism snapped. "Get them both out of my court before I do it myself."

32

HEATH

The chaos had carried on in my head. People came and went. Liam disappeared then returned. Questions were asked of me, but I couldn't answer any of them. Hours passed, and I only realized it when I was finally loaded back into a police wagon and the sky around me had turned to night.

Back at the prison, I had to go through several checks to make sure I hadn't picked up any contraband while out in the real world, and my stomach growled its emptiness at missing dinner.

I somehow doubted there'd be a three-course meal waiting for me back at my cell.

Eventually, a guard hustled me down the empty hallway toward solitary, my feet heavy, my body numb.

"Wait."

I tensed at Rowe's voice.

The guard paused, forcing me to stop as well, since he had an iron-tight grip on my arm. I couldn't look at Rowe, though. Didn't want to see the expression on his face now that the world thought me a convicted killer.

They were only seeing what I'd known all along.

The darkness of my past now consumed me, seeping out through my pores and tainting my face, my body, my clothes with the blackness of my soul.

"You're needed in Gen Pop. I'll take Michaelson."

The guard nodded, letting me go and disappearing around a corner.

Rowe didn't touch me, but he didn't need to. His energy poured from him in waves, crossing the small gap between us. "We need to talk."

I shook my head. My throat was too tight, and the vise around my chest too constricting. I could barely breathe, let alone talk. The judge had handed me a one-way, express ticket to death row. And all I could think was I deserved it.

Rowe's fingers clamped around my biceps, cutting into my flesh with the force of his hold. "Yes, we fucking do. Wherever you are in your head right now, put the fucking brakes on."

I glanced at him. He stared straight ahead as he marched me toward my cell, but his concern was etched into the pull of his eyebrows and the fierce determination in his eye.

"Death row," I muttered numbly.

"Just keep walking."

I did because what else was there to do? We rounded the corner of the Gen Pop hallway, and I stiffened at the noise coming from inside. Rec time had just finished, and the men were all still lingering in the doorways, using up every last minute of their perceived freedom before they were locked down for the night.

"Dead man walking," a voice drawled from the doorway.

Rowe stopped. "What did you say?"

It was Zye, lounging against the wall, watching with those impossibly blue eyes that never seemed to miss a trick. Randall stood beside him, looking every inch the dumb thug he was, backing up Zye who had clearly cemented himself the position of alpha in DeWitt's absence. Instinctively, my fingers closed into fists at the sight of them together. I hadn't forgotten what Randall had done to me during the riot, setting me up for him and his friends to attack. It didn't surprise me that he'd buddied up with Zye.

Zye let his gaze sweep me from head to toe before landing on Rowe's face. "I said... Dead. Man. Walking."

Rowe's body went entirely stiff beside me. "How did you even hear about the trial already?"

Zye eyed me, his smile wide. He lifted one shoulder in fake nonchalance. "I didn't."

Rowe stepped forward. "Then what the fuck did you mean by that?" His hate for Zye poured off him in waves, and he kept advancing. "Are you threatening him? Or me?"

Tension crackled in the air around us, and not the good kind. Zye straightened, pulling himself to his full height to go eye to eye with Rowe. "Threaten a guard? That'd be pretty dumb of me, wouldn't it?"

"It would," Rowe growled.

Zye leaned in even closer. "Thing is, why would I threaten you?"

Rowe didn't say a word.

"Got a guilty conscience, Pritchard? Can't blame you. I would, too, if I was in the habit of stealing other men's families."

Rowe lost his grip on his composure. He grabbed Zye by the shirt and slammed him against the door. "You stole my family, Zye. Let's get that straight. Not the other way around. You stole them both when you killed her."

Zye glared at him, his light-colored eyes suddenly soulless. "I just took back what was mine." His gaze slid to me, before it focused back on Rowe. "And *now* I'm going to take what's yours. All of it. Every single person you love."

Rowe roared at the threat, slamming Zye against the door. With my hands cuffed I couldn't do much to help, but another officer ran out from Gen Pop and got between them. He shoved Rowe away from Zye who laughed his head off maniacally, like Rowe's reaction was hilarious.

"Stop," I said to Rowe quietly. "You're just giving him what he wants."

Rowe's chest heaved as the other guard shoved Zye back inside Gen Pop.

But his laughter echoed back. And so did his threats. "You can't be here to protect your boy twenty-four seven, Pritchard. That's all I'm saying. At some point, he's either gonna get out of solitary where I'll be waiting for him." He chuckled. "Or I guess the alternative is he stays there 'til a lethal injection gets him. Either way. Might as well say your goodbyes now, gentlemen. You're done."

Rowe looked like he wanted to run in there and kill

him with his bare hands, but I blocked the entrance, forcing him to face at me. "Hey. Stop. Let it go."

"Can't."

"You have to." I sighed. "Come on. Just take me to my cell."

He forced himself away from Gen Pop, and we walked the rest of the way in silence. He popped the door on my cell and pushed the door open.

Two people stood on the inside. My gaze skirted right past Liam and landed on Mae.

Fuck. Her eyes were red-rimmed from crying, and she stared at me with such desperation it broke the wall I'd been trying to erect around myself. A lump rose in my throat over all the things I'd lost today. My life seemed insignificant until it meant losing her.

Losing them.

She smashed through my crumbling defenses, throwing herself at me. I lifted my arms and let her into the circle made by my handcuffed wrists. She had no tears left, but she trembled as she held me.

"What are you doing in here?" I murmured into the top of her head, inhaling the familiar scent of her shampoo. If this had been another life, if I'd been another man, I could have been waking up with that scent on my pillow. Instead, it would probably be the last part of her I got to have before I was marched down death row.

How the fuck had I gotten here?

It wasn't really a question. Because it had only ever been a matter of time. One bad decision. One lifetime of regret. One end to it all.

I looked over her head at Rowe. "Did you do this?"

"She needed you."

I nodded. Rowe undid my cuffs, and I wrapped my arms around Mae properly, holding her tight to my chest, not wanting to let her go.

"We'll appeal," Mae said determinedly into my chest. "We'll appeal for as long as it takes."

I turned to Liam. But the expression on his face told me everything I needed to know.

We could appeal all day long. It wouldn't change anything.

"When?" I asked him. "She said she wanted it expedited."

His mouth pressed into a grim line, and Mae twisted in my arms to look at him. Rowe stared in horror as well.

"Liam, when?" I forced the words out, though my chest felt like it was caving in.

"Could be a few months. More likely weeks. Days at worst."

Nausea curdled in my gut, but I fought the sick feeling away. I'd been here before. On death's doorstep, and I hadn't even cared. But I did care now. Because now I had something I hadn't had back then. Now I had something...someone...to live for.

Rowe flattened himself against the wall, his gaze pinning me, his head shaking 'no' ever so slightly.

I laughed bitterly. "It's probably for the best. If I stay here, Zye will get to me eventually. I think I'd rather go out with a lethal injection than by being shanked in the showers."

"Don't fucking say that!" Rowe yelled, exploding the grip he'd had on his emotions. "That's not happening! None of it."

I stared at him, wishing I could hold him the way I

held Mae. Wishing I could promise them all that this was going to turn out all right.

Liam's face contorted in agony, watching Mae cry in my arms. Rowe's expression was full of identical torture.

"Liam! Isn't there anything you can do?" Mae asked between heart-wrenching sobs that cut through me like a knife.

"Short of digging him a tunnel out..." He swallowed hard. "No. This was never going to be a fair trial. They had him convicted before we even started."

Mae's quiet sobs echoed around the tiny cell as the last flicker of hope I had inside me died.

This was it. I needed to tell them goodbye. I couldn't draw this out. I couldn't ask them to keep coming here, sneaking in, risking their lives and careers every time just to see me. I was the anchor, pulling down their ship in a stormy sea.

It was time for them to cut the rope and let me go.

"Hit me," Rowe said suddenly.

"What?" I asked.

"Hit me," he repeated.

"What the fuck for?"

Rowe closed the gap between us, Mae stepping to the side to make room. He took in Mae's defeated face, before his gaze locked with mine. Something burned bright there. But it wasn't the defeat and devastation that fixed in Mae's and Liam's eyes.

Rowe's burned with something more. He kissed me hard, slamming his lips against mine in a touch that was bruising, and owning, and one I immediately wanted more of.

But he pulled back as fast as he'd come in and said it

again. "Hit me! Take my access card and get the fuck out of here. Find an exit. Leave." He started shrugging out of his clothes, unbuttoning his shirt.

When the three of us stared at him in shock, he shoved at my chest, yanking at my shirt. "We need to swap clothes."

"Are you fucking insane?" I sputtered.

Mae's eyes were huge. "Rowe, he can't!"

"What she said!" I confirmed. Rowe had lost his fucking mind. But he was still determinedly shedding clothes and staring me down like he expected me to do the same. "Rowe! I'm not doing this!" I turned to Liam. "Talk some fucking sense into him!"

I could almost see the wheels whirring in his head.

Then Liam turned and threw a fist into Rowe's face.

Mae let out a cry, covering her mouth with her hand.

Shock punched through my gut as hard and fast as Liam's fist had connected with Rowe's cheekbone. "What the fuck, man?"

Rowe clutched his face, then straightened. Something unspoken passed between them, then Rowe squared his shoulders. "Again."

Liam's fist smashed into Rowe's mid-section.

"Stop!" I demanded. "Just fucking stop!"

But Liam's arm reared back, and his fist took another crack, this time at Rowe's ribs. Then he looked at me while Rowe groaned in pain. Everything inside me yearned to go help him, but everything in his expression told me to stay back, and that my help wasn't wanted.

Liam's chest heaved as he squared off with me. "What do you have to lose? They can't sentence you to death twice."

"But—"

Mae stepped in front of me once more, a new determination in her eyes.

I shook my head. "Mae, no. Don't tell me you agree? And when you all go down for assisting?"

"At least you won't be dead." Her eyes glittered. She scooped Rowe's shirt from the floor and held it out to me. Her fingers didn't tremble, and there was fire in her words.

"Don't make this all be in vain. Take it. Escape."

The end...for now.

The story continues in Fatal Felons. Read the epic conclusion to Mae, Heath, Rowe, and Liam's story.

Make sure you check out my website for bonus scenes and a free novella! www.ellethorpe.com

ALSO BY ELLE THORPE

Saint View High series (Reverse Harem, Bully Romance. Complete)

*Devious Little Liars (Saint View High, #1)

*Dangerous Little Secrets (Saint View High, #2)

*Twisted Little Truths (Saint View High, #3)

Saint View Prison series (Reverse harem, romantic suspense. Complete.)

*Locked Up Liars (Saint View Prison, #1)

*Solitary Sinners (Saint View Prison, #2)

*Fatal Felons (Saint View Prison, #3)

Saint View Psychos series (Reverse harem, romantic suspense. Complete.)

*Start a War (Saint View Psychos, #1)

*Half the Battle (Saint View Psychos, #2)

*It Ends With Violence (Saint View Psychos, #3)

Saint View Rebels (Reverse harem, romantic suspense. Releasing in 2023)

*Rebel Revenge (Saint View Rebels, #1)

*Rebel Obsession (Saint View Rebels, #2)

*Rebel Heart (Saint View Rebels, #3)

Saint View Strip (Male/Female, romantic suspense standalones. Ongoing.)

*Evil Enemy (Saint View Strip, #1)

*Unholy Sins (Saint View Strip, #2)

*Untitled (Saint View Strip, #3)

Dirty Cowboy series (complete)

*Talk Dirty, Cowboy (Dirty Cowboy, #1)

*Ride Dirty, Cowboy (Dirty Cowboy, #2)

*Sexy Dirty Cowboy (Dirty Cowboy, #3)

*Dirty Cowboy boxset (books 1-3)

*25 Reasons to Hate Christmas and Cowboys (a Dirty Cowboy bonus novella, set before Talk Dirty, Cowboy but can be read as a standalone, holiday romance)

Buck Cowboys series (Spin off from the Dirty Cowboy series. Complete.)

*Buck Cowboys (Buck Cowboys, #1)

*Buck You! (Buck Cowboys, #2)

*Can't Bucking Wait (Buck Cowboys, #3)

*Mother Bucker (Buck Cowboys, $#4)

The Only You series (Contemporary romance. Complete)

*Only the Positive (Only You, #1) - Reese and Low.

*Only the Perfect (Only You, #2) - Jamison.

*Only the Truth - (Only You, bonus novella) - Bree.

*Only the Negatives (Only You, #3) - Gemma.

*Only the Beginning (Only You, #4) - Bianca and Riley.

*Only You boxset

Add your email address here to be the first to know when new books are available!

www.ellethorpe.com/newsletter

Join Elle Thorpe's readers group on Facebook!

www.facebook.com/groups/ellethorpesdramallamas

ACKNOWLEDGMENTS

Ah, Solitary Sinners. The book that truly lived up to its name because I wrote the entire thing while I was pretty much in solitary confinement myself haha. It will forever be my 2021 lockdown book, the one that was written before the sun came up, because all my normal working hours got eaten up with homeschooling three kids.

I did not enjoy those 5am starts, but I hope you enjoyed this second installment of Mae, Liam, Heath, and Rowe's story! One more to go!

Big thank you to the people who support me with each and every book. Emmy and Karen, my awesome editors. Jolie and Zoe, my author besties. Louise, Dana, Shellie, Samantha, Kirsty, and Tamara, my beta readers. My beautiful promo and ARC team, as well as my Drama Llamas readers group.

And of course, thank you to Jira, Thomas, Flick, and Heidi. I love you guys more than anything. Wouldn't want to do a pandemic lockdown with anyone else.

ABOUT THE AUTHOR

Elle Thorpe lives on the sunny east coast of Australia. When she's not writing stories full of kissing, she's a wife and mummy to three tiny humans. She's also official ball thrower to one slobbery dog named Rollo. Yes, she named a female dog after a dirty hot character on Vikings. Don't judge her. Elle is a complete and utter fangirl at heart, obsessing over The Walking Dead and Outlander to an unhealthy degree. But she wouldn't change a thing.

You can find her on Facebook or Instagram(@ellethorpebooks or hit the links below!) or at her website www.ellethorpe.com. If you love Elle's work, please consider joining her Facebook fan group, Elle Thorpe's Drama Llamas or joining her newsletter here. www.ellethorpe.com/newsletter

facebook.com/ellethorpebooks
instagram.com/ellethorpebooks
goodreads.com/ellethorpe
pinterest.com/ellethorpebooks

Made in the USA
Middletown, DE
22 October 2023

41261007R00198